IT'S ALWAYS BEEN YOU

Bethanie L Kramer

ISBN-13: 9798753941374

Cover Picture - Copyright © 2018 by Alexa Vandemark, licensed from Jenna
and Brent Campbell
Cover design by: Victoria Wright, PublishingWright.com
Library of Congress Control Number: 2018675309
Printed in the United States of America

This book is dedicated to my little family. Thank you for putting up with the lack of attention some days. For allowing me to bounce how men react to things off you. For being my biggest cheerleaders. For allowing me to follow my dreams. And Chase, please don't ever read any of these books. I mean it.

To my friend, Donna, for reading and giving it to me straight when I had things wrong. For always being willing to read weird excerpts at the drop of a hat, even while you were dealing with things.

To my beta readers who are now dear friends. I adore you and your dedication. Thank you.

To God for letting my brain work in strange ways. If it wasn't for your plan, my life would be bland.

CONTENTS

CHAPTER ONE

Rose pulled into the driveway of her new home with the moving truck following her. Looking through the car window, she saw two young children playing in the front yard next door. It made her smile. She had forgotten what it was like living in a small town. Living in downtown Charlotte, North Carolina for the last eleven years, she only ever saw kids playing at the park or in the street.

She climbed out of her car and stretched. The kids were now staring at her, so Rose gave them a tiny wave before turning her attention to the movers.

Rose knew the movers were only here for a few hours. One of the primary goals of hiring them was so they could place all the heavy furniture where she wanted it. After the movers left, it would be hard for her to move any of it herself.

Once everything was out of the truck and the furniture where Rose wanted it, the movers packed up their supplies.

A confident smile set on her lips as she said, "Thanks for all of your help, guys." Slipping the movers a tip as they left, she wandered to her car to finish grabbing the last few items from her trunk.

Holding her last moving box, Rose stared at herself in the reflection of the storm door of her rental house. Five foot five inches, with long blonde hair tied in a ponytail, she was twenty-eight years old and moving home. Not home to her childhood home. The closest she could find to her dad was this rental, two blocks away. The small distance was fine with her, though. She still wanted some privacy.

Coming back to her small hometown in Michigan wasn't what Rose had envisioned. She had left after high school, moving to North Carolina for college with dreams of settling in Charlotte and teaching in the city. North Carolina had always been one of her favorite places when she was younger. The mountains, the cities, it had it all and seemed like a dream world.

Moving had been an escape from high school heartbreak but had been an exciting adventure as a young college student. Her dad had rented a U-Haul, packed her up and helped her move to the dorms at Appalachian State University that first year. The trip had been full of horrible food, stinky hotel rooms and beautiful scenery. But it was still one of the best trips of their lives. He had cried the day he had to leave her but had known that Rose would be ok.

Rose had met her two best friends, Alaina, and Grace, at college. They had been her roommates. The three of them had been inseparable since that first day on campus.

Rose only ever came home again for holidays and the occasional visit, despite missing her dad. Instead, she stayed with Alaina's family each summer during college.

After college, the three friends had moved to Charlotte to start their careers, renting a two-bedroom apartment together. Rose and Grace were still sharing the same apartment in downtown Charlotte eleven years later. They had walked down the aisle with Alaina four years prior as their friend had married her prince charming. Her friend now had a little boy and a baby girl who was due in three weeks. The thought of missing the arrival of sweet Beatrice saddened Rose, but returning home was now more important.

Rose had seen her dad's number pop up on her iPhone one day in

May and immediately answered "Hey daddy! What's up?"

"Hey Rosey girl." He sounded tired, but that was to be expected. His disease caused that. "Rosey, I need you to come home."

"What dad?"

"I need you to come home. I need a little more help. Your cousins are involved with so much at school now, that your Aunt Bri is getting stretched thin. She doesn't have as much time as before to take me places and to appointments." He was quiet for a minute. "The doctor says my Parkenson's is progressing faster. I get tired quicker, the tremors are getting worse. We just... just need more help."

Rose was completely still, not sure how to answer. Her dad was her world, but Charlotte was her home now. "Are you there, Rose?"

"Yeah, dad, I'm here. Sorry. I, um, of course I'll come." Her voice was gentle, though her heart was breaking. "I have to finish the school year, though, ok?" Her head was spinning, unsure what was happening, but her dad needed her.

"Of course, sweety." When he paused, Rose wiped a tear from her cheek. "Rosey, what's the hesitation?"

"Dad, you know I'd jump through any hoop for you."

"But?"

"But I just really don't know how I'm going to avoid... him."

Rose heard her father sigh, "Eventually, Rose, you need to just rip the band aid off. It's been ten years."

"I know," Rose tapped her finger on the back of her phone, "I'll figure it out. Love you daddy."

"Love you too, Rosey. Tell Grace the same." Her dad had taken on the fatherly role with Grace early on. Her family life was less than subpar and he knew she needed a father figure.

"I will." She ended the call, setting the phone on the counter, still reeling from the request. The pit in her stomach grew.

Rose had been a daddy's girl since birth. Her parents had been two peas in a pod until she was born. Then for reasons unknown to Rose, things between her parents became more and more tense each year.

Right after Rose's seventh birthday, her mom decided she needed a break, and took a trip to Tijuana with her best friend, Lilly. Lilly had returned. Rose's mom had not. Her dad had begged and pleaded with her mom to come home to no avail. Her mother had a stubborn soul and didn't want to be tied down anymore.

It broke Rose's and her dad's hearts, but what could they do? After a couple months, it didn't matter anymore to Rose, or so she told herself. She and her dad had done fine and now, twenty-five years later, her dad was her number one fan and one of her best friends.

After the phone call with her dad, Rose and Grace sat down to discuss what was happening. "I know it isn't ideal, Grace, but my dad..."

"I know Rose. I'm not mad. How long do you think you'll be gone?"

"I have no idea. I'm hoping not for more than a year, though. Maybe Bri and I can come up with something long term for him. I can still send money for rent if you want. It won't be the full amount, but I can help."

"No, don't worry about it. I'll figure it out. You need to worry about your pops, Rose. Do what you have to do. Your room is here when you come back."

After that conversation, Rose immediately started looking for jobs and had been lucky to find one right at the same elementary school she had attended as a child. Since her dad wasn't to the point of needing twenty-four hour care, Rose decided to get a rental. She finished the school year and drove home that weekend.

Now here she was, standing in the little town in Michigan that she never dreamed of moving back to. Sighing, Rose opened the door and walked into the living room, setting that last box on the floor. Home... for now. Closing the door, Rose sank to the floor. The twelve-hour drive had rocked her, as did her overactive mind, but she had made it. And so far she had not had any run-ins with her ex. Day one, almost success. Luckily, she had a great playlist on her phone, and Alaina and Grace had checked in with her throughout the drive. As much as she wanted to nap now, that wasn't an option. It was time to face reality. She had to get herself in order and go see her dad.

After a quick shower and digging through some boxes to find clean jeans, Rose threw on her favorite blue "Kane Brown" t-shirt and boot cut jeans. Only able to find flip flops, she threw them on. She had tried to prepare herself, but she still wasn't ready to see what toll Parkinson's disease had taken on her dad since Christmas. Rose talked to her dad daily. She could hear the tremor in his voice, but seeing him was going to make it real.

Walking out the door, her eye caught something moving next door. Looking to the neighbor's driveway, the two kids were still out playing, a little boy and girl, both with the most beautiful curly brown hair, and they were staring at her again from their driveway.

Shielding her eyes from the sun, she gave them a smile and a little wave. "Hi there!"

They both giggled and the little boy asked, "Did you just move into mean Jack's house?"

"Oh my, Jack sounds scary. Did he used to live here?"

"Yes, and then one day... POOF... gone!" The boy said, throwing his hands into the air.

"Well then, yes, I did," and then Rose whispered, "But I promise I'm not mean." The kids both giggled again. "My name is Rose. What are your names?"

"I'm Oliver and this is my baby sister Chloe."

"I'm not a baby," Chloe responded, crossing her little arms across herself.

"No, you are definitely not a baby," Rose smiled at her. "Well, it was very nice to meet you both. I'll try to come meet your parents later this week, ok? I gotta run to see my dad now," Rose said with a little wave.

Something about that little boy was so familiar. She shook her head as she turned, walking in the direction of her father's house. After the long drive, some fresh air and a walk were exactly what she needed. It would give her a little more time to prepare herself for seeing her dad.

Gibson

Chloe waved frantically watching Rose walk away and Oliver turned to walk back up the driveway, kicking a stone. Just then, Gibson came out to call the kids in for a snack. He had hoped he would be quick enough to meet the new neighbor.

"Who was that, guys?" Gibson asked.

"Oh, just a lady," Oliver said

"She was beautiful, dad! She looked like a real princess!" Chloe said, skipping towards him. These kids were no doubt his, as they both had his curls and hair color that matched his dark brown eyes. Oliver could be Gibson's twin because he looked just like him, right down to the dimples in his little chubby cheeks. They were the best part of him. The best thing he had ever done in his life.

"Well, I'll have to meet this princess," he said laughing, "Let's go get some rice crispy treats, bozos."

"Dad, can we make her cookies?" Chloe pleaded.

"Yeah dad. She's new! Mom always says to be nice to the new kids," Oliver added.

"Sure, we can make some for her. We can bring them over later." *This ought to be an adventure,* he thought as he glanced back to the house next door, wondering about the mysterious neighbor.

CHAPTER TWO

When she turned the corner onto her dad's street, she saw him waiting on his front porch. The sight jarred her. His hands were in his lap, but the trembles were not allowing them to sit still. His head was doing a bit of a sway that had not been there at Christmas.

As a little girl, Jason Harper was her Iron Man. Most people called their dads superman. That didn't describe her dad at all. He wasn't some chemically changed person. He was a real guy who, when the need came, put on that suit of armor, and protected her. In Rose's world, he was the smartest and strongest man ever, creating and adapting as he went after becoming a single dad. Superman would never be strong enough to do what her dad had dealt with, which is why she always described him as Iron Man. He could do just about anything.

At five years old, she had wanted a swing set with a fort and sandbox because little Emmy down the road had one. He went out that weekend, bought lumber and built one from scratch. At sixteen, after being asked to prom for the first time, her dad had figured out how to use a sewing machine to add the little camouflage details she had wanted to her dress.

Jason stood and smiled. Raising his hand, he waved at his daughter. He gingerly walked down the front steps and held his arms open. Rose ran up and hugged him tightly, not wanting to see how the disease had eaten him already.

She had known that there seemed to be something wrong almost seven years ago, but being in North Carolina, nothing was real. The doctors weren't sure what was happening to Jason at that point. All Rose knew was that he was experiencing joint pain and some mental slip ups. Maybe he had downplayed things for her sake.

Over the last few years, the tremors had started, and it was hindering his ability to drive. He retired early from the dairy farm and Aunt Brianne had cut back the hours at her job to help him as his mobility slowed. He didn't need a full-time caretaker as he could still do almost everything on his own, but there were things that were becoming increasingly difficult to do and his mind was starting to slip a bit more.

"Rosey girl," he said into her hair, "I prayed you would make it here before dinner."

"I'm here, daddy," she responded, keeping her face pressed into his shoulder.

"Rosey!!" a voice called from behind her dad.

"Aunty Brianne!" Rose said, raising her head.

"Get over here and give me a hug before I leave. I have dinner out on the counter for you both." Her aunt said. Rose was her aunt's doppelganger. Everyone said so. They did look similar, except her aunt was about three inches taller than her. After a few minutes of idle chit chat, Aunt Bri left, leaving Rose and her dad to talk. "Ok, you two. Have a great evening. Jason, I'll see you in the morning for your appointment."

Jason waved his sister away, "I know, Bri, go home." Chuckling, he pulled his daughter into a side hug. "Let's go inside."

Entering that front door brought back her entire childhood. The smell of a previous life, lavender, and vanilla, mixed with the smell of burning leaves. It made her feel sad for all the time she had lost with her dad, but also made her want to run. The feeling of falling back into her old life scared her.

As she walked through the living room, she glanced around. Her senior picture hung on the wall with a new teacher picture of her from Charlotte tucked into the frame. Running her finger across the last family picture they had taken before mom had left, she still didn't know why her dad left the picture up. She stopped in front of the picture of her and her dad that had been taken two Christmases ago at the tree farm just outside of town. Bending down, she saw a new picture frame holding the selfie she had posted on Facebook of her, Alaina, and Grace the last time they had gone hiking. Smiling, she turned away and walked to the kitchen, grabbing two plates and two glasses from the cupboard. Walking over to the table, she noticed the medicine bottles on the counter, causing her to take a sharp breath.

I don't want to do this. I'm not ready to let my dad go. I should have never left. "Dad, can you grab some napkins and the silverware?"

"Sure. Brianne has something in that crock-pot. I don't know what. I know she told me, but..." He scratched his head. "We both know that's the only way she knows how to cook," he said with a little laugh. Rose smiled back at him. Well, he wasn't wrong. "She must be getting better. You seem to have gained a few since I was home in December." Rose teased her father.

"What!" he patted his belly. "This is my keg; the beer keeps me strong." They both laughed. "Besides, it's actually all those ladies from church who keep bringing me dishes of food. Bri means well, but most of the time I have to toss what she makes." He winked at his daughter, bringing back a memory of how it was after mom had left.

Bri had tried then too, but unless it had come out of a crock-pot or the frozen food aisle, it never tasted right. Her dad had learned how to cook over the years. Jason could take any meat and randomly throw seasoning at it. It always ended up perfect, but he never could remember what he used, so it was never duplicated.

"Go sit dad, I'll dish your plate." She removed the cover from the crock pot and the most amazing smell penetrated the air, but nothing could cut the thickness of her thoughts.

After dishing two plates of pork and vegetables, she hurried over to the table, placing a plate in front of her dad and one in front of her seat. Jason said grace. While they ate, Rose told her dad about the trip and unpacking. He raised his eyebrow at her when she told him about the kids next door, causing her to wonder what that meant. Around eight o'clock, she saw that her dad was getting tired.

Not wanting her dad to feel badly if he asked her to go first, Rose said. "Dad, I'm going to head to the rental. I'm tired from the trip and still have to find my sheets and blankets."

"Rosey, I'm so glad you are home. Go, get settled, I'll be fine," he replied.

She finished the dishes quickly, watching him head to the living room and into his recliner. She heard the TV pop on, and the sound of the Tigers' game blared through the house. Planting a kiss on her dad's balding head, she said, "I'm going to go see my new classroom tomorrow at the school. Do you want me to come grab you after and we can get lunch?"

"That sounds nice, sweetie. Just let me know what time."

"Ok, love you dad."

"Good night, Rose. I love you too."

And with that, she was out the door, making a quick stop at the local market to grab a few things. She knew her refrigerator was empty, and that coffee was going to be necessary to do anything worthwhile in the morning.

She pulled into her driveway, opened the garage, and pulled the car in. Other than a few larger items for her classroom, the car was the only other item in there. Shutting the garage door, she walked into the breezeway and turned to lock the door behind her. It was a city thing that was unshakeable Growing up in this sleepy town, they never locked the door, but after living in Charlotte, it was the first thing she always did after getting in the house.

Gibson

Gibson had just finished tucking the kids in when he noticed a light turn on in the house next door.

Dang it, he thought, *missed her again.* The kids had watched for her off and on the entire evening, but it had gotten late. Before putting them to bed, Gibson had promised his sad eyed children, "I'll bring the cookies to her this weekend guys. Your mom is supposed to pick you up while I'm at work tomorrow." *And she'd better be on time.* His sitter, Brandi, had to leave early the next day, and Gibson had to work late.

He had put the cookies on a plate and covered them with plastic wrap earlier. They didn't look perfect, so he had only added the ones that were least burnt. The kids had tried mixing the best they could before they had gotten bored, and Gibson had tried to remember they were in the oven. The fifteen minutes had gone faster than he had expected though, and in Titus family form, only half were salvageable. It didn't matter, though. The kids wanted to give them to the new neighbor. Gibson decided he would not drop them off after he got back from the farm the next day. He knew he would be tired and would want to relax. Shaking his head, he hoped he wouldn't look like a weirdo knocking on her door with cookies on Saturday, but secretly hoped she was as pretty as Chloe had carried on about.

CHAPTER THREE

Waking up the next morning, Rose stared at the ceiling of her bedroom while lying in bed, thinking about how her day would go. Smelling the coffee brewing downstairs, she was thankful that she had unpacked the coffeemaker last night. Rolling out of bed, she headed to the kitchen, grabbing the eggs from the fridge.

Just as she was about to reach for the seasoned salt, she heard the screen door slam next door. Rose peeked out her kitchen window, catching only the back of a man walking down the driveway carrying trash bags. But that back and those shoulders was all she needed to see for her to get those butterflies moving in her stomach. Her knees felt weak. Boy, she was a sucker for a muscular upper body. It was obvious to Rose that he worked on a farm. The back of his neck and his arms were tan, and that ass was delicious. From what she could tell, he was dark-haired, tall and…

"Oh shit," she whispered, pulling her hand to her face as he turned back up the driveway, "Gibson!"

She shut her eyes and flopped to the floor. This couldn't be happening. That little boy had to be his son. He looked just like him. "How did I not see it before?"

They had met in high school. Rose had stepped off the school bus the first day of her freshman year and missed the bottom step.

"Argh!" she yelled, hitting the ground. Her backpack flew out of her hands. Everyone around laughed.

She pushed herself up from the cement and inspected her knees and hands. A hole in her favorite jeans glared back at her, but other than her knee throbbing in pain, she was ok. Searching for her backpack; she found it had landed in front of the most gorgeous boy she had ever seen. He was talking to a football player and hadn't seen the backpack in front of him. Watching as if in slow motion, she saw him catch his foot in the arm strap and then trip, placing him flat on his face with his right arm under him. He jumped up, giving a slight wince as he grabbed his arm.

Rose ran over to him. "I'm so, so sorry. I tripped and then I couldn't hold on and..." Rambling was something she did in front of guys, but this time she was tongue tied. He was gorgeous. Tall, dark hair, bigger than most, but not overweight. He was built like a football player with broad shoulders and arms of muscles. His eyes were a shade of brown, almost like chocolate, and those dimples...

"Hey, it's ok. You didn't do it on purpose." He smiled at her, still holding his arm. The smile swirled her stomach.

"Are you ok? You're holding your arm." She reached to touch him, but hesitated.

"I think so." He couldn't take his eyes off her. Noticing, Rose blushed and looked away. The heat wasn't something she was used to, at least not from a boy's eyes.

Interrupting the heat wave, the school nurse ambled over to them. "Gibson, are you ok? Tanner said you fell and were holding your arm. Football season has barely started."

"Uh, yeah, I think I'm fine." Gibson tried to brush the nurse off.

"Well, looking at the angle of your arm, I'm fairly certain that you are not." The nurse was examining his arm with a twisted face.

Both Rose and Gibson looked at it then, too. He had broken it that day, but according to him, he didn't feel the pain at all. All he felt was a connection to Rose.

Before the nurse could whisk him away, he turned to look at Rose again. "So, I didn't catch your name, and I know I've never seen you before."

"Rose, and actually my dad works for your dad on the farm. I'm a freshman this year." *Why am I blushing?*

"Well, Rose, can I get your number? I'd like to talk to you some more but apparently I'm headed to the hospital." Shocked, she nodded and fumbled through her backpack for some paper. She scribbled her number down and shoved it at him. He shot her that smile again with those dimples, sending a shock through her body. "Thanks. I'll call you later." She could only nod as he turned, walking inside.

Rose looked around at everyone who was still standing there. Her best friend Holly was staring at her, and Rose froze.

"Holls, what just happened?"

Her friend grinned at her, "Sounds like you just got picked up... by a JUNIOR ON THE FOOTBALL TEAM!" Holly let out a little squeal, causing Rose to roll her eyes.

"We'll see if he actually calls." Rose hiked her backpack onto her shoulders and walked into the building, praying she wouldn't trip anyone else. She already felt horrible. Starting her freshman year by taking out one of the football players was definitely not her plan.

That night around seven, Rose heard the phone ring. Her dad carried the cordless receiver to her room, peeked in and said with a confused look, "Um, Gibson Titus is on the phone. Why is he calling you?"

"Dad, give me the phone. I'll tell you later." She grabbed at the receiver and shut her door before stammering into the phone, "Uh, hello?"

"Hey, Rose. Um, Gibson here, the guy that tripped over your backpack? How was the rest of your first day?"

"After almost killing you, it was pretty uneventful. How's your arm?"

"Oh, ya know, cast for 6 weeks, means I'll miss most of football season, but I can deal with that."

"Gibson, I'm so sorry."

"Say that again."

"I'm sorry?"

A soft chuckle came through the receiver. "Not that."

"What?"

"My name. It sounds different when it comes out of your mouth."

"Gibson?" When she said it, her entire body flushed.

"Phew, girl. Tanner was right."

"About what?"

"You're going to be the death of me." He was laughing, and to her it was the best sound ever. They talked for another forty-five minutes before Rose's dad picked up the other phone and interrupted.

"Um, guys, I do need the phone tonight."

"Dad," Moaning, she heard him hang up again then said, "I guess that's my cue. Thanks for calling."

"Rose, wait, before you go. Uh, are you busy Saturday night? I was thinking that I could maybe take you out on a date?"

"Oh. Um, I'll have to ask my dad first. Can I tell you tomorrow?"

"Sure, night."

They were a couple from that moment on. Even at a young age, they had discovered the secret to a balanced relationship. Balancing family, friends, and time with each other. He was her first kiss. They were each other's first lovers. Everything about them screamed forever. He doted on everything that she did, and she was his biggest fan. After he graduated, he had stayed working at his dad's farm. He was a corn fed, farm boy who was slated to take over his dad's farm when the time came. Rose and Gibson were each other's fiercest friend, standing up for each other in such uniformity that no one could break them. Or so Rose thought.

Halfway through her senior year, there had been a party. Rose wasn't huge into the party scene, but any other time, she would have gone. She had caught the flu though, and that weekend stayed flat in bed. Gibson had stopped by before going, bringing her some flowers and a box of her favorite tea. He hadn't cared if he got sick, he just knew he wanted to make her happy and hopefully feel a little better. After kissing her forehead, he headed to the party. As usual, he had gotten drunk, but that wasn't even the worst part.

Holly had called Rose that next morning, "Rose, I know you're sick, but I have something you need to hear."

Rose was lying in bed, still feeling the effects of the flu. "Holly?" she groaned.

"Yes, geez, Rose. What are you dying over there?" her friend asked.

"I kinda feel like it," she responded.

"Whatever, I take it you're lying down then. You're gonna want to be when I tell you."

"Could you stop rambling and get to it, please? I'd like to go back to being dead." Rose's head was pounding, and all she wanted to do was sleep.

"Ok, last night at Cody's party, Lacey showed up." Lacey was a sophomore that Rose and Holly had taken under their wing during Lacey's freshman year. She was kind of nerdy, but super sweet. They didn't want her to get trampled on when she had joined their junior math class three weeks after school had started.

Holly continued, "I have never seen her look the way she did. She had her hair done, makeup on and that outfit was tight!"

"So what, Holly? Lacey went to a party. She goes with us all the time." If eye rolling was a tone of voice, Rose had just used it.

"Not looking like this. Anyway, that's not the news. She followed Gibs around like a puppy dog, filling his cup whenever it was empty, trying to hang on him. Then Gibson said he was leaving and walked out the door."

"This sounds like nothing. What part of 'I have the flu' don't you understand?" Rose had her pillow over her head now.

"Ok, so still not the news." Rose threw her arms up, even though Holly couldn't see her. Holly rambled on. "Lacey followed him outside. And then Cody started hollering at us, so we went to the window, well me and Kendall and Cody did, everyone else was still partying."

"Holly, please! Get to your point already!"

"Sorry, Rose. The news is that Gibson, YOUR Gibson, was outside with her and we caught them making out!!" Rose sat up straight in bed.

"Excuse me, what?" she responded. "I don't think I heard you right."

"Oh yes you did, girl. Your gorgeous, perfect, sexy ass boyfriend and Lacey were making out and then they wandered off a little out of sight. Well, no one could see what was happening, but they were out there for a full hour. ALOOOONE… When he came back in, he looked… I mean, he was drinking a lot, and he looked ruffled, shirt untucked, hair messy, something wet on his crotch. He said he had put Lacey in her mom's car and sent her home."

Rose couldn't believe what she was hearing. Her heart started to race, and the bile in her stomach began creeping into her throat. "Wait, Holly, are you sure it was Gibson? I mean, he wouldn't do this to me." She felt tears burning her eyes. "He wouldn't, I know it."

"Rose," Holly started again, "unless there is another twenty-year old guy who's tall with brown curly hair and brown eyes that hangs out with us…" her friend trailed off. "I'm sorry to have to tell you this, Rose. Shit, maybe I shouldn't have said anything. I'm so sorry."

"No, you were right to tell me, Holly. I'm glad you did. I haven't heard from him today. I just assumed it was because he was hungover or because he knows I'm sick. Which I think I'm actually going to throw up now. Bye." She flipped her phone closed and sat there on her bed, rocking in place, grabbing her pillow, and screaming into it. She flipped her phone open again and shot off a text to Gibson. Hitting each number to get the words out took forever, and because she was mad, occasionally, she had to erase a few letters and start again.

Don't ever call me again.

I cannot believe you cheated on me.

And then the next text said it all.

I thought you loved me.

I'm done.

She turned her phone off and threw it across the room. The tears were flowing wild now down her cheeks and her chest was heaving while she sobbed.

"DAD!!!!!" she yelled. She heard her dad running down the hall.

"What's wrong, Rose?" he said, busting through the door. Seeing his daughter's face, Jason rushed to her. "What happened?"

"He… he… cheated on me!" she forced through her sobs.

"Wait, what?" Jason said, looking at his daughter.

"Gibson. He cheated on me." She looked at her dad starting to sob again. Jason grabbed his daughter in a bear hug and sat with her until she had cried herself to sleep.

After closing her bedroom door, he stormed down the hallway and grabbed the house phone. He dialed John Titus' number. When John answered, all Jason could get out of his mouth was, "Tell your kid to leave my daughter alone." He didn't even wait for a response from John before slamming the phone back into its cradle.

Appalachian State University in North Carolina had accepted Rose earlier that year and until that day, she hadn't been sure what she was going to do. She needed out of this town and away from the man who she had thought was the love of her life. Gibson's deception had catapulted her out of Michigan and into North Carolina. In Rose's mind, what you do when you're drunk is what you want to do sober but don't have the balls to. There wasn't anything to talk about.

For weeks afterwards she would hear the house phone ring, her dad answering it, and growling into the receiver before slamming it back down. After about a month, he had gotten softer about it, but still would tell Gibson that she wasn't home.

Since Gibson had graduated two years prior, Rose didn't have to see him at school, although Cody would occasionally try to give her a message from him. She accepted nothing. She had ignored his calls on her cell phone, sending them straight to voicemail, letting it fill up so that he couldn't leave anymore. When graduation day came, she saw him in the crowd but didn't acknowledge him. She told her dad that as soon as campus opened, she wanted to go, and he had agreed. The day before they loaded her up and left for the long trip down south, Jason had told Gibson to stop calling.

She left her small town in Michigan that year, hoping to never have to return for more than holidays. Sure, she had come home from time to time, but always stayed clear of any place that Gibson might corner her. She had found a life that she loved in North Carolina, dating here and there, spending time in the mountains and at the beach. North Carolina had all the things she loved about Michigan, plus those gorgeous mountains that seemed to call to her almost every weekend. And now here she was back in Michigan and her neighbor was the man she had tried to run from.

Rose knew she had to work through the rest of her day with this new knowledge of him living right next door. Having lost her appetite, she dumped the eggs in the disposal and went upstairs to get ready to meet the principal.

CHAPTER FOUR

Rose

She pulled into the elementary school parking lot, still shaken from seeing Gibson. Shutting her car door, she adjusted her skirt and checked her hair and teeth in the side mirror. She took a deep breath and walked towards the door. When she got to the door, she rang the bell and a nasally sounding woman answered, "Hello?"

"Hi there. It's Rose Harper. Your new first grade teacher."

"OOOh ROSE! It's me! Kendall! Hang on, I'll buzz you in," the bubbly voice from the speaker yelled.

When she heard the buzz, she pulled the door open, met with a loud scream and the thundering sound of high heels running down the hall. Kendall Spring. They had been pretty close in school, but Rose had heard little about her since moving.

"Rose, I was so excited to hear you were the new teacher. I never thought you would be coming home. Not with Charlotte and all that big city craziness! I thought for sure some southern boy would have swept you off the market too, but I saw you're still using your maiden name! And here you are in the hallway!" Kendall was never at a loss for words. Rose laughed as her old friend carried on.

"Kendall, you have not changed a bit." she said. It was true. Except for those few pounds of what Rose could only think was baby weight, Kendall looked exactly like she did the day they had graduated. Red curly hair, bright green eyes, shorter than Rose, but bubbly and happy. "And nope, no southern boy charm could fool me into falling in love. I wanted to stop in and see my classroom and maybe meet the principal in person. Is he around?"

"He sure is. Right this way. I'm so excited to see you." Kendall kept jabbering away as she walked Rose to the principal's office.

In the front office, she introduced herself to the principal, Mr Highland. Mr. Highland showed Rose around the building, finally ending in her classroom.

When that classroom door opened, everything that she loved about teaching came rushing back to her. The smell of the classroom, like library books and candy. This was what Rose needed after the rough couple of days she'd endured. She walked to the desk and sat down. Scanning her room, she made mental notes of things to change and written notes of what she needed. She would have to look for the boxes of books she had brought with her when she got home later.

The class list was in front of her on the desk. Rose glanced over it, finding last names she recognized, wondering if any of them were children of people she knew or not. Her eyes landed on one name. Oliver Titus. She felt her blood run cold. Gibson's son was one of her students. She put her head in her hands as a single tear ran down her cheek. *How am I going to do this?* She would have to face her ex at home AND at school. For some reason, it had never crossed her mind that having his kid in class was a possibility until now.

CHAPTER FIVE

Gibson

Saturday morning, Gibson prepared to head next door. "Ok, I'm showered. Favorite white shirt, khaki shorts. Hair... eh, so so. Breath check" he puffed into his hand. He shrugged to himself, walked to the kitchen, and grabbed the plate of cookies, then walked out the door. Whistling to himself, he walked down his drive, the sidewalk and up the neighbors' walk, trying to stay off the lawn in case this new person was particular about that type of thing.

It was a little weird walking up to this house after the last few years of turmoil with Old Jack. He knew it wasn't Jack's fault that he was ornery; the man was old and didn't like kids.

Taking a deep breath, Gibson slowly exhaled and knocked on the front door.

Rose

Rose was still working on unpacking her Charlotte life into her hometown rental when there was a knock on her front door. Startled, Rose turned. She pulled the curtain back a little to peek at the porch. There he stood. *What's he doing here?*

Her hand hovered over the doorknob, but then stepped back, standing in silence. Gibson knocked again. *You knew you would be faced with him at some point.* Shaking her head, she slowly opened the door and peered up at him. The look of surprise on

Gibson's face made her realize he did not know it was Rose that had moved in next door. It appeared that his family had not informed him of his neighbor, just as her own dad had not told her. He stood there with a plate of cookies in his hand. The smile that sat on his lips turned down.

"R... Rose??" he whispered.

"Oh, um, hi Gibson," she said in the most nonchalant way she could handle.

"I... I... didn't realize.... what... no wait, why...?"

"My dad," was all she could muster. That face. She wanted to punch it and kiss it all at once. That was a feeling she didn't expect. She had harbored all that hate towards him for years, and now she wanted to sink her tongue deep into his throat the first second she saw him.

"Oh, yeah. Jason isn't doing the best. I'm sorry," he said, rubbing the back of his neck. "I guess I didn't realize you were coming home."

"And yet here I am." The annoyance in her voice was not lost on him. "So what can I do for you?" *I know what you can do for me, drop off the face of the earth... or throw me over your shoulder and take me upstairs. Stop it, Rose, he's a bastard.*

"Right, sorry. Um, so my kids said that a, um, pretty girl had moved in next door, and they had wanted to bring you cookies, but they had to go to their mom's yesterday, so they made me promise to bring them over." He realized he was rambling, so he stopped talking and thrust the plate at her. *How is it possible that she's more beautiful now than she was all that time ago?*

"Oh, well, thank them for me," she said, reaching for the plate. She looked up at him again and pushed a stray hair from her face.

"Um, yeah, so, here you go. How long are you in town?"

Pulling the plate towards herself she replied, "Well I took a teaching job at school this year so at least that long, I guess."

"I see. Rose, I'm sorry," he stammered.

"I don't want to talk about us," she said bluntly.

A smirk crossed his lips. "Uh no, I also wanted to ask if you needed someone to mow your lawn at all? I mean, I know Old Jack had a mower, but I'm pretty sure they sold all of his stuff when he moved into the home. I had been mowing his lawn for him, anyway and I was going to mow mine today so I could get yours done, too. I mean, if you would like." Gibson stumbled over his words, rambling again. *What is wrong with me?*

"Oh, I hadn't even had a chance to think about that yet. Um yeah, I mean if you have time. Doesn't look like it's been touched in a while and I haven't gotten anything for yard work yet. I'm not sure when I will be able to." The dimpled smile that crossed his face made Rose's inside tighten. *God those dimples are... snap out of it.*

"Yeah, it's been a couple weeks since the lawn service came by. I'm thinking they... never mind. Doesn't matter. I'll do it this afternoon. I'll let you get back to whatever you're doing." He turned and started walking down the steps. At the bottom, he stopped and turned back to her. "It's really nice to see you, Rose. You look great. Maybe we could go get a bite or coffee sometime soon? Try to catch up?" Again, with the rambling.

"We'll see, Gibson," she tried not to sound rude, but she wasn't sure what she was feeling.

"It's just, you left. I didn't even get to tell you my side of the story."

"I can't get into that right now, Gibson." She moved her hands to her hips. "I'm here for my dad, that's it."

"Yeah, I get it." Gibson turned to walk across the lawn but stopped short. "You know at some point, you really should hear my side of the story. It's only fair."

"There is nothing fair about the situation, Gibson. And I told you I didn't want to talk about it. Not right now." Her voice shook.

Gibson nodded, turning again leaving her yard for his own.

Rose closed the door again and shook her head. Why did he still have to make her weak in the knees? And how is it possible that he was more handsome than he was when they were younger? And two kids? He had always wanted kids. Lemonade. She needed a glass of lemonade and maybe a little vodka in it.

Gibson

"What in the actual fuck," Gibson mumbled to himself, opening the door, "She's back, and living next door, and I don't know how to act. I'm freaking thirty years old. I should be able to handle myself." He slammed the screen door behind him. "Why her? I might have to look for a new house. I can't live next to her. She still sounded like she hates me." He pulled his tee shirt off and put on the ACDC shirt he usually mowed in, then changed into his work shorts. Stomping back through the house, he had the sudden realization that he was acting like his six-year-old. He would not let her get to him, except that he had just now when he couldn't pull himself together.

He walked out to the garage and pulled the mower out, starting it up with a quick pull. His mind was running wild. *Maybe I can finally get her to listen to me.* After he mowed his lawn, he ripped his shirt off. It was WAY too hot to mow another lawn in that black rag. Gibson quickly grabbed a beer and chugged it down before moving next door to help his new neighbor out.

Rose

Moving from the front door to the kitchen, Rose grabbed her phone to call her voice of reason, Alaina.

"Wait, Rose. You're saying he came to your door with cookies, and you didn't throw them in his face?"

"Alaina," Rose knew she sounded like she was whining, "he looked so good. And he smelled so good. And he just... ugh what is wrong with me?"

"I know what's wrong with you, you've never stopped to work through your feelings. You just up and ran down here to good ole North Carolina and thought your problems would just go away," her friend always spoke with reason and was almost always right. "You'd better be careful up there. Sounds like the pulls of old fires are already burning you."

"I know, Laney." After a sigh, Rose said, "I gotta go. I wanna finish a couple things up here before I go back and see dad. Love you."

"Love you too, Rosey." Alaina would no doubt call her later to be sure nothing happened and would surely be on the next plane if she even smelled any sign of trouble.

Just as Rose was about to head up the stairs, she heard the lawn mower start out front. She peeked out the front window.

Oh, good lord, seriously? He couldn't wear a shirt while mowing? She felt her stomach tighten as he walked toward the road. Her tongue slipped across her lips. *Why did those shoulders and that back have to be so perfect?* Every muscle was popping out and those arms just looked so... so... *yummy.* She could feel herself slipping, and was that drool? She touched her chin to be sure. *Stop it, Rose. Get your shit together. Your dad needs you and you have a school year to plan for.* Rose tried to pull herself from the window but couldn't move. *Ok just one more look*, she promised herself. She pulled the curtain back again, but this time, he caught her and waved with a dopey smile on his face. She had never been turned on by a dad bod before, but his was perfect with the muscles on his chest and shoulders just enough, and that little bit of a beer tummy. This is not what she would have found attractive in Charlotte.

What is wrong with me? She stared a bit too long. Feeling her cheeks turn red, Rose gave a quick wave back before flying up the stairs.

She called Brianne, "Can you meet me at dad's?" She needed to get away from the inferno Gibson was causing her house to become.

"Sure, what's up?" Her aunt asked.

"I, um, I just want to go over things before you leave for vacation." Rose needed all the information she could get on how to help her dad.

An hour later, she was pulling into the driveway behind Brianne. With a quick hug, they walked up the front steps and into the house.

"Dad," Rose called. The sound of the TV was all the response. "DAD!"

"What, what, who." The sputtered response came from her old man. "I was dreaming that the Tigers won the world series."

"Well, that's a dream in its own right." Brianne said under her breath. Rose laughed. Her dad and his sister were always good at bantering with each other. She remembered when her mom left, Brianne was the first to jump in. Even though Bri had a brand-new baby, she still sent meals and babysat Rose when Jason was at work. They were one big, happy family.

"What brings you two over here? Am I in trouble?" Jason was looking up from his chair. Stubborn man wasn't getting up for anyone, wake him up from a nap, he'd tell you.

"I wanted to get some idea of what I needed to do while Bri is on vacation next week."

"Bri ain't allowed to be gone next week. I don't do vacations."

"Too bad, Jay. We promised the kids a trip this summer, and darn-it, they are getting it," Bri pushed back with a smirk, walking toward the kitchen. She beckoned at Rose to follow, who planted a quick kiss on her dad's balding head before following her aunt.

On the counter was a notebook. Bri opened it and pulled Rose over to her. It was all there. All the doctor's information, all the diagnosis paperwork, all of it. In big letters, the words "Parkinson's Disease" stood out, sending a small shudder through Rose. Bri leaned over to squeeze her.

"He's fine. Just slowing down a bit. He really only needs a little bit of help. We already bought one of those automatic pill spitter outters with an alarm on it from Amazon, so he remembers to take his pills. You know your dad; he thinks he's a superhero."

Because he is, Rose thought to herself. *He's Iron Man.*

"Here is the list of food that he shouldn't have. See canned fruits and veggies, no cheese, no matter how much he asks. He gets his Crunch ice cream bars and even that probably shouldn't be allowed. But you can't deprive the poor guy. Removing this stuff has seemed to help some." Bri glanced at Rose and continued, "Doctor's phone numbers. My cell, which, of course, you have. Melanie and Jacob's number from down the road in case something comes up."

"But what do I need to do? I know, cook or take him out to eat.

How is he with cleaning and everything? I mean, I don't have to bathe him, right?" She gulped.

"No sweety," Bri giggled, "He's fine. Ted installed a bar in his shower down here for him. We moved his bedroom down to the first floor as well."

Rose's eyes glistened with tears. "Brianne, I knew he was sick, but seeing him... his hands, his head. I could hear it in his voice, but..." she trailed off.

"Oh Rose. I can't imagine being away and not being able to see things change over time." She grabbed her niece's chin in her hand and looked her in her eyes. "You are going to be fine. You are your father's daughter. I know you can do it, or we wouldn't have made the decision to call you." She swiped the tear off Rose's cheek and smiled at her.

Rose grabbed her aunt and hugged her. She could do this. It would be excruciating and heart breaking, but she could do it.

CHAPTER SIX

Rose

The week that Brianne was gone sped by. Between dad's laundry, cleaning, dinners and preparing for her first day at the school, she was bushed. Brianne had called when they had gotten home on Friday afternoon to see how things had gone.

"Well, I discovered he won't eat anything I make him. Somehow, I found a pizza box in the trash on Tuesday, no idea how that got there. Other than that, it went fine, just like you told me it would."

"Well, good. I didn't figure there would be any issues."

"Was the trip fun?" Rose asked.

"It was. It's a lot to tell on the phone though. And I now have a mountain of laundry to catch up on."

Knowing Brianne was home allowed Rose to relax a bit. Enough that she thought it would be fun to head to the tavern in town. She hadn't been there since she went with her dad at Christmas a couple of years ago. Who knows who she'd run into. Holly for sure, and maybe Kendall. She hoped so, anyway. She was missing Alaina and Grace and the nightlife of Charlotte. Seeing some old friends might soothe her restlessness.

Dressing up to go to the bar in Charlotte was always a huge, extravagant activity. Find the right outfit, do the hair just perfect, the makeup was always on point. Getting ready to go down to the honky-tonk in her hometown wasn't as daunting, but still felt that way. Rose found the new peasant top she had bought just before leaving North Carolina. When she put it on, the fabric slipped off her shoulders, settling exactly where it should. She paired it with her favorite distressed shorts. Mascara, some light eye shadow, and a stroke of pink lipstick were all she put on her face before throwing some big loose curls into her hair that she prayed would stay there all night yet knowing they would fall out before she left the house. She dug her strappy sandals out of the box on the floor of her closet and double checked herself in the floor-length mirror that was still sitting on the floor. She had to get that hung before school started.

The tavern was only a couple of blocks away, so instead of driving, she decided she would walk. This time of year it stayed light out until at least nine thirty and the town was so calm, anyone would be safe walking alone after dark. It felt a bit strange heading to the bar at nine, though. In Charlotte, she and the girls wouldn't be heading out the door until ten at the earliest for a night on the town.

Taking a deep breath, she pulled the door to the bar entrance. It didn't move. Confused, she pulled again. Stepping back from the door, she found the 'open' sign blinking, and she could hear music playing inside. She pulled again. Nothing. Just then, a hand reached above her and pushed the door.

"Oh my god, I'm so dumb," she said, looking up to see who was behind her. Gibson's brown eyes stared back at her. "Oh gosh hi," she said

"Hey yourself." His eyes sliding up her body, meeting her eyes. "Gosh, huh? That's a pretty tame word from a city girl." She swallowed and turned back to walk through the door, her body still warm from his gaze. The bar was full, but not packed. Old country was playing on the jukebox. She heard laughter and smelled the fryer and old beer. With her head down, she walked to the bar.

"Let me get your first drink," she heard Gibson's low grumble say behind her.

"No thanks, Gibson, I've got it," she replied.

"Whatever you say," he said before asking the bartender, "Can I get a Budweiser?"

"I'd like a rum and coke when you get to it, please," Rose said. "And start me a tab please... if we can do that.

"Rough week?" Gibson asked, turning to her.

"I'm not sure rough is the word but I'm hoping things get easier this week."

When the music stopped for a second between songs, Rose heard a yell from the other end of the bar, "Holy Shit! Rose Harper!" and sure enough, there was Holly strutting towards her.

"Holly! Is that you?"

"Duh. I know, I know. I look good," her tall friend said, motioning around her curves. She swooped Rose into a hug. "I had heard you were home, but didn't want to bother you yet. And here you are, so we are going to get DRUNK!" Her friend had not changed. Tall, beautiful, thin, mouthy! Every guy had wanted her when they were younger, but no one could ever nail her down until Rob had moved to town. She was the wild to his calm, the high to his low, the yin to his yang.

"Let's dance, biotch." She pulled Rose onto the tiny dance floor in the corner of the bar. Laughing, Rose danced with her friend, yelling above the music for ten minutes before telling Holly that she needed to sit. She had wanted to drink a bit that night. Try to relax. Just enjoy being home in her Podunk town.

Climbing onto a bar stool at the bar, she took a sip of the sweet drink she had ordered. It tasted too good, so she took a longer pull. She scanned the room, seeing some other familiar faces. There was Thomas and Cody playing pool. Cara and Jimmy feeding each other fries in the lone booth. Some of the older folks in town, parents of kids from her class and grandparents, were playing euchre at the circular table. Small town life was such a warm lifestyle.

She got up from her seat and started to wander over to the pool tables to say hi to the boys. Just as she took her first step, her sandal strap broke and sent her flying backwards. Her glass went flying, but she didn't hit the ground. Someone's arm was around her waist. When she righted herself, she turned to thank her savior. Of course, it was Gibson. It was always Gibson.

"Whoa there. I see those feet of yours are still thinking on their own," he said laughing, "Are you ok?"

"Yes," she said, shrugging away from him. "Thank you for catching me." She forced a small smile.

"Well, I couldn't let you fall on this nasty floor looking like that," he said slyly.

"Gibs, enough."

"What?"

"The flirting. I can't take it."

"What flirting? All I'm saying is that you looked nice, and I didn't want you getting dirty. Is that all it takes to pick a girl up in big old Charlotte?"

"I just... never mind. Thank you again. I need another drink now and then I want to play some pool." she said, turning back towards the bar. "BUT I guess I'd better figure out my shoe issue first."

"Sam, you got some duct tape back there?" Gibson called to the bartender. Sam threw a roll of tape at Gibson.

"Sit," he directed Rose. Hobbling over to a table, she sat as instructed. He took her sandal in one hand and her foot in the other. The touch of his hands lit her skin on fire. She couldn't take her eyes off his hands as he worked to repair her sandal the best he could. Each gentle pull and twist sent flames up her legs that stopped at the top of her thighs. "There, that should hold it for now," he said, setting her foot on the floor. Taking her hand, he pulled her out of her seat. "Go play with those boys. I know you can whip 'em. You always could."

"Thank you again." she said, looking up at him. Trying not to be rude, she gently pulled her hand from his, for the first time realizing that the music had stopped, and everyone was staring at them. Her face flushed the hottest she had ever felt, so she quickly made her way to the pool table and said "Cody, how about you play against someone who knows what they are doing." The music started up again, and the night continued, but she was aware of the fact that she was now a part of the small-town soap opera. In fact, she was now one of the major storylines.

Gibson

Gibson returned to his barstool again and tossed the tape back across the bar. "Thanks, Sam." The bartender nodded at him as Gibson grabbed his beer. Making a little small talk with someone next to him, Gibson couldn't keep his eyes off Rose. He put an elbow behind him on the bar as he watched her smoke Cody in her first game. He laughed to himself when even Jimmy had come out of his booth with Cara to play a game. Poor Jimmy was unsuccessful too and had to be consoled by Cara.

The smile and laughter coming from Rose made him shake his head and smile, too. When she threw her head back, he imagined kissing that neck again. God, she hadn't changed much.

He shook his head to get out of the daydream just as Leggy LeeAnn strode up to him. Gibson knew what she wanted, but it would never happen. At least not in this lifetime. Sure, LeeAnn was pretty. Those legs went from the floor to the ceiling, but she wasn't anything he had ever thought about. Apparently, she had thought about him, though... a lot. She climbed onto the stool next to him and leaned in, placing a hand on his thigh.

"I've got a plan," she whispered so close to him he thought her lips brushed his ear.

"Not today, LeeAnn," he responded, not taking his eyes off Rose.

"It's not that kind of plan, silly," LeeAnn said, playfully tapping him on the arm, leaving her hand resting there, "Although, I would love that sometime. No, I think you should pretend to have a good time with me," her voice was almost a purr, "and just see how little miss flower petal over there responds."

"Nah, Lee, I'm good." The woman was closer than he felt comfortable with, and he watched as Rose put her pool stick down catching the action at the bar. "Come on, back off a little bit, huh."

"What's wrong? You got a reaction." LeeAnn laid her hand on his arm.

Gently pulling his arm from her grip, Gibson responded, "Not the way I want to get a reaction. You're a nice girl, LeeAnn, but there are plenty of guys in here that will give you the attention you want." His eyes trailed back to Rose hoping she had returned to her game. What he caught was Rose pulling what was remaining of her sandals off. She said something to Cody, who quickly went and bought three shots of tequila and what appeared to be another rum and coke. Rose, Thomas, and Cody downed a shot each. She chugged her drink, evidently asking for another, because this time Thomas ran back to the bar. Turning back to the pool table, she aimed and shot the eight ball in by mistake.

Definitely not what he wanted. LeeAnn wasn't backing down though, so Gibson pushed out of his barstool, trying to maneuver away from her.

———————————

Rose

Around one, Rose decided it was time to go. Her feet hurt not only from dancing but because she wasn't wearing shoes anymore. She felt a bit wobbly, knowing that while the first shot with the boys was fine, the second and third round was probably not a great idea. She settled her tab, gave Holly a hug and headed for the door, stopping before she got there. Rose spun to look for Gibson.

The leggy blond she had never seen before was still trying to get his attention. The feeling of jealousy attacked her out of nowhere. The girl reminded her a little too much of Lacey and she was just buzzed enough to make a fool of herself, so she did. Swinging the remnants of her sandals over her shoulder, she walked over to him, positioning herself between the blonde and Gibson and grabbed his hand. "I need you to walk me home." Her eyes were sultry, burning into his soul. His eyes widened.

"Um, I'm not heading home yet." he said, nodding toward his full beer.

"Yeah, but I'd feel better if you walked me. You know, I still kinda feel like I'm in Charlotte. It's not ok to walk home alone there," she was slurring her words slightly and stuttering.

"It's Main Street. Nothing happens on Main Street." He was smirking now.

The look he gave her caused Rose's heart rate to hit new peaks with the wave of anger and embarrassment that hit her. "I just... argh... never mind," Whipping back around, she flew out the door. *You're so stupid, Rose. You don't want him. Hell, you don't even care about him anymore. You're such a drunken harlot!* As she walked down Main Street, she heard heavy footsteps behind her.

"Wait, Rose, stop." His voice pulled at her, causing her feet to stop. As he reached her side, he continued, "I'm sorry. I'm honestly confused. One minute you're hating on me, then the next you need me to 'walk you home'," he said, flashing air quotes as he mimicked her.

"I don't know, Gibs. I just... I just saw you with legs in there and something in me fired up. Don't worry about it. I'm fine."

"LeeAnn? Rose, she's a friend. And no, you're not fine. You wouldn't have done that if something wasn't up. Talk to me Rose."

"I can't Gibson. I closed the wound you made, and the scar tissue has grown all over it. I can't bust that open again." She felt a tear slip down her cheek.

He stepped closer and lightly wiped her cheek. "Can't we try to be friends?" he asked in a low voice. He took her hand and stared at her in the light of the streetlamp.

"I can't," she said through her tears.

"Why not? Why can't we just try to be friends? Why can't we talk?" He knew he was pushing her with his questions, but she had started it.

"I just can't Gibson. I don't trust myself and I can't," she yelled. Her tone took him back, and he dropped her hand.

"I don't get it. It's been over ten years. We should be able to sit and chat things through," he responded. "Please, Rose. Evidently, we're going to be seeing a lot of each other living next door, and I just found out that you're Oliver's teacher this year. Don't you think we can just be adults and talk? That way we can at least not feel uncomfortable around each other."

Rose started walking in the direction of her house. He was still following her. Her voice shook when she said, "I'm not sure I'm gonna be able to do that. I think I'm going to have to look for a new place." She paused, stopping her steps again. "You broke me that day, you know. I try not to, but I still think about it. I didn't even hear what happened from you. I had to find out through Holly." Her voice was almost a whisper. Gibson was beside her in an instant, and she could feel him throughout her entire being. He said nothing, so she stole a look. His eyes were fixed forward, but a sadness was there.

The amount of alcohol she had consumed, allowed her brain to spew almost every thought she had about their past."Everything I knew was ripped out of my soul. All of my dreams were dashed. My heart died," she continued, "You were my everything, my entire existence. I didn't know who I was without you, and I didn't want to know. You made that choice for us, and I couldn't figure out why."

"You never let me tell you, Rose. You wouldn't take my calls, never responded to my texts. There's more to the story, Rose." His eyes were pleading with her. She turned and started walking away from him again. He followed her, determined to tell his side of the story. "More than what everyone sent around the rumor mill. I want to tell you my side. I've wanted to for all these years. Please, can't we just sit and talk?" he questioned. He remembered the regret he had felt that night. But she didn't know everything.

"What do I NOT know, Gibs, WHAT?" she said, stopping at the front walk to her house. "What could be so important that I would want to change my opinion. You literally did what I told everyone you would never do." She threw her arms forward, pointing at the houses as if they were people. "I assumed that my boyfriend wanted a real future, that he only had eyes for me. Boy, was I a stupid girl. You broke my heart like I didn't matter."

She shoved her finger into his chest.

He lowered his head and stood still. In a gruff voice, he said, "It wasn't my fault, Rose. You've gotta understand that." She huffed and turned to start walking up her front steps.

"I need a drink," she huffed. "Do you want a beer?" Her response surprised him.

"I'd better just head home. It would be better to discuss when we aren't drinking," he said. She turned and looked at him with her mouth hanging to the ground. "And see I walked you home, no boogie man got you either." He bowed then, knowing he crossed the line. He was so fed up he didn't care.

"You're ridiculous," she yelled, unlocking her front door. Then she turned back to him, flipped him the traffic finger and slammed the door behind herself. That's when she let her tears flow.

Rose didn't go to the kitchen for that drink. She went to her room. Stripped off all that she had on and put on her biggest tee shirt she could find. She just wanted comfort. As she climbed into bed, she clicked off her bedroom light and cried herself to sleep. She hadn't felt like this since that day her heart had been broken.

Gibson

Gibson walked across the lawn to his house, and then turned around again, back to Rose's porch. He did this four times before he just sat down on her porch steps. He wasn't sure why and didn't even care. His mind was a whirlwind of emotions. *First, she tells me she doesn't want anything to do with me, then she plays like I'm hers. Then back to not wanting to be around me.* But he felt the chemistry was still there. Judging by her reaction tonight, he could only guess that it was there for her, too. He sat down and put his head in his hands, drifting in and out of sleep.

Rose

The sun poked through her bedroom window. She hadn't closed her blinds before climbing into bed last night and now regretted it. Laying there, Rose replayed everything that had happened the night before. The pit in her stomach grew as she remembered the last moment. Flipping him off was probably not the most mature thing for a first-grade teacher to do, but it had felt so empowering. She pulled her cotton shorts on and walked downstairs. As she passed the front door, she glimpsed something outside. She unlocked the door and opened it to find Gibson sitting on the step.

"What are you doing?" she asked, peeking her head out and looking around.

"I'm not sure," he replied, scratching his head. "I tried to go home last night, but I kept coming back. I wanted to get things out. I couldn't leave. I'm not sure."

"That's your own fault. YOU were the one who didn't want to talk when we were drinking. OW, I need Tylenol and coffee. Do you want some?" Rose said, rubbing her head.

Gibson rose from the step and followed her into the house. He wasn't sure this was the smartest thing to do, but he couldn't stop himself.

She pulled a filter out and filled it with coffee grounds before filling the reservoir of the coffeemaker and setting it to brew. She threw a box of Entenmann's coffee cake on the counter and pulled two forks out of the drawer. Opening the package, she slid a fork to Gibson and took a huge forkful and ate it. Shrugging, he followed suit. The kids weren't around, and he wasn't trying to be a role model at this point.

"So, talk," she demanded.

Gibson tried to put into words what he had wanted to say the night before. But his head was pounding, both from the beer and the argument. He conceded.

"I think I'd better just go home. I really want to talk this through, Rose," he stood and walked to the sink where he dropped the fork, "But I have two kiddos that will be coming home soon from a week with their mom, and I need to get some sleep before they do. Oliver will want to ride bikes and Chloe, well I'll probably end up with makeup on my face before the end of the day." He turned to look down at Rose. She still took his breath away, the same way she had when she had fallen into his life all those years ago. It almost hurt his heart. Absent-mindedly, he lifted a hand to his chest. He wanted to touch her, to hold her, but he knew that wasn't happening anytime soon. When she forced herself to look up at him with those blue eyes, the hurt oozed from them. He raised his hand and put it on her shoulder. "Just think about it, ok?" and sauntered through the house and out the door.

The second the door closed, Rose threw up in the sink. Alcohol and stress had her a mess.

CHAPTER SEVEN

Rose

For the next few weeks, she went to her dad's every day with her curriculum and classroom plans in hand. She wanted to spend as much time with him as she could this summer before the school year started. She also wanted to avoid her gorgeous neighbor. Embarrassed with how she acted and unsure if she was ready to discuss anything.

Each day, Rose learned more about the disease that was taking Iron Man away, but also enjoyed spending so much time with him. The banter that they had was so normal, and she felt like home was becoming home again. He was putting on a facade that he wasn't ill, but Rose noticed that the tremors were definitely more severe and his movements were starting to slow. The research that Rose had done at the first diagnosis of his disease told her this and the fatigue he dealt with were all symptoms of stage three Parkinson's. One day, after being home for about a month, her dad asked, "So Rosey, how's it going living next door to Gibson?"

"Well, dad, the good thing is farm work tends to be crazier this time of year, so I don't see him much." She let out a sigh. Her dad smiled and nodded.

"Ugh, dad, I didn't tell you this. But we had a fight just after Bri got home from vacation." Rose's voice hinted at regret.

"Wanna tell me about it?" Jason asked.

Rose told the story to her dad. He laughed at the sandal problem and frowned at the use of the traffic finger. But never once did he say she was wrong, although he didn't say Gibson was wrong either. It was almost like old times telling her dad these things.

"So actually, you're over here every day just to avoid what's happening there? I see," Jason said, quizzically.

Rose's head snapped to her dad, "You know that's not true! I'm here to be with you."

"I know, I know, but come on, it seems pretty convenient, doesn't it?"

"I mean, I guess. But I don't want you to think that way. You are not a distraction. You're the reason I'm here, the entire reason I came home, remember?"

"Rosey, you don't have to get defensive with me. I know your reason to come home was for me. Maybe I had a little side plan myself." He didn't look at her, but he knew that there was some sort of response to that.

It was true, if looks could burn down a city, hers would in an instant. "Excuse me?" she all but yelled. "Side plan?" she stomped in front of her dad. "What do you mean by 'side plan'?"

"Rose, you weren't settling down with anyone. You and Grace haven't found anyone in that huge town. I know how you tried, though. I thought maybe bringing you home and letting you and Gibson reintroduce yourselves would solve two of my problems."

"And what two problems are those, Jason." She only called her dad by his first name when he pissed her off and when he acted like a child. Both were happening right now.

"Well, I wanted you to be here with me, to spend some quality time while I still had quality time left in me."

This made her sad to hear him say, and she immediately felt bad for getting mad at him. "And?" She pushed in a gentler tone.

"And I would love to be able to walk my daughter down the aisle, while I can still walk, and maybe have some grandkids to keep me smiling."

"Awe dad," Rose started feeling a lump in her throat, "But you can't force that second part. You know as well as I do, he broke me. I don't know if that's repairable. I don't know if I WANT it to be."

"Even if it isn't, there are a lot of other farm boys around here. My daughter is beautiful, intelligent, and kind. You could get any guy and then stay around for the rest of my days." The look on her dad's face was almost boy-like. She had known that eventually there would be some words of wisdom. She just wasn't ready for those words when they came.

"You know Rose," he started, "when your mom left us, it was hard at first. The betrayal and broken heart. I never thought I would heal. I had thought she and I would be like your grandparents, together forever." He sighed, and she opened her mouth to say something.

He held up his hand. "She was wrong for leaving, but we were young. I'm not happy with how she left us, but I wanted her to be happy. When you were about thirteen, she called to talk to you." Rose's eyes widened. This was news to her. "You weren't home, but she promised to call back the next day. I didn't tell you so that you didn't get your hopes up. I waited by the phone that entire next day to be sure we didn't miss that call. She didn't call. I don't know what I'm trying to tell you."

Jason shook his head before he continued again. "I forgave Dana the day she let me know she wasn't coming home because if I didn't I would have festered the anger and hurt and you would lose two parents. I wanted you to have a happy childhood and me being angry would have kept that from you." reflectively he said, "All I wanted was for her to be happy. Rosey, you need to be happy."

CHAPTER EIGHT

Rose

A few days after that conversation with her dad, she had thrown a roast in the slow cooker with some carrots and potatoes. Rose knew she could never eat it all. She wanted to apologize for how she had acted the night after the bar but didn't want to give him any thought that there could be a reconciliation. Pacing in front of the refrigerator, she picked up her phone only to set it down at least three times.

"Grow up, Rose." her own voice startled her. "You need to try to get through this. You're not going to be able to avoid him forever." *Besides, the girls are right, you've never let him go.* So she extended an olive branch to her old beau, calling Gibson's cell phone. "Thank god" she muttered when his voicemail picked up. "Uh, Gibs, um Gibson, it's Rose... Um I just wondered if you'd... I mean, I made a roast for dinner, dad already had dinner, there's too much here for me to eat... I mean it will probably spoil before I can... erm, wondered if you wanted to stop after work and grab some." her hand met her forehead, "If you aren't too tired, feel free to stop over and get some. I mean get some roast. Yeah, so bye." Ending the call in a fury, she laid her head on her arm. *So smooth, idiot.* Food had always been the way to his heart when they were young. She'd hoped that hadn't changed.

Around seven thirty that night, there was a gentle tap on Rose's front door. When she answered, Gibson was standing there in his jeans, dirty shirt, and work boots, but looking oh so yummy to her. He slowly entered the house, turning sideways to pass her. He gently brushed her body with his, looking down at her face. A volcano erupted in her body.

"Hey, I heard there was food," he said with a sheepish smile. His voice was smooth and dark, sending a shiver through her.

"There is," she replied, gathering her thoughts, and walking to the kitchen, "Sit down, I'll get you a plate." She grabbed a beer from the fridge as well and sat them both in front of him.

"So, how's life on the farm?" she asked, not knowing what to say and feeling completely stupid for the question.

He tilted his head a little. "Life on the farm?" But then took a bite of the roast, letting out a moan, "Oh my god, what did you do to this? It's amazing!"

"My secret recipe." Please, God, don't let him moan like that again.

They made small talk for about ten minutes, and then she broke Alaina's rule. "So, I think we need to talk." "Ok... about?" he said mid bite.

Rose took a deep breath before locking her eyes on his. "About how I was drunk a while back. About how I just assume things and never let you explain. About how we will be living next door to each other for a while." She dropped her head before finishing. Looking up at him through her eyelashes, she whispered, "About how we both know there's still an ember that hasn't burned out."

His breath hitched at the last sentence. After a second, he said, "Well, first, drunk you is someone new to me. She's wild, and to tell you the truth, kind of hot. Second, you were right and have always been right to be mad. But I need you to know the whole story." He stopped. Gazing into her eyes, he said, "Third, you're not moving? I mean, I knew you wouldn't be able to find anything, but who knows what Jason can do when it comes to his daughter." She smiled, hearing him talk about her dad like that.

"Let's talk about the fourth subject when we're ready." Gibson's eyes smoldered when he said it, sending a wave through her body. He took another bite and leaned back, rubbing his stomach.

"Woman! That roast!"

"Woman, huh," she said, grabbing his plate.

"Ok, sorry, ma'am." He took a swig of his beer, watching her walk through the kitchen back to her seat. His eyes dragged across her body. The switch of her hips pulled at his groin.

"Alright, sir, speak. I want to hear what you say is the full story."

Her voice snapped Gibson back to the conversation. "Huh, oh right," he replied. "See, Rose, I was drunk, but I swear to you I didn't initiate anything. Lacey kissed me, but I pushed her back and told her no." Rose wanted to cover her ears. It made her stomach knot up and she thought she was going to puke, but she kept listening.

"I had tried to walk away to my car to go home but Lacey stopped and tried to kiss me." He stopped, and voice saddened, "I did kiss her back the second time she came at me but then realized what I was doing. Then she dropped to her knees and tried to, well let's just say my zipper stuck, thankfully." Quickly he added, "Not that I would have let that happen, anyway. Rose, I was young and drunk, and I don't know, dumb."

"Well, dumb is the understatement of the year." Rose said, annoyed, feeling her anger well up again. "Holly said you guys were gone for a long time. What happened then if you guys weren't screwing in the weeds?"

Gibson's eyes widened. "You think we... ha, not even close. Lacey had thrown up. I was trying to be a friend, holding her hair back. I swear to you, Rose, nothing happened." He stopped his story, and they sat in silence for a few minutes.

"I'm not sure about your story, Gibson. It's hard for me to believe you when everyone told me otherwise."

"I know, Rose, but they weren't all there. No one was outside with us." He was determined to have her understand. "I was so drunk. I knew I hadn't, you know, gone that far. But I wasn't sure what was real."

Gibson shook his head, and quietly said, "It wasn't until after you left that Lacey finally came clean about what had happened. No one wanted to believe her, including me, but she was adamant. Rose, she insisted I told her to stop it because," he stopped. His eyes grew intense when he looked at Rose and finished, "Because I only wanted you, Rose." He breathed a sigh from his mouth, looking away. "Even if I had known before you left, I wouldn't have stopped you from leaving, though. You have always been the one of us who would be able to go and make something of yourself. Once you made the decision to go, I couldn't get in your way."

Rose couldn't believe what she was hearing. "Wait, hold on. We could have had everything we wanted... And you let me go?! Even after you knew, you could have said something. I would have come back home after school instead of staying in Charlotte!"

"Would you, though, Rose? Jason told me how happy you were there. How you had made some great friends and how you were living your dream life. I couldn't rip that out from under you. Did I wish that maybe you would come home? Yes, God, yes. But at that point, I knew it was over and time for me to move on."

"I don't ... I don't understand."

"It was all for you, Rose. I loved you so much... I still love you, although I didn't realize it until you came home a month ago. It's always been you."

Rose felt a stray tear fall down her cheek as she pushed up from her chair. She started pacing around the kitchen. "No, this isn't happening. Gibson, not now. I have so much going on with dad and school. Why are we doing this now?"

"You wanted to talk," he stupidly said. But she nodded. He was right. She had brought it up tonight.

Her head was spinning. Mindlessly, she started running water to do dishes; she didn't know what else to do. Soap in, bubbles growing, heart pounding, brain spinning, heart pounding... heart pounding. She felt him move behind her. He didn't touch her at first, but she knew he was there. The air was thick with his scent and her want. He touched her shoulder, letting his hand slide down her arm. She froze, feeling the lightning pulse through her. As his hand moved back up, she cautiously turned to look at him. His face turned down to look her in the eye, causing her to lift her chin up to look back.

He dipped toward her but then his lips slipped toward her ear, and he whispered, "I'm sorry I let you go."

His breath in her ear made every cell in her body scream for him. "I'm not sure what to think, Gibson," her tone teetered on breathy. He had her pressed against the sink, both of his hands on either side of her, their faces close, his desire pushing against her stomach.

"I need to know how to prove this to you, Rose." She could feel every part of her insides tighten at the lowness of his voice. His breath was hot on her face, and she was suddenly aware of her shallow breathing. Her skin was tingling. She closed her eyes as she shook her head.

"I don't know," she said with a sigh, looking at him again. He leaned closer to her mouth.

"It's always been you," he repeated. His gaze darted to her lips then back to her eyes. A small sound came from her mouth and that was it. His mouth met hers with ten years of built-up need. She let it happen, hell, she wanted it to happen. Closing her eyes, her mouth moved with his, dipping their tongues together, moans escaping from both of them. It lasted all of twenty seconds, but both of their hearts were pounding.

She broke away first, shocked at herself for letting it get to that point. His hand was still on the small of her back, holding her tightly to him. She looked at him with too much need but said, "We can't do that again. You don't know how hard I worked to put you in a box in the back of my heart, Gibson. This isn't what we should be..." and he kissed her again.

This time she melted into his arms, grabbing the back of his head, and wrapping his hair in her fingers. He lifted her with the one arm that was around her and started towards the living room. Unconsciously, she wrapped her legs around his waist. In that moment, Rose realized she was throbbing against his body, and it was intensifying with every step he took towards the couch. He never left her lips. When he set her down, he laid her back and spread on top of her. His member was ground against her, rubbing in the spot that she wanted it to. The second she started to enjoy it was the second that panic flashed across her and she pushed him back.

"I can't do this," she blurted. "I mean I can, but I can't. I cannot let you just waltz in here and say those things, and everything is all better. That's not how it works."

Gibson sat back against the arm of the couch, rubbing his temples. "I know, I'm sorry, Rose. I really am. I just... couldn't we try again? We can't start all over from the beginning, but maybe we can carve a new start."

She sighed. More than anything, she wanted to be with him, be able to fall back into what they had before. It had been ten years, though, and she was a different woman than she was then. She reached across the couch and took his hand. He looked at her inquisitively.

"I'm not saying yes," she said. "I'm saying prove your version of the story and maybe we can try to work through this. I wish I could just believe what you say, but..." The sides of his lips turned up slightly, making those dimples pop again. He nodded.

"Ok." He squeezed her hand, brought it up to his mouth and dropped a small kiss on the back of it. His eyes met hers causing her body to light on fire again.

She quickly stood. "You should probably go before things get out of hand again," she said sweetly. Gibson nodded and rose from his seat. He put his hands on both sides of her face, leaning down to kiss her forehead. She closed her eyes to cherish the warm feeling that was left there. Walking to the door, Gibson looked back at her, still standing next to the couch.

"Thanks for dinner and dessert," he said with a wink.

"Get out of here," she said, laughing, throwing a couch pillow at him. He closed the door behind him, and she locked it. She stole a quick peek through the curtain before turning out the living room light.

Heading back to the kitchen, Rose grabbed her phone, shooting a text to Grace. She needed to talk to someone who wouldn't judge her or talk sense into her. She started washing the dishes, still mesmerized by what had just happened. Praying that Gibson would find a way to prove his version to her, but also praying that he didn't. Confused, she was in a place in her heart she hadn't visited in a long time. The ring of facetime shook her out of her trance.

"Hey Grace," she said, answering and setting the phone on the windowsill in front of her.

"Hey yourself. You must be in a pickle if you need my single ass to talk to," Grace replied, smiling. Rose missed her friends dearly, and seeing Grace's sweet face with her wild, curly hair pulled into a ponytail made her heart hurt a little.

A sigh escaped her lips, "Grace, tonight went wrong."

"Oooo tell me all about it," her friend squeaked.

"Ok, but you CANNOT tell Alaina!" Rose warned her friend.

Grace's smile was more mischievous with the warning. "This sounds better than I was hoping. Spill."

Rose spilled the beans about the events of the evening. Seeing Grace's facial responses throughout the entire story looked like she was watching a romance movie. After she finished, Grace was just staring at her.

"So, wait," Grace shook her head, "you're telling me you let this hot ass man into your house to eat your famous pot roast and didn't expect sparks to fly? Girl, that roast makes ME want to sleep with you and I don't swing that way!"

"I didn't think roast was a turn on," Rose shrugged with a little smile.

"Rose! Seriously, I know you think you have him in this little box packed away in your mind, but do you realize that since you moved here ten years ago, you have compared every guy you've dated to him. Hell, you've compared every guy Alaina, or I have dated to him."

Rose flinched at that. "No, I haven't," she said firmly.

"Yes... you have," Grace responded, "Think, Steve not tall enough, Rod not corn-fed, George no dimples, that guy from the frat. What was his name? Anyway, he didn't look as good in a flannel. I can keep going if you'd like."

Rose's hand flew to her mouth. "Ok, Grace, I get it," she said, but after a minute she conceded, "Maybe you're right."

"Of course I am. No one else has had a chance, Rose. You've never given up on the dream life with Gibson. Now tell me about the whole makeout session. You KNOW I love the dirty details."

"Nu-uh Grace. All you get to know is that my clothes stayed on and so did his."

"No hands wandering? No grinding?"

Rose glared at her friend until a small smile touched her lips. "Fine, there was inappropriate touching that I might have started. But I stopped it before his hips could…"

"Oooh, don't stop now, his hips could what?" Grace wanted to hear something she wasn't going to get.

"Nothing. Just know that the fire… still very much there."

"You suck, Rose. Why won't anyone give me more details." Grace shoved back into her seat in defeat, pulling a laugh from Rose.

"Because Grace, no one is as casual about sex as you are. I swear if you got offered a spot in a porn you'd jump at the chance."

"Not true. But if Chris Hemsworth asked… let me hang up your hammer so you can…"

Rose threw her hands up at the phone, laughing, "Stop. I know what you're going to say. Let's change the subject now." The rest of the twenty minute conversation revolved around Rose's dad and Grace's obsession with the new guy in her building. The entire conversation, though, Rose's mind was next door.

CHAPTER NINE

Rose

The next week, Rose was at the grocery store picking up some items for her dad. As she reached for the shredded wheat, she heard a timid, "Hey" behind her. She spun around and was face to face with Lacey Evans.

"Um, hi," Rose said, curtly.

"I'm glad I ran into you here, Rose." Lacey looked a little more run down than most of the friends from school Rose had run into over the last few weeks. She had four kids in her shopping cart, a huge stain on her shirt that looked like some sort of spit up and bags under her eyes that made her appear older than she was. "Ok, I'll bite. Why?" Rose asked.

"I ran into Gibson the other day," her foe said. Rose must have had a look of disgust on her face because Lacey said, "He begged me to talk to you. I told him I guess I could. Then he asked... well, I have something I need to show you sometime."

"Do you? Well, I'm not sure I want to see anything you want to show me, Lacey. And I'm not sure that I can continue to talk to you cordially in front of your kids here."

"Rose, I'm serious. I feel bad and Gibson asked if I still had this. I didn't think that I did. A video from eleven years ago taken on a flip phone? But then I remembered I had stored it on the cloud, or whatever, because it reminded me of when I was young and dumb. And that I had kissed the hottest... never mind." The blush on Lacey's cheeks did not go unnoticed by Rose. "He asked if I had it and I do and I guess I have to show it to you."

"What are you talking about? And what does Gibson have to do with this?"

"The video, Rose. THE video of me and Gibson making out," she replied bluntly and a little too loudly.

Rose's mouth dropped to the floor. The video that Gibson had mentioned that night last week. *Could it have been true? Did I just waste eleven years of what would have been the perfect life being mad about something that could have been fixed right away? It was his fault I left, though. He didn't try to stop me... or did he? He had called every day until I moved. Oh god, did I sabotage myself because I was stubborn like my mom?* Her internal struggle was showing on her face.

"You ok, Rose?"

"So, how do you want to do this?" Rose asked Lacey.

"Well, we obviously both have grocery shopping to finish, and then I have all these dang kids to get home and fed. I can see if Henry will watch the kids tonight, and I can come to you. It'd be a chance to get some time in the car alone."

"I have to help my dad tonight," Rose said defensively. She wasn't sure if she wanted to see that video or if she was ready to feel the pain.

"Ok then, tomorrow? It won't take long, I promise. And I won't stay. I'm just doing this to make Gibson happy and maybe apologize after all this time?"

Just then, a woman's voice came from behind Rose. "I should have known it was you, Lacey. Are you still talking about my Gibson?" Rose turned and was face to face with Lorna, Gibson's ex-wife.

"I'm sorry? Your Gibson?" Rose noted Lorna was swaying a bit and had a cart full of liquor. It seemed like an odd combination, but then again, she was a mom.

"Yeah, Lacey here's been after my Gibson since high school. Oh, wait," A note of recognition covered Lorna's face, "I remember you." She pointed at Rose. "You're the girl that left him. Ha, thanks, babe. You have NO idea what you lost."

"Rose, you remember Lorna Jacobs, don't you? She was in the grade below me." Lacey was shaking her head at the condition the woman was in.

"Oh right, yeah. Hi Lorna."

"That's Ms. TITUS to you." Lorna gave a vicious smile. "Lacey, don't you think it's time for you to let your Gibson fetish go? And, Rose," Lorna drew her name out longer than it should have been, "welcome home." The woman turned, and with a little stumble, pushed her cart towards the checkout. Rose looked at Lacey with a questioning look.

"Boy, she looks like shit today." Lacey looked concerned.

"Yeah, what's that all about?"

"Looks like she fell off the wagon again. Not really sure, but I've heard other rumors too."

Rose shook her head, trying to make sense of what she had just seen. Turning her thoughts back to the conversation she had been having with Lacey, "So, uh, where were we? Oh, right, can you be at my house around seven tomorrow? Don't expect us to become friends again, though, Lacey."

Lacey nodded. "Seven it is. Thanks, Rose." She turned back to her cart of kids and walked away. Almost like anything that was just said didn't matter.

Rose let out a huge breath and held herself up with the cart. Her legs were like jelly, and she felt her heart pounding.

Driving from the store to her dads, she passed the school. She caught a glimpse of two kids on the swings with their dad pushing them. It was Gibson and his kids. The little girl was laughing, and the little boy was trying his hardest to pump his legs. She could see the overflow of dimples on all three faces all the way in the car.

After pulling into her dad's drive, Rose opened the trunk. Her dad gingerly descended the front steps.

"Did you remember my crunch bars?" It was always the first question when she got his groceries.

"Do I ever forget them, dad?" she said with a giggle. "Now grab those front bags and I'll get the frozen inside. It's freaking hot out today. I'd hate for you to lose your crunch bars to the heat."

Together, she and her dad unpacked the groceries. When they finished, Rose made some lemonade and gave Jason his second dose of medication for the day. The doctor had him up to three doses per day now. There had been minor improvements in the shakes and the stuttering, but the disease kept him slow.

She ripped the Band-Aid off to ask her dad a big question. "Dad, how do I know if it's best to follow my heart or my mind?" she said suddenly, "I mean, I thought I was doing what my heart wanted living down in Charlotte, but the more I'm home, I feel like I never should have left."

"Well, kiddo, sometimes we do something that at the time is the right thing. You had to go. I was so proud of you for going. You needed that space from me and this place to find yourself. Then it runs its course. I know coming home wasn't what you were planning on doing, but I'm not sorry I asked you," he said, looking at his glass.

"Dad, I'm glad I came home. I want to help. I was lucky to find a job so close too," she said. After a brief pause, Rose asked her next question. "Did you ever find it hard to love after mom left? I remember you dating some of the single moms and I thought for sure that Holly and I were going to be sisters at one point," she giggled, "She and I used to sit up at night playing out your and Mindy's wedding when we were twelve." She shook her head at the memory. "But you never settled down. Why?"

"I don't know. No one did it for me like your mom. Sometimes I wonder if she waltzed through that door today, would I take her back? I don't know, maybe. Don't get me wrong, I still hate that she left us. It makes me angry at least once a day. But we turned out ok. I got curious once though. I looked her up on Facebook a few months ago."

He looked at Rose with a sheepish look, scratching the back of his head, his cheeks a little pink. Rose's mouth opened and then closed, not sure what to say. "I found her, still as beautiful as the day I met her in high school. A little older, but that smile took my breath away... still... even now talking about it makes my heart jump a little." He looked down again at his glass and wiped a drop of condensation away.

"Dad, I didn't realize this was how you felt," she whispered.

"I messaged her." Jason looked as surprised at his admission as Rose.

"What?!?! Dad!" Her eyes were the size of half dollars. She couldn't believe she was hearing this for the first time.

"I know. I know. I was feeling vulnerable." Jason put his hands up. "The doctor had just told me I wasn't allowed to drive anymore, and I was starting to feel like I would never have a chance to reach out to her or see her again. It was a dumb move, I know."

Softening her tone again, she asked, "Well, did she respond?"

"Yes," he looked up at Rose, "She told me she missed us but that she wasn't leaving her life in Mexico. She also said she... she stopped loving me long before she left. Said she realized she never really wanted to be tied down." His voice was sad.

"When she left us, dad, I never wanted to talk to her again. I never have. I just don't know how to react to this. She broke our family, dad. She broke you and left me without a mom!" Rose huffed . "I can't believe this."

She stood and walked to the counter to pour another glass of lemonade, before walking out the back door to the patio. She heard her dad sigh behind her. Staring at the backyard, she re-played what had just happened. Sputtering to herself, Rose said, "What was he doing? Why wouldn't he have told me this? It was a good thing I came home when I did. It's obvious he still doesn't act like an adult. What in the world was going on in my life? First Gibson, now this?"

She yelled out, "What the hell, dad!" She sat down at the patio table and put her head in her hands. She heard the screen door open with a creak, heard the chair scrape across the concrete next to her, and felt his hand on her shoulder.

"I'm sorry I didn't tell you, Rose," he said in a strong tone, "But I didn't think I needed to tell you if nothing was going to come of it. But now that you're here and I know I'm the one who asked you to, I wanted to be one hundred percent honest with you," he sighed, "I just, it's always been her, Rose."

She lifted her head and looked at her dad. "What did you just say?"

"It's always been her. My heart couldn't be with any other woman because it's always been her." He looked at his daughter, seeing her mother in her eyes.

"That's exactly what Gibson said to me the other night," she said in disbelief.

"The other night?" Jason tilted his head. "What? Rose? What happened?"

"He said it just like that. Gibson said his marriage to Lorna didn't work out, and he was sure it was because he never stopped loving me. He said it, just like you did, it's always been me." She said, realizing she was smiling.

"I knew that too," Jason said sheepishly.

She snapped her head to look at her dad. "What do you mean you knew that too?"

"Come on, Rose. You were asking me about this exact issue in the house. Besides, I've thought since your freshman year that you two were good together. A little too good at that point in your life. It was another reason that I knew you needed to leave and fly on your own. If it's meant to be, it's meant to be. You flew back to your nest, not just for me, but for your heart, too. I'd like to think I've had a hand in this. See, my second problem is getting solved too!" Her dad sat back in his chair, a look of pride crossing his face.

She couldn't believe what she was hearing. She knew she had broached the subject, but she wasn't sure if she was ready to get the answer she was getting.

"Dad, I'm not ready to do this. Not with him. I can't just forgive and forget."

"Rose, just listen to him. Please, do it for me?"

"If I do this, I'm not doing this for you. I'm doing it for me and my happiness. I'm the one who has to live with whoever." Jason sighed, knowing his daughter was right. The second he shot her a goofy smile, Rose groaned. "Let's go inside, dad." She pulled herself out of her chair and helped her dad up. Rose could tell this conversation had taken a bit of a toll on her dad. He looked tired. So, after cleaning up the kitchen, and leaving a few notes for her aunt, Rose settled her dad in for a nap, kissed him on the cheek and drove home.

CHAPTER TEN

Rose

The kids were out front playing when she pulled into the driveway. "Hi Rose!" Chloe yelled, waving her tiny little hand at Rose.

"Hey kids. What are you up to?" Rose said, walking to their driveway.

"Dad bought us CHALK!" Oliver showed her the blue piece he was holding in his chalk covered hand. Rose smiled at him.

"I see this. What are you drawing?" She looked at the driveway that was covered with rainbows, horses (or what she thought were horses) and people.

"I'm drawing you a flower!" Chloe proclaimed. She looked up at Rose, who was trying hard not to laugh. Chloe's little face was covered in chalk, as were her little yellow tee shirt and her jean shorts. Gibson was going to have a hard time getting those clothes clean. The kids were laughing and having so much fun.

"You guys are doing such good work," she said to them both. "I've got to go work on my school stuff, though. I wish I could stay out and draw with you both!"

"Stay, Rose!" Oliver pleaded.

"I can't bud, I've got a lot of work to do."

"Pleeeeaaaassseeee, can't you stay? Just this one time?" Chloe asked.

Rose smiled. "Oh, ok. You've got me for a half hour," Rose said, squatting down and grabbing a piece of pink chalk.

"YAY!!!" both kids yelled. It was so sweet that Rose giggled, but it also made her heart break a little. These kids could have been hers if she would have just let the full story come out all those years ago. As she scraped the chalk against the sidewalk, she heard the screen door open on the side of the kids' house. When she looked up, Gibson was staring at them with a weird smile on his face.

"Well, hey there," he said to Rose.

"Hi, Gibson." She looked back at the concrete.

"Daddy! Rose is drawing with us!" Oliver said excitedly.

"I see that," he said, walking over to them, "I was just coming out to tell you both to wash up for dinner." The kids both groaned but did as they were told and walked to the house.

Oliver stopped part way to the house and looked up at Rose. "Rose, can you play after dinner?" His brown eyes wide as he asked.

"I'll have to see what I can get done before then, kiddo," she said, ruffling his hair as he sulked past her.

Gibson squatted down next to Rose. "Are you hungry at all?"

"Actually, I just got back from dad's and need to work on my school stuff," she looked at him. Those deep brown eyes melted her every time, but she had to stay strong. She had to wait and see what was on that video. "I saw Lacey today," she whispered to him. His hand stopped short of the piece of chalk he was reaching for.

"Oh, yeah?" he said.

"Yeah, for some reason I agreed to her coming over tomorrow," she said, grabbing a piece of chalk and putting it into the bucket, "She says there is something that I HAVE to see.... oh, and that you had talked to her and was forcing her to show this to me?" She turned her face to see his response.

Gibson let out a small laugh. "I wouldn't say I'm FORCING her to show you, but I may have implied that if she didn't, my life would be over. Oh, and I offered to paint her front porch for her since her loser of a husband won't do anything."

Rose smiled, "A little dramatic, don't you think?" Turning back to the chalk she said, "Well, I'll be interested to see this old-fashioned flip phone video." She stood up and twisted from side to side, trying to loosen the stiffness that the stooping had caused. Gibson stood too and brushed a stray hair from her face. His hand lingered on her a moment too long.

"Hopefully that old-fashioned flip phone video helps me get what I want," he said in his low voice. She felt her cheeks flush.

"Um, I also saw Lorna today."

Gibson's body froze. "Did you? Where?"

"The grocery store, same time I saw Lacey. She was a hot mess, swaying all over, and she had a cart full of liquor." She searched Gibson's face.

"She was probably shopping for her mom." Gibson paled a little but shrugged it off. Rose was still worried. His face said more than shopping for her mom.

"DAAADDDD, Oliver threw water at me!" Chloe's shriek came from inside the house, breaking the moment, and both Rose and Gibson laughed.

"I'd better get in there before there is a full-on water fight in the kitchen again."

"Again?" she laughed

"You have no idea." He was rolling his eyes with a smile. "Maybe we'll see you after we eat?"

"Maybe," even though inside she was yelling, *YES!*

Working on her classroom decorations was the only thing Rose could muster after today. She pulled the Amazon box out of her bedroom closet and let it slide down the stairs to the living room. Grabbing her label gun out of the entryway closet, Rose sat down on the living room floor. Opening the box put a smile on her face. Creating new storage for her new classroom was something that she was excited about.

She had taught for so long in the inner city of Charlotte that teaching in her small town was a brand new, exciting adventure. Rose went down the list of kids' names, labeling a storage bin for each of them. Being a new teacher six years ago, she had only been able to find substitute teaching gigs for the first six months. The big break came for her when an elementary school in downtown Charlotte called, needing a first-grade teacher. She had gone immediately for the interview, and they handed her the job the next day. The school was as desperate as she was.

That first year, she questioned her decision of choosing that school and also choosing her profession. Those kids pushed and pulled her heart all over the grid. By the end of that first year, she was tired, but found it was a good tired. The year after that was easier, as she had found her groove. The ebbs and flows of the family dynamics for each child became the music to her life.

Now she was in a whole new world of teaching. These kids were a stark contrast to the families in the inner city. Rose was excited, but she truly missed those kids. They were where her heart had learned to want to be. She thought that there was no way these kids would need her as much as the kids she was used to teaching. Her heart felt homesick for the normalcy of Charlotte. While some things were tough there, at least it was home.

Looking at the picture next to her couch of the last class she'd taught before moving home, her heart hurt. Every class she had taught had always come back to see her the following years. They were all special to her.

Last year's kids wouldn't be able to come see her, they wouldn't be able to rely on her for support anymore. It was the second time since she arrived that she regretted moving home. No, she didn't regret it. She just wished she was still there, helping the kids who truly needed her.

She had grown thicker skin each year and had her heart broken many times by kids coming in with new bruises or unbathed, or in tattered clothing. The list was endless. On more than one occasion, she had to report child abuse to the authorities. Even through all those heartbreaking moments, she would never have changed a thing. Those kids were why she went to work each day. She knew this year was going to be a lot different, but there would be struggles. She was ready for anything.

CHAPTER ELEVEN

Rose

Around seven, she peeled herself off the floor to grab a beer from the fridge. It was then that she remembered the kids had wanted her to come back over. She felt her heart drop. Timidly, Rose peeked out the kitchen window, but there was no movement outside.

"So dumb, Rose," she said out loud to herself. She knew she had to finish what she was working on, but still felt like she had let those kids down a little. Or maybe they didn't even remember that they were playing outside with her... yeah, right. She knew better. Kids that age don't forget anything. She peeked out the window again and saw Chloe's little face looking out the side door.

Crap, Rose thought, *they're heading to bed*. She slipped on her flip-flops and all but ran across the lawn to the side door of Gibson's house. She lifted her hand to knock. As she did, she heard the pitter patter of feet charging towards the door.

"You forgot about us!" Chloe said, swinging the door open, pushing through the screen door to stand in the driveway. She was already in her pajamas and had a splatter of toothpaste on her shirt.

Rose bent down and squeezed the little girl. "I didn't forget you, doll. I just got carried away getting things ready for your brother's classroom. I'm so sorry,"

Chloe moved her hands to Rose's face, pulling it in front of her. Looking into Rose's eyes with the same color brown eyes that her dad had, she asked quietly, "Do you think you can read me my bedtime story, Rose?"

"Who are you talking to, Clover?" Rose heard Gibson's voice from somewhere in the house. Chloe turned in response to her nickname.

"Clover?" Rose asked.

"Yeah, that's my nitname." Chloe's eyes danced when she responded.

"Your NICKname, Chloe." Gibson came into view just then, wearing a white tee shirt and grey sweatpants. The sight of him made Rose swoon a little. "Well, hey there," he said, a smile creeping across his face, flashing his deep dimples.

Chloe started jumping up and down in the driveway. "Look, daddy, Rose is here! She's gonna read me my bedtime story!"

"Wait, I didn't..." Rose tried to interject.

"Oh, is she?" he eyed Rose. "We thought you forgot about us," he said warmly.

Rose felt her face flush. "I know. I was just telling Chloe that I got wrapped up in getting stuff ready for Oliver and his classmates and lost all track of time."

Gibson leaned forward, pushing the screen door open. Chloe scampered inside. He nodded his head to the side, motioning for Rose to follow. "She already has her princess book picked out. You'd better follow her to her room."

"Um, ok," she said, lifting her eyes to his. His smile still sat on his lips. As she brushed past him, his woody scent wrapped around her. It was almost intoxicating how everything about him made her lose all sense of herself.

Evidently, Rose was moving too slowly because Chloe grabbed her hand, pulling Rose with strength that no little girl should have. "Come on, my room is this way!" she said with a squeal. Gibson followed as the little girl guided Rose through the house.

"Is that Rose?" she heard Oliver yell.

"Yes, and she is going to read me my princess book!" Chloe responded in a way that sounded a lot like "Na na boo boo". Gibson released a tiny snicker, causing Rose to glance behind her. His eyes flicked to hers, the deep brown of them drowning her soul.

"Good luck," Gibson said as he walked into what she assumed to be Oliver's room.

After reading what ended up being Cinderella and tucking Chloe in tight like a burrito as she had requested, Rose walked back into Gibson's kitchen. He was just pulling two beers out of the fridge. He turned, waving one at her. "Wanna go sit on the patio?"

"Sure," she shrugged, grabbing the beer from his hand.

"Go pick your seat. I'm gonna check and make sure Chloe isn't trying to sneak reading another book."

Rose pushed open the door, heading to the patio, settling into one of the chairs. The sound of crickets singing to each other filled the air as the first fireflies of the night were dancing to the music. She closed her eyes and took a deep breath. The smell of hay and cow manure was something that she had hated when she was younger, but now that she was home, it brought a sort of nostalgia.

The screen door creaked, causing Rose to open her eyes. Gibson was lowering himself into the chair on the other side of the table, "Hey." His eyes warmed her body. The shock of the feeling pulled her gaze back to the sky. They sat in silence for a few minutes, watching the sun settle lower in the sky and the first stars peek through the flawless sky. Breaking the silence with a sigh, she took a pull on her beer before blurting, "How did I walk away from all of this? Living in the city, you forget how beautiful the stars are. My apartment in Charlotte is right downtown and it's so bright from the lights that you just can't see them this clearly, it takes a drive out of town." A hint of sadness hung in her voice.

Gibson looked over at her, "You just had to get away and see it all first to know what you were missing."

She fiddled with the label on her bottle, nodding. "Yeah, but it's amazing how quickly you forget the beauty of this." She looked up at the sky again, catching a falling star flash across the sky. A sad laugh left her lips as she took another quick swig. "So how did Chloe get that adorable nickname?"

"Clover?" Gibson laughed quietly, "Oliver didn't quite understand how to say Chloe when she was first born. He just kept calling her Clover everywhere we went. I guess it just stuck."

Rose smiled, picturing tiny Oliver and baby Chloe. "That's cute. I guess I could see his point as a little kid. I used to call giraffes, gaffs." She shrugged, shooting Gibson a sideways smile.

"Gaffs huh," he said, grinning. "Yeah, Oliver's loved Chloe since day one. Sure, they argue, but I know she's his favorite person right now. I just hope they stay this close forever. My brothers, sisters and I aren't super close anymore and it makes me sad."

"Life does that sometimes. I'm jealous of anyone who has siblings." She pulled her eyes away from him to look up again. Still not able to drink in enough of the beauty above her.

"Yeah, I remember you always used to say you wanted to have more than one kid because of that."

Rose quickly turned her face back to him, "I'm surprised you remember that."

"I remember a lot of things. You'd be surprised." He winked at her before changing the subject. "What time is Lacey coming over tomorrow?"

"I guess around seven. Why?"

"No reason. Just want to make sure I'm ready for you when you come running back to me," he laughed at his joke, drawing a scowl from Rose.

"What makes you think that even if she proves you right, I'll want to come running?" she asked sarcastically

Gibson's fingers tapped on his thighs for a second before he pushed up from his chair. Walking around to stoop in front of her, he tipped her chin to look her in the eye. "I may not know much about the new city girl you've become, but I do know the country girl that you were. She was a romantic, always wanting the good feeling ending to a story. Maybe you won't come back to me, but just knowing that the air is clear and that you are right here, right next door, will be enough for me." He brushed his thumb across her cheek and kissed her forehead. Rose closed her eyes, relishing in the touch. When she opened them, he was starting to stand, but she grabbed his hand and pulled him back down to her.

"Gibson, wait," she said, pulling him closer. He put his hand on the arm of her chair, stopping himself just in front of her face.

"Rose?" She didn't let him finish before she closed the space between them. The kiss was brief, but enough to make her insides tighten again.

When they separated, Rose was flushed. She couldn't believe she had just done that, but it felt so right. "I'm sorry." She quipped.

"Don't be sorry." He pulled his chair over next to hers. When he sat, he took her hand, strumming his thumb over her fingers. "I liked it."

She stole a look out of the corner of her eye. His eyes were gently dancing over her face. "So, um, what made you let the kids play with chalk today?"

"Ah, the old 'change the subject' move." He squeezed her hand as they fell into more conversation.

After another beer, Rose told Gibson good night with a quick peck on the cheek and headed home.

Closing the door behind her, she heard the ding of her voice-mail and realized she had left her phone behind. Punching in her password, Rose's heart sank when her aunt's frantic voice started in her ear. "Rose, I need you to call me right away." Then another voicemail from Brianne. "Rose, you need to come to the hospital as soon as you can!"

Her heart was pounding as she grabbed her keys and jumped into her car. Speeding through town, Rose prayed that the county cop wasn't anywhere in the vicinity. She made it to the hospital in record time and ran to the emergency room entrance.

"Bri!" she yelled, walking through the automatic sliding door. Then turning to the intake nurse, "My dad was brought here. Jason Harper. Do you know where he is?"

Rose's high emotion made the woman appear to move at a snail's pace. "Miss, what is your name? I can't give any information un-less you are on the list," the woman behind the window said.

"Rose, Rose Harper. I need to know where he is. Oh my god, why didn't I take my phone with me." She was frantic, feeling tears starting to well up.

After what seemed like an eternity, the receptionist nodded. "Ok,

I see you're on the list. I'll have an orderly come up and bring you back to see him." The door next to Rose clicked and slowly opened. A young man, about nineteen years old, told her to follow him. She felt like everything was running in slow motion.

When she got to her dad's room, Bri was sitting in a chair. The beeping of machines filled the air. Rose couldn't move past the door, unable to move her feet forward. Her aunt looked up then, catching Rose's eye. Noticing the lack of movement, Bri walked over and took Rose's hand, tugging a little, moving Rose forward. This all seemed like a dream. Not a dream, a nightmare.

Rounding the corner of the room, she sucked in a sharp breath. Her dad was sitting in bed, a bruise forming on his left eye, his arm wrapped, and his leg was being held up in the air in a sling, but he was alive and awake.

"Hey Rosey," he said softly

"Dad! I was so scared. I'm so sorry I didn't have my phone with me!" She glanced between her dad and her aunt. "What happened?"

Her dad lowered his head. "I wanted to clean my gutters. I always clean my gutters and I haven't done it in over a year. I felt great today, so I pulled the ladder out of the garage."

"Dad," Rose sighed, "You know that wasn't a good idea."

"Well, I realize that now," he said with a sheepish smile.

"So, what all is..."

"He broke his collarbone for sure. His arm and leg are too swollen to know if there is a break or just some bone bruising," Bri started, "He hit his head, so concussion, and that black eye," Bri pointed at Jason's face, "that was from trying to get up." Rose pinched her nose between her eyes, then rubbed her temples before looking up at her dad.

Jason was still sporting a stupid grin, the same one he gave when he thought he could do something, but failed miserably. Like the time when she was fifteen, and he tried to fix the shower but forgot to turn the water off first. The water had shot across the bathroom, causing a minor flood that leaked through the living room ceiling. She just shook her head at him.

"So, what were you doing that you didn't have your phone, young lady?" her aunt asked jokingly. Rose shot her aunt a look that said maybe not the time.

"Spill it, Rosey," her dad said

"Hey! Ok! I had to run next door to apologize to Oliver and Chloe for losing track of time if you MUST know," she replied

"And that took three hours?" he pushed in a tone that she knew was meant to be funny.

"Well, I read Chloe her bedtime story and then..." she trailed off.

"Go on. This sounds juicy," Bri said.

"Well, it's not," Rose said with a huff. "Gibs and I had a couple of beers after the kids went to bed. That's all. I mean, I am here at ten. Come on, you two. Quit it," she said with a little laugh. Then shooting her dad a sideways look, "We're here because my DAD decided to climb a ladder."

Rose stayed all night in the hospital with her dad. She had pushed Bri out the door around eleven thirty and thankfully at around midnight they had moved her dad to a private room upstairs. Fortunately, the new room had a chair that reclined enough so she could catch a few minutes of shut eye between vital checks.

Around six in the morning, her phone pinged. It was a text from Gibson:

Um why is your door wide

open? Are you ok?

She shot off a fast response.

Shit, I forgot to lock it.

Dad's in the hospital.

Do you want me to

go check inside?

Do you have time? Shouldn't

you be at the farm already?

Well, I'm already late, what

would a couple more minutes

mean? Hang tight.

Her heart pounded. Not only was she worried that someone had broken in, but she was nervous that she had left something out that would embarrass her in front of Gibson. She didn't know what that was, but at this point, anything was possible.

Other than a mess of craft

supplies on the floor, house

looks good. Should I lock it?

Thank god. Yes, can you check

the back door too, please.

Both doors are secure. My

work here is done. How's

your dad? What happened?

Thank you, Gibs. That's a relief.

Talk to you this evening? I owe you.

Sure

She smiled to herself, then looked over at her dad. He looked worse than the night before. The bruising was blue, but the swelling looked like it was stable. Hopefully, they would hear something today. Rose hated seeing him hooked to all the machines.

The doctors had to take special care, though, because of his disease. The bones of a Parkinson's disease patient become increasingly fragile over time and while her dad wasn't that far into the disease (by her calculations), the doctors still wanted to be careful. Besides, he had just fallen off a ten-foot ladder. Jason's eyes opened and looked around, landing on his daughter. He smiled and closed his eyes again.

"Dad. How are you feeling?" Her voice was gentle.

"Oh, I'm fine. You know me." But a wince crossed his face, shooting his eyes open. "Where's the pain meds?"

"Should I call the nurse?" she asked. He raised his hand to show he was hitting the call button. The door swung open, revealing the night nurse just finishing her rounds before the day shift came on. She put two small cups on the bed table, one with pills and one with water.

"Did you order breakfast, Mr Harper?" she asked as she looked over his vitals.

"I have no idea. You all had me so hopped up on these pain meds last night," he said with a tiny laugh.

"I filled the menu out for him while he was sleeping," Rose replied.

"Good, that should be up soon. On a scale of one to ten, what's your level of pain this morning?" the nurse turned back to Rose's dad.

"I'd say right now, an eight." he said, throwing the pills back with a swig of water. "Soon to be a zero."

"Alright. Well, I'm about to clock out. I'll add this med to the chart and hopefully you will be gone before I come back tomorrow night." With that, the nurse turned and left.

The rest of the day nurses were in and out, sending her dad down for x-rays and one visit from the doctor to discuss the results of said x-rays. They already knew about his collarbone, but his left arm was broken as well. Luckily, his leg was just bruised. The doctor wanted Jason to stay one more night just to monitor everything which had made her dad groan.

Around four in the afternoon, Bri showed up to relieve Rose for a bit. Promising to be back around nine, Rose pecked her dad's cheek. It was at that moment she remembered Lacey was coming and there was no way for her to reach out to reschedule. She hugged her aunt and rushed out of the hospital.

CHAPTER TWELVE

Rose

Rose took a quick shower when she made it home. Throwing a microwave dinner in, she started picking up her craft supplies. The distinct sound of a car pulling into the driveway next door caught her attention. She heard the door close, but she didn't hear the side door open. Grabbing the vacuum from the front closet, Rose bent over to plug it in before hearing a whistle from behind her. Whipping her head around, she twisted her back just right. The pain shot through her, and she collapsed to the floor. Her door opened and slammed shut.

"I'm sorry, Rose! I didn't mean to startle you!" Gibson was holding his hand out to help her up. She reached for it, but her back twinged so hard that she stayed where she was.

He stooped down in front of her with the most concerned handsome face she had ever seen. He wrapped his arm around her waist, pulling her arms around his neck. As carefully as possible, he moved to stand, trying his best to not jostle her too much. Rose cringed as they stood, but it wasn't as bad as she thought it would be. He helped her over to the couch and lowered her to the cushion.

"What are you doing here?" she asked, handing him a throw pillow to put behind her.

"I wanted to see how your dad was doing and find out what happened. But you were leaning over and... well, I'm sorry, I couldn't control my man brain." She smiled at him. He meant well. His brain, though, was crazy.

"Thanks for asking about dad." She couldn't stop gazing at his face, the smolder of his eyes, the concern he showed. "Yeah, so he fell off a ladder. He was trying to clean his gutters, not sure why, and the ladder flipped backwards," she explained "He broke his collarbone and arm and has a concussion. They want to keep him again tonight."

"Holy shit! What in the hell was he doing on a ladder?"

"He said he was having a good day and wanted to do something for himself." She shook her head, trying not to picture the scenario.

"I'll go over there tomorrow or sometime this week and finish the gutters for him," Gibson said. "That man still thinks he's..."

"Iron Man, yes. I mean, I get it, but he knows he shouldn't be doing things like that anymore." She picked at her fingernails.

"You know your dad, Rose. It's in his nature to want to do things on his own."

Rose sat still for a minute before looking at Gibson. "You don't have to go do that," her eyes darted across his face, "clean his gutters. I know that you have the kids. I'll call someone to come and do it."

"Like hell you will. I can do it, I WANT to do it," he pressed.

"Ok, ok," she said, putting her hands up and cringing because that movement sent pain up her back. "Ugh. Lacey is going to be here soon, and I look like crap just like my house."

"I'll call her and tell her to come another day."

"No, no, Gibson. I want to get this done. I don't want to wait any longer to have her here because if I'm being truthful, I really don't want her here in the first place," she said urgently. "I just need an ice pack and some ibuprofen. I should have both in the kitchen." She started getting up.

Gibson stepped in front of her. "Sit. I'll go get both," he demanded and started towards the next room.

"The ibuprofen should be in the drawer next to the sink," she hollered.

After he brought everything back to her, Gibson started for the door. "I gotta go relieve Brandi before the kids eat her alive."

"Hey, thanks, Gibson," she said, "I'll text you when she's gone."

Gibson's lowered his chin gently, the hint of a smile on his lips.

Thirty minutes after his retreat, Rose heard a car pull into the driveway.

Well, here goes nothing, she thought.

There was a knock on the front door, but Rose didn't move from her spot.

"Come in, Lacey," she yelled from the couch.

The door timidly opened, and Lacey entered the living room. Rose still didn't get up, which she could tell made Lacey feel uncomfortable.

"Sorry, I just hurt my back and can't seem to move right at the moment," Rose said. "Otherwise, I would have come let you in." Lacey side eyed her a bit. "I also have lemonade I was going to get for us both but apparently my neighbor likes to be creepy and scare people into hurting themselves." She rolled her eyes while thumbing next door.

Lacey smiled, knowing who the neighbor was. "I've heard he can be a bit of a nuisance," Lacey responded with a tiny smile. The ex friends shared a small smile.

This was going better than expected. Lacey looked a little more rested than she did the day before, but maybe that was because of the tremendous amount of makeup that she had caked on her face. She looked around the living room before taking a seat on the rocker across from Rose.

"Thanks for coming, Lacey. I'm sure it was hard to get away from the family for a bit. Especially for something like this."

"No, I really think it's better this way. I feel more sincere sitting here with you." Lacey's cheeks flushed a little, "Plus, it gives my husband a chance to see what I deal with every day. I like reminding him from time to time." A small chirp came from Lacey's throat and she winked at Rose. "So, how do you want to do this? Do you want me to tell you what happened, or do you want to just see the video?" Lacey asked.

"I mean, if I'm being truthful, the last thing I want to do is watch the video, but Gibson is dead set on that being how I find out 'the truth'."

Lacey smiled and responded, "Let's start slow then." She folded her hands in her lap and her leg started to bounce.

"So, you had to know the crush I had on Gibson. The first time I saw him walking with you in the hallways, I almost couldn't breathe. Why else would I be tagging along with you and your friends?" she shrugged. "Anyway, I had heard that you were sick, so my sixteen-year-old self-decided to devise a plan. I was going to try to seduce Gibson that night. I had actually been trying to break you guys up for weeks."

"What? How?" Surprised to hear this, Rose couldn't remember any time that she had felt like there was an attempt like this.

"I purposely put myself in places where Gibson was without you, the ice cream shop when he was with the guys, or at the farm. I tried working there, only lasted a week. Um, what else?"

"Huh, I guess I didn't see that as any kind of play on your part. Maybe that's because I knew Gibson was mine." Rose shot back, realizing exactly what Gibson had said the other night was how she felt too.

"Hell, Rose, I tried to 'inspire' him to sleep with me one time at another party by wearing some, er, risqué clothing. You know the kind that showed off my goods." Lacey shimmied a little then, hoping to get a laugh. Rose didn't laugh. "Do you know what he told me when he saw me?" Rose sighed, and shook her head. "He had told me you were his love and girls who dressed like that weren't anything he'd ever think about going home with anyway." Rose smiled a little at that.

Lacey shook her head sadly, and Rose knew the main story was coming.

After releasing a breath, Lacey continued, "Well, when I found out you were at home sick, I had borrowed some tight jeans from my older sister and a pink shirt that Gibson had commented on at some point. I added a little light makeup, trying to mimic what you wore. Maybe if I looked a little like you, he would either mistake me for you or realize how hot I was," Lacey confessed, her eyes brimming with tears. Rose cringed.

"I just kept feeding Gibson beer every time I saw his glass was empty. I had to get those beer glasses focused on me. And then I saw him heading for the door, so I ran after him. I knew he shouldn't be driving, so I thought it would be the perfect chance to corner him and take him home."

Rose cringed and she knew her thought was mean but all she could think was *What a hussy!*

Lacey continued. "I stopped him next to his truck and tried to take his keys. He had held them up in the air, and of course he towered over me. I pretended to jump for the keys, but then when I was coming back down, I wrapped my arms around his neck, pulling him down to my level and kissed him. But Gibson wasn't having it. He pushed me off of him and reminded me he was dating you and that no one else could take your place." Rose's cheeks flushed at that.

"I told Gibson I was sorry and that I had tripped or something like that, and that I really just wanted to see if I could drive him home. He said ok and then I lunged at him again, this time not taking no for an answer. He was so drunk that he let it happen for a few seconds. It made me feel like I had won. I ran my hands up his chest, then pulled his hands to my chest. I just pushed more and more with that kiss. It was everything I wanted. I even tried to grab him over his pants. I'm sorry Rose. I know I shouldn't have, but he was just... ugh, you know. He pushed me off after a few seconds. Well, more like shoved me. Then, because I was down there, I reached for his zipper..."

"Ok stop. I don't want to hear any more." Rose put her hands over her ears.

Lacey reached out and touched Rose's hands, pulling them off her ears. "He stopped me, Rose, before I could even touch him and then the way he said your name, well, it literally made me puke... all over him," she said, "I had way too much to drink which is probably good that I didn't talk him into letting me drive him home. He held my hair. You know how sweet he can be. Made sure that I was cleaned up and then called my mom to come pick me up. He waited with me to be sure I got in mom's car safely." Lacey stopped and looked at Rose.

Rose wasn't sure if she wanted to punch Lacey right there or feel bad for her. No, she wanted to punch her more than when she had found out about the kiss.

"This is a lot, Lacey." Rose was reliving her senior year in a way that she had never wanted to.

"I know. I should have told you the truth from day one. I just was so happy you guys had broken up. I thought it meant I might have a chance with him. God, you know how gorgeous he was. How gorgeous he still is," she almost mumbled the last sentence.

Rose shook her head. "How about this video you have? Let's see it before I go off on you."

Lacey's hand shook as she pulled her iPhone out of her purse. She got up from the rocker and walked over to the couch. "May I sit next to you?" Rose shrugged, pointing at the seat. Lacey maneuvered to the cloud and scrolled through a million pictures and videos of what Rose assumed were Lacey's family.

"Here it is," Lacey said after an eternity, handing the phone to Rose. Rose tapped play and there it was... well, most of it... in grainy flip phone video. It was a first person view of Lacey following Gibson out the door. Her whiny voice pleading with Gibson, the kisses (well as much as could be recorded clearly) and Gibson's voice both times, clear as day, saying Rose's name. The video ended with Lacey hurling on the ground. Rose would have to take Gibson's and Lacey's word that it ended there in real life as well.

Sitting back, Rose handed the phone back to its owner. Taking a deep breath in and letting it out, she tried to let her brain make complete sentences. Her blood was boiling. When she turned to Lacey, all she puffed out was, "You might want to go back to the rocker now."

Taking the cue, Lacey quickly stood and rushed back to her seat. As she rocked, she tried to apologize in many ways. Her eyes were sad, her posture limp, the tear on her cheek and then the words. A genuine apology came from the same lips that had tried and succeeded in breaking Rose's heart.

"Rose, I am so, so sorry."

That's when Rose realized again that Rose herself had broken her own heart by not listening to Gibson, the only other man besides her dad, who was her top supporter and best friend. She had done this to herself.

"Lacey, I would like to thank you for coming over. I kind of still want to kill you though," Rose started.

"Totally understandable," Lacey responded. She was shaking a little at the look in Rose's eyes.

"I thought you were my friend, Lacey. I would have done anything for you. So, I don't understand why your head thought this was right. But what I really don't understand is why you wouldn't tell me any of this until someone bargained with you." Rose took a breath. "It literally took Gibson, MY Gibson, to talk you into telling me the truth. Like, why is that? Why couldn't you have just said something at SOME point on your own?"

Lacey looked stunned at first and took a minute to respond. "I don't have a good reason, except that I thought you were gone for good. I know that sounds bad, Rose. When Gibson called me the other day, it surprised me he hadn't told you already. How was I supposed to know that it would have hit you so hard that you wouldn't even talk to the love of your life?"

That took Rose back. She had only just thought of that, and Lacey had thought it all along.

"Lacey," Rose started, and stopped. She looked over at the window to see if there was any movement next door. "Lacey, I think I've heard enough. Um, thank you, um, for finally growing some balls and letting me know the truth." She knew she sounded rude when she said it. She even saw Lacey flinch a little, but she didn't care. Even though it hurt her back, Rose stood and motioned to the door. Lacey stood moving towards the door, knowing not to push the issue.

"So, who did you end up marrying, Lacey? Some rich dude with a flashy smile?" Rose said condescendingly. "Did you steal him from someone else?"

"Actually Rose, I married Teddy. We got married nine years ago and have four kids. I had thought that my apology would help smooth things over, but I guess I was wrong," Lacey huffed. "I sure hope that you can at least forgive Gibson, Rose. You've always been the one for him. Even Lorna couldn't take your place, and compared to you, she was a freaking supermodel." Lacey threw the last stab, turned, and was out the door before Rose realized it. Letting out a sigh, Rose felt her back tensing up again. She made her way to the refrigerator and grabbed a beer, never opening it. Gazing out the back door, she replayed all the gruesome details that Lacey had just spilled.

What a disgusting excuse for a woman. She thought. *What a rude snitch. What right did she have?* And then the realization came back that in the long run, no matter how wrong Lacey had been, Rose was just as wrong not even letting Gibson explain anything all those years ago. She wanted to run next door right then and hold Gibson. To tell him how sorry she was and how wrong she had been, but she didn't have time. She was due back to the hospital soon.

She put the beer back in the fridge and grabbed her phone. Gingerly walking back to the living room, she shot off three texts.

One to Gibson:

> *Can we talk tomorrow?*
>
> *Gotta go see dad.*

One to Alaina:

> *OMG girl I need to talk to you*
>
> *and Grace in a bit are you free?*

And one to Grace:

Three way call in a bit???

All 3 responses came at once.

Gibson:

Sure. I'll be home after 6.

Her two friends both responded with the same answer:

Duh.

Grabbing her keys and holding her back, she walked out the front door... this time remembering to lock the door behind her.

On the way to the hospital, she called her friends, telling Lacey's story to them.

"So what are you going to do with this information?" Alaina asked.

"I know what you should do. Take him back!" Grace all but yelled.

"I just don't know how to restart things. Like we were one person until that day," she whined to her friends, "And now."

Grace broke in. "And now you've already started taking those steps to rekindle. Rose, before you even knew the whole truth, you started falling again."

"Ugh, I know. God he makes my heart flutter."

"But?" Alaina pushed.

"But now I think I'm even more pissed at Gibson. He literally could have run after me. He could have found me anytime I came home. He could have had dad talk to me. There are so many things he could have done and he didn't. It's almost like he didn't actually care."

"Rose, stop." Alaina's mom-voice stopped the rant. "Remember what he told you the other night. He did it because he loved you. He wanted you to have more than what he thought he could give you."

"I never wanted anything more than him and our happily ever after." Sadness dripped from her tone.

"So, maybe you're about to get it," Grace piped in. "Maybe now is the time! Everything happens for a reason, Rosey. Maybe this is when this relationship is supposed to happen."

Alaina interjected again, "You need to slow it down, though, girl. You can't just jump into bed with him. These make out sessions, they need to stop or slow down."

Rose sighed, "I know. We've had ten years of separate lives to overcome. And I don't want to break the kiddos' hearts either."

"Think before you jump in the sheets," Alaina said matter-of-factly.

"Jump in the sheets before you think," teased Grace, always the risqué one.

Rose shook her head, "I gotta go. I'm pulling into the hospital parking lot. I can text while I'm here, but I'll talk to you both tomorrow." The girls all said their goodbyes, and the call disconnected.

All night at the hospital, Rose split her time between her dad while he was awake and her thoughts about the entire ordeal with Lacey and Gibson. Around eleven, the familiar ding of her iPhone rang out. Looking at her dad, she hoped the noise hadn't disturbed him. Seeing no movement, she pulled her phone out of her purse. It was Gibson.

I know you said we would talk

tomorrow. I just want to make

sure you're ok.

Rose shook her head and texted back

                                Well my back feels like a herd of

                                    elephants ran over it if that's

                                      what you're wondering.

Again I'm sorry about that.

Chloe told me I was a jerk. :)

                                      Chloe might be right. ;)

How was the convo with Lacey?

She turned her phone so she couldn't see the screen and considered her text back.

                                      I really want to talk in person.

                                      Dinner tomorrow?

Ok but has to be here. And you

may have to read another princess

story first.

                                      Deal. Give the kids a hug for me?

Done.

Just like that, she was alone in her thoughts again.

CHAPTER THIRTEEN

Rose

Rose woke up with a start and couldn't figure out where she was at first. The beeping of the heart monitor righted her head. She looked at her phone; it was three in the morning and the night nurse was quietly trying to take her father's vitals. He looked grumpy and ready to go home. Rose didn't blame him. The worst part of being in the hospital was that as many times as the doctors or nurses said to rest, they came in to bug the patient twice as much. She prayed silently that they would discharge her dad tomorrow. He needed to be home so that he could rest. Settling back into her blanket, she fell asleep, back into the dream she had been having. She and Gibson, tumbling around her bed.

The next afternoon, the doctor did indeed discharge Jason. Rose pulled up to the front door of the hospital, scrambling out of the driver's seat to help her dad. She had called her aunt before they left, so when they pulled up to her dad's house, Bri was already there with her husband and kids. After getting Jason in the house, she grabbed the paperwork and his prescription from the front seat of the car, thankful that the hospital had filled it and that she didn't have to run to the pharmacy. Giving the paperwork to her aunt, Rose filled her in, "They gave him a painkiller right before we left the hospital. So, he won't need another one for four more hours." She and her aunt had become good at throwing information at each other over the last month.

"Go home, Rose. Get some sleep, some Rose time. We've got it from here." Brianne hugged Rose before turning her and gently pushing her out the door.

Rose hated leaving her dad behind, but the prior night had tired her out and she wanted to take a shower before heading over to Gibson's.

Gibson

"Shit," Gibson said under his breath. He had seen Rose pull in and wasn't near ready for dinner to be done. The chicken was in the oven and the kids were so excited that they were trying to help him. Chloe had put on a dress that she had worn for a wedding earlier in the summer and was prancing around the table, putting forks down at each seat. Oliver was just as excited watching the vegetables he had put in the microwave and folding paper towels into napkins. It wasn't five stars, but it was the best that a single dad, working full time, could throw together.

He stole ten minutes to take a quick shower and put on some clean clothes. When he came back out, Chloe was dancing and singing some song she had made up about the princess who lived next door. He smiled at his daughter and said a quiet prayer that things would end up how he hoped in the end. Rose's heart was the last thing he wanted to break, or his own heart, but more importantly, he didn't want to break Chloe's or Oliver's heart. He heard the microwave ding and helped Oliver pull the veggies out. He had about ten minutes before Rose was supposed to be there.

Rose

Rose was dragging. So much had gone down in the last few days that she was mentally and physically exhausted. She forced herself into the shower, then forced herself to blow dry her hair. She got dressed before sitting on the edge of her bed, closing her eyes for just a second. Or so she thought.

Next thing she knew, her phone was ringing her awake. She had fallen asleep. Grabbing her phone from her bedside table, she noticed she was running late.

"Shit," she breathed, hitting the accept button, "I know, I'm sorry. I'm walking down the stairs right now."

"Are you ok?" Gibson asked.

"Yeah, I just fell asleep for a minute. I didn't even try to. I just sat down. I'm sorry. I'm coming. Be there in a minute." She hung up, sprinted down the stairs and out the front door. She hurried across the lawn and knocked on the side door of the Titus house. The pitter patter was fast and furious running towards the door. Oliver made it to the door first.

"Hey Rose!" he said excitedly, "I helped dad make dinner tonight!"

Giggling, Rose said, "Hey, Oliver, I can't wait to see and taste what you guys made!" Oliver grabbed her hand and pulled her in the door. Chloe was behind Oliver and grabbed Rose's other hand, looking at her with a huge smile.

"I got to help daddy put the forks and spoons on the table!" she squeaked.

"Well, that's very helpful," Rose responded. When they rounded the corner into the kitchen, Gibson was finishing setting the table and looked up at a sight that took his breath away. Rose holding hands with his kids. It was like the dream he had let go of so long ago. Rose smiled at him and, as if reading his mind, looked down at the kids.

"I gotta go grab the chicken. Take a seat." Gibson said once he shook himself back to the present.

"SIT BY ME, ROSE!" Chloe hollered.

"Chloe, lower your voice a bit," Gibson hollered.

"SORRY, DAD," she yelled back. "Please, Rose?" Rose smiled at the funny exchange.

"Of course, just show me where to sit."

During dinner, Oliver pointed out the vegetables that he had "made" in the microwave. Rose oohed and ahhed over the green beans. Gibson had turned out to be a pretty good cook. Although she was certain that there was nothing but the chicken that was homemade on the table.

"Let's go get ice cream!" Oliver said when they finished up.

"Not tonight, buddy. Rose has had a rough few days and I think she would rather just stick around here for a bit." Gibson looked at her to gauge his response to find Rose nodding, mouthing 'Thank you,' to him. He winked at her.

After clearing the table, they all went into the backyard so the kids could play a bit before bedtime.

Gibson motioned to the chairs at the patio table. The same ones they had sat in two nights prior. Lowering herself into one, Rose watched as the kids ran to their swing set. Gibson sat himself in the other chair and looked at Rose.

"How are you doing?" he asked.

Turning to him, she sighed. "I'm tired. My body and my brain hurt. My heart hurts. I can't even describe where I'm at right now."

He nodded in understanding. "I can only imagine. How's Jason?"

"He's home. He's tired too, currently not in a lot of pain, thanks to his meds. Bri and her family are over there right now."

They both looked over towards the kids, who were happily

swinging and carrying on. "Gibs," she started. He turned to her. "I'm so sorry," her voice was sincere. He started to respond, but she held up her hand. "Let me finish. I wasn't sure I was going to want to have this conversation tonight, but I'm here and I need one thing off my mind." He nodded, quickly looking at the kids to be sure they were still ok.

Rose took a deep breath and began. "Let me start by telling you how badly I feel about how things ended with us. I should have been wiser and realized that my best friend would never do any-thing to hurt me." She struggled to continue. "Lacey told me everything in unwanted detail. In a kind of sick way, it felt like she wanted to rub it in my face again." Gibson grimaced. "I know she didn't. She was actually kind of sincere. But nonetheless, she told me everything. Gibson, I'm so sorry for not believing in you." She continued in her apology but stopped short of telling him how she felt about him. She hung her head, shaking it sadly.

Gibson let out a long breath. Then, reaching across the table, he took her hand. "Rose, I have to say, I'm glad that this is out in the open now. I was so pissed at you. You just wouldn't even listen to me. We had four years together. I wanted to hate you, but I was never able to. I forgave you the minute you left town, but it's nice to hear you say it." He smiled at her and then pulled his hand back and checked the time. "Can you stay for a bit yet? I gotta get the kids ready for bed." Rose nodded, feeling a bit relieved that she had gotten most of what she wanted to say out.

Of course, Chloe wanted her to read another princess book at bedtime. And, of course, Rose obliged. After they tucked both kids in, Rose and Gibson wandered back to the backyard. She wanted to word what she had left to say clearly and concisely.

"Gibson, Alaina told me not to but I have to ask." she looked at her hands. Before lifting her eyes to his. "Why didn't you... run after me? I mean it was like you didn't care."

"I wanted to. God, I've told you that, Rose. I also didn't know if we really knew what we wanted at that point. I mean you threw us away too, when you wouldn't listen to me. I just figured that maybe it didn't matter as much as I thought it did."

Her heart broke. "I still don't get it though. You could have easily told dad, or even came down to find me. You know the big romantic gesture that's in the movies."

"Young, stupid, idiot…. I don't know. All of those things. I don't really know the answer other than I hoped that by letting you go blow off steam in another state that you would realize that you needed to come back. That we would be able to talk after separating." Gibson sighed before looking at the sky. "I guess I just… I just hoped that something would happen and you would hate it and then come home and then we could figure it out then. But you found new friends, and fell in love with North Carolina. You were happy. Who was I to interfere then?"

Rose hung her head feeling a tear travel down her cheek, but then felt a giggle start to rise. "I just can't believe that we both thought the other…" the giggle became stronger. "We both were so stupid. I mean if you had just stayed with me that night. Or if I had taken your phone call. Shit." The laughter choked back down her throat. "I'm glad that we had this little chat. I'm glad I know what really happened. I'm just sorry it took so long." She leaned forward, resting her elbows on her knees before turning to look at Gibson again. "So there's something else.""Ok," he said, smacking a mosquito off the back of his neck.

"I know that you're hoping now that I know the entire story, that we can just pick up where we left off… or at least that's what I've gathered over the last, um, heated moments." She stopped to take a breath.

"But you think we need to take it slow?" he finished for her.

She was fiddling with something on her arm that wasn't there. "Well, I'm not sure slow is the word I'm looking for, but I don't think we can just jump into... a relationship. We're both older than we were. I mean, ten years is a long time to not really know someone anymore. I've had a few relationships since you, but nothing that worked. And I mean, you're a dad!"

"Rose, my kids are my first priority. But even they can see and feel our chemistry." He stopped, taking a breath. "I get it though. I do." His voice got warmer, "I'll work for this. And I promise you, we will make it this time." He leaned over, pulling her chair towards him.

"What are you doing?" she asked.

"Just getting you a little bit closer." he replied with that goofy grin that she loved. "You've been thousands of miles away for a very long time. I hope you don't mind if I want to close the distance." The brown of his eyes seemed to get darker. Like they were undressing her, causing a stir in her stomach.

"Let's take it a day at a time, like we have been." Drowning in his gaze, she whispered, "I have missed you, though." Leaning over just in front of his face, she tugged the little goatee that he had started growing a few weeks earlier towards her, and brushed her lips over his. Her cheeks felt warm realizing what she had just done. Pushing away gently, she stood and said, "I need sleep. I can't even think straight, especially when I'm around you."

He grabbed her hand, pulling her into his lap. "Don't leave yet." Their faces were so close, there was barely room for air. His fingers ran through her hair. Her eyes dipped to his lips again."I would love to finish out the evening with you, but I just can't keep my eyes open," she whispered with a sigh. "And I'm not sure that I can keep myself from doing something we're not ready to do."

"That's ok, I understand. Get up, my leg is asleep anyway," he said with a snort. She rolled her eyes at him. As she stood, he smacked her on the butt, and she slapped him on the arm.

"I'll talk to you tomorrow," Rose said with a smile.

"I'll start making plans for a proper date, Rose. I told you I'm all in at making this work. Go home and sleep. Oh, and hey, tell your dad I'll be over soon to clean those gutters," he flashed that gorgeous, dimpled smile again, warming her body.

CHAPTER FOURTEEN

Rose

The next week, Rose spent most of her time with her dad and with her classroom preparations. School was right around the corner, and she had a lot to do to be ready in time. Gibson had gone over to clean the gutters for her dad, something that Jason welcomed but wasn't overly happy about at the same time. It made him feel inept.

Thursday of that next week, Rose got a text while she was putting up decorations in her classroom. It was Gibson.

Hey gorgeous, dinner tonight?

Just us.

Sure!

Ok, I'll pick you up at 6.

Sounds good.

Rose looked at the time and set her phone on the desk. She still had a good couple of hours before then. She could easily get a few more items done. The classroom had to be perfect for her first hometown class. This was huge for her. So many of her classmates' kids would be in her class and she wanted to make a good impression and prove what an excellent teacher she was.

Around four thirty, Kendall popped her head through the doorway. "You're still in here?" and then, taking in the room, exclaimed, "Wowsers! This looks great! Oh, my goodness!"

Rose smiled, turning a full three hundred sixty degrees in the room to look at everything. "You think it's enough? I'm thinking I need more."

"No freaking way!" Kendall's hand jumped to her mouth. "Sorry about the curse word. This looks amazing. Every first grader in town will want to be in your class."

"Freaking is not a swear word," Rose laughed

"Well, if you know what it's derived from..." Kendall started, but Rose cut her off.

"I know. I know," Rose lifted her hand laughing which in turn made Kendall laugh.

"But seriously, this looks awesome!"

"Thanks, Kendall. I'm worried I missed something. I have a couple of things to add yet, but I think I'm mostly done. First grade is a hard year for some kids." Rose grabbed her purse and phone from the desk and walked towards Kendall. "We should have a drink sometime."

"You... you want to go do something with me?" Kendall asked.

"Um, Kendall, yes. I want to catch up! I need to rekindle my friendships if I'm going to be here," Rose chuckled, "I wasn't great at it when I lived out of state, but I have missed most of you."

"Yeah, yeah, I think girl's night is coming up again. We usually sit around and drink while the dads take care of the kids."

"Well, I'm thinking more like shopping, nails, food... and then maybe drinks."

"Ooohhh that sounds fun. I'm not sure I can talk Joe into watching the kids that long, but maybe!" Kendall's eyes were dancing with excitement.

"Let's talk about this soon. It needs to happen. But I have to run, I've got... dinner waiting." Rose couldn't come up with anything better to say.

Kendall nodded, a knowing smile sitting on her lips. Rose knew that the small town had been gossiping about her and Gibson since the night at the bar.

"Stop it." The giggle from Kendall that followed Rose's response made her roll her eyes gently. "I'll see you later, Kendall."

"Have fun, Rose!" Kendall chirped as Rose hurried past her friend.

———————————

Rose and Gibson

A little after six, Rose was still sitting on the couch, alone, in her body clinging black mini dress. Her blonde hair was curled, and her makeup was spot on. She looked at her phone to be sure she hadn't missed any texts. It wasn't until around six thirty that she heard Gibson's truck pull in his driveway, the door slam and then the house door slam. Her phone rang with a text.

Girl I'm hurrying. I'm so sorry.

Dude, I only wait so long.

I know, I got caught up on a

broke down tractor.

Whatever. I'll wait 15 more

minutes and then I'm putting on

pjs and The Notebook.

Stop texting me so I can shower.

Ok, but I'm starting to walk

up my stairs...

She smiled through the exchange. Ten minutes later, she heard his screen door slam and his feet running across the pavement. Silence. Then he was pounding on her door. She slowly got up. More pounding on the door. Rose moved like a sloth across the room. Another knock and then her phone dinged.

I made it in 11 minutes. Come

on. You told me 15!!

She laughed as she opened her door.

Gibson said, "I'm so sorry I'm late." Then his hand shot to his heart. "Rose," he said, breathless, "You look... look...sexy as hell!"

"Oh, this old thing?" Her hands traced over her curves, his eyes following.

Gibson held his hand out and spun her in a circle on the porch. "I'm not sure I can make it through dinner. Girl, you look... mmm. You did this on purpose, didn't you? We're supposed to be going slow." He was rambling again. *Dammit, why does she make me lose my mind?*

"Stop it you weirdo, but thank you," she said, batting her eyelashes, "You look pretty good yourself." She looked him up and down. She always loved him in wrangler jeans and a button down. *Button downs are easy to rip off...* wait, she shouldn't be thinking that far ahead. Like he said, they weren't trying to hurry things. She gave him a quick peck on the cheek, and they walked to his truck.

"I really am sorry I was late."

"I would wait all night for you," she breathed.

Dinner was always good at Chuck's Bar and Grill. It wasn't where she had expected to go but did not know what to expect. The conversation between them flowed and there were a few comfortable silences. After dinner, they took a walk to the park near the restaurant. Rose sat in a swing and Gibson pushed her as they talked more about life.

"So, how did you and Lorna end up together? She was what, two years after me in school?" she asked.

"Yeah, I think she was. We were both at the bar one night and it just clicked. She liked a lot of the same things as me. I've known her forever. Remember her grandparent's farm was right there next to my family's. I don't know. I never saw her as anything until that night. Are you sure you want to hear this?" He had stopped pushing the swing so he could look at Rose.

"I do. We have ten years to learn about. Lorna was a big part of that."

"Ok," he began pushing her swing again, "so we just clicked that night for some reason. I had dated a couple of girls from Clarksville. They weren't really my type, but something to do, I guess. Anyway, maybe a year after you left, we saw each other at the bar. We spent the whole night drinking and talking. I woke up at her house the next morning with a headache." He stopped again, looking at her and then finished, "That was the night Ollie was conceived." He hung his head at the memory.

"So, you guys weren't married yet?"

"No, we, um, we were supposed to be a one nighter, but the one nighter turned into a few dates and then she found out she was pregnant. I wasn't OK with it at first, but the thought grew on me. You know I've always wanted a big family." Gibson glanced at Rose as she nodded "Plus, I knew she was good for me at the time. We always had fun. It felt a little off, but I wanted to be sure we brought our baby up with two parents. I proposed when she was six months pregnant, and we got married a month later at the courthouse."

"Huh. That's totally not what I expected to hear." Rose was still swinging, allowing her feet to drag across the ground. "Did you enjoy married life?"

"Well, like I said, it never felt right, but I guess we loved each other enough. We had chemistry. I mean, we did have Chloe a couple years later." He was looking at the moon, trying to keep his words PG. He wasn't sure that Rose needed to hear all the sex-capades that he and Lorna had tried to keep their marriage alive.

"But in the end?" she pushed

"Chloe was only a year old. In the end, Lorna and I decided to take a break. Well, she decided. She said I wasn't as attentive to her as I was in the beginning. I just never felt it as hard as I did with you. I tried, for the kids, I tried so hard. But in the end, I was losing myself. I know it sounds cliché. Then she started drinking more and had met some friends who were into some harder drugs. She told me she was only smoking pot, but I think by then, she was already starting down the path to destruction."

"So, the kids are with you almost every day. Doesn't the mom usually get the kids?" Rose asked.

"Well, that's sexist," Gibson said and then laughed. "Actually, Lorna had full custody at first, but about three months after the divorce, she got wrapped up with the wrong guy. She started using the wrong drugs and drinking entirely too much. The guy she was dating hit Oliver, and that was it."

Gibson was now staring at his hands. "She called me one day, and we went to court. The court ultimately handed the kids over to me full time. Lorna had to leave the guy and clean herself up as stipulations for visitations, which she did. And then she had supervised visits for a few months. We agreed to every other weekend after that. To this day, it still scares me to send them with her, but she has come a long way in the last year. She's been sober and has a great boyfriend. I'm not giving them back though." He looked at Rose, sadness spreading across his face. "Truthfully, I'm not sure that Lorna ever wants them full time again."

"Wow." That was all Rose could spit out. How could anyone willingly give up their kids? She was grateful that Gibson was the kind of dad that he was.

He turned the conversation to Rose and how things went in Charlotte. "So, tell me what I missed. Any dudes I need to beat up?"

"Ha ha, very funny. But no, there is no man back home... I mean, in Charlotte, that is pining away for me."

"That's hard to believe." Gibson's voice was low.

"I mean, I was serious with a couple of guys in Charlotte. One guy I dated for six months before he told me I was his favorite side dish. I had thought we were going somewhere when actually he was using me behind his wife's back. Using me." She hung her head this time, trying to hide the sadness. Gibson let out a small growl. "The second guy I thought was it. He was sweet, country, stable. A lot like you actually." She shot him a quick grin. "I don't know. I woke up one day and couldn't bring myself to text him. That's when I knew then that I wasn't in love with him. I was in lust." She stopped short of telling him how the sex was great, and that they hadn't ever gone on actual dates because they could never get out of the bedroom. "I was looking for all the things that weren't good for me, I guess." What Rose didn't say was that no one could stack up to Gibson in her heart. She had given herself to Gibson in high school, in every sense of the word.

They talked for hours. It wasn't until midnight that they decided they needed to head home. While they hadn't made it through ten years of missing time, they had made it through some of the hardest parts to talk about, their other relationships.

They held hands in the truck the entire way and, after pulling in his driveway, Gibson walked her to her door. They stood holding hands for what seemed like forever. His thumb strummed the back of her hand as he ran the fingers of his other hand through her hair. Rose looked at him with those doe eyes, screaming at him to kiss her.

Grabbing her by the waist, he covered her mouth with his. Letting a sigh out, Rose melted into him, their tongues dipping in and out desperately, almost like they had never done this before. He let out a moan and started walking her backward towards the door. Frantically, she felt for the door handle and opened the door as Gibson's hands moved up her back. When she twisted her fingers into his hair, he released another low groan. The sound made her plunge her tongue into his mouth again. Once they were inside, Gibson reached behind him without leaving her mouth to close the door. They were fumbling around like two high schoolers.

They stood in the entryway, mouths moving against each other. While he kissed her neck, he moved his hands over her shirt, kneading her breasts. She found her hands traveling up his chiseled front before she pushed him back a little. He stood back, looking at her. His jeans were starting to feel tight with desire. Her hands traveled to the first button on his shirt. She slowly started unbuttoning it, stopping to look up at him. His eyes were molten. He stood still and let her open his shirt completely before shrugging it off. Then she stood back against the wall, both of them panting.

He placed his hand on the nape of her neck and pulled himself against her. His length rubbed against her stomach. Moving his hand down her neck, he found her zipper, sliding it down her back. So slow that it was almost painful.

"Gibson," she whimpered with pain in her voice, causing him to stop and look at her.

"Do we need to stop?" he asked.

She looked at him with sad eyes and nodded. "I'm sorry," she whispered. He nodded and slid her zipper back up, kissing her softly on the lips as he did. She smiled and again mouthed 'I'm sorry.'

"Don't," he said, "You're right. We said we were going to take our time. I promised I would be good." She felt tears in her eyes, and he gently took her face in his hands. "We will get there, Rose. I'm not going to push this, though. I want you to be ready and for us to be in the right place."

Rose nodded, stood on her tiptoes, and kissed him again. She bent down and picked his shirt up off the floor. He shrugged it back on, covering the body that she wanted so badly. Taking his hand, she walked him back to the front door. But then, without taking her eyes off him, she locked it, before turning to the stairs.

"Rose, what are you doing?" he asked. She surprised herself, too.

"I thought maybe we could at least sleep together... in a clothes on sort of way. I think that might be safe."

"I don't know if that's a great idea," he said softly, "My main man down there might try to take over again."

She let out a shy giggle. "I just want you to hold me. It's been an almost perfect night," she said in a breathy voice.

"Rose, I'm serious," Gibson tried to argue with her, but then as he looked at her gorgeous face, he gave in and followed her up the stairs. When they climbed onto her bed, he wrapped his arms tightly around her. She fit perfectly in them, almost like his arms were made just to hold her. Rose fell asleep, holding the hand that he had laid around her.

He awoke as the sun was rising and grabbed for her, but she wasn't there. The aroma of coffee and eggs filled the air, and he stumbled out of bed and down the stairs. She looked ravishing in the kitchen with her cotton shorts and tank top on, hovering over the pan on the burner. The floorboard creaked, grabbing her attention. When she looked up at him, he caught the sleep still in her eyes. How she looked at that moment made his heart melt. This was something that he'd had to miss all these years. This is what he had wanted to wake up to but hadn't had the chance. She gave him that sleepy smile and went back to scrambling the eggs.

She flipped some eggs onto a plate, grabbed two mugs of coffee and sat down at the table. Gibson followed like a puppy dog. She had two forks, but sitting next to each other, they took turns eating off the same fork. It was almost like sitting in a Nirvana. The two of them, having breakfast together. Rose snuggled in close to him, laying her head on his shoulder as he wrapped an arm around her. Nothing would take this time away from them. Nothing until Gibson looked at the clock.

"Shit," he said, "Lorna's going to be at the house shortly with the kids." He looked at Rose. She was mid bite looking at him.

"I thought you didn't have the kids this weekend." Rose knew that the way she said it came off crass but didn't mean it to. He narrowed his eyes at her, and she raised her hand. "That didn't come out right. I was just really hoping we had the whole day to be together and, I don't know, talk more." Her tone was sad.

Gibson's eyes softened as he stroked her cheek. "I know, me too. I just remembered, though, that Lorna has to drop them off early. She called yesterday while I was working with a lame excuse. I know it's because her boyfriend is home. Don't worry, we'll have time like this again soon. She's taking them Thursday instead of

Friday this week and keeping them through Sunday." He picked her chin up and kissed her. Then he stood up, taking her hand, walking to the door together.

He left a gentle kiss on her lips, embracing her before he left. Rose's heart was on fire, but her mind was a mess.

CHAPTER FIFTEEN

Rose

Rose spent the rest of the day with her dad instead. He helped her repaint the book nook she had brought from her classroom in North Carolina. It was shaped like a tiny house, and she had bean bags that went inside. A place for kids to hide away and read. All of her classes had loved it, so she could only hope these kids did too.

There were only two weeks left of her summer break, and Rose was feeling nervous for three reasons. First, she wouldn't be able to be as hands on when it came to caring for her dad during the week. She had told Bri that she would do dinners and bedtimes, hoping to have her weekend evenings free. Second, she was starting this new job. Even though she had taught for many years, it still gave her butterflies. Some of these kids were the children of her old classmates and friends. They would all be judging her ability. Third, Gibson. She knew she was going to have to learn how to split her time again, but this time, she wanted to. It differed from any other relationship she had so far in her teaching career.

Watching her dad dip his brush into the paint again, Rose sighed.

Jason's eyes pulled away from the paint to look at his daughter. He knew that sigh from when she was young and wanted to say something but couldn't find the way to break the silence. "What's up, sweety?"

"Dad, I can't believe I've been here nine weeks already. I never thought I'd be back here."

"And yet here you are," her dad said. "How are things going with Gibson this week?" Jason chuckled to himself. He knew it had been a struggle for her to keep herself together.

Rose and Jason's relationship had returned to the father-daughter relationship they had before she left. Though now there was the added friendship that sometimes happens with parents and their adult children. She was back to telling him everything... well, almost everything. She left out certain details, but he knew that she and Gibson had been spending time together.

"Things are going ok, I guess. A bit confusing because I want things to be where they were, but I know we need to work to get there. It's hard, ya know?" Rose had stopped and stood back from the paint job to see if there were any glaring mistakes. "I think we're good here, dad. How about lemonade?" She walked around to her dad, who was sitting on the driveway.

"That sounds good," he said, reaching up for her to help him to his feet. Jason still had the cast and sling on his arm, so she tried to be as gentle as possible.

Walking to the porch, Rose got her dad settled into the porch swing and then went to get the lemonade before settling herself into the swing next to him, handing him a glass.

"Ok, Rose. I see it on your face. Spit it out," Jason pulled the glass to his mouth. The trembling was getting worse again.

Taking a breath, Rose said, "I'm nervous, dad."

"About?"

"About everything right now. I'm nervous about you and your health," she started eyeing him as she said, "It's getting easier, dad, but watching my dad struggling, it's the most heartbreaking thing I've ever done." Rose took a breath, letting her words set in. She didn't want to tell him, but he was her best friend. You don't keep things like that from your best friend. Truth be told, it was more than heartbreaking to her. She knew this was the beginning of the end, but did not know how long it would drag on, or how much time she actually had with him.

Her dad nodded, "Mm-hmm, I know, honey." He cleared his throat as he set his glass down. Turning to look at her, Jason took her hand and squeezed it.

Rose's eyes softly darted across her dad's smiling face. "I'm so incredibly glad that you called me home, dad. We needed this time to get back to where we were. I needed to be here with you, and I'm not going anywhere. I just need you to know that there may be times where I just... I don't know... I just can't mentally handle things. I'm not even sure if that's what I mean."

"Rosey," her dad said in his gentle voice. The same voice he used any time her heart had been broken when she was young. "I'm not going anywhere anytime soon. I know this is tough for you. It's tough for all of us. Any time you feel you've had too much, tell me, or tell Bri." Rose's head dropped a little, so Jason put a hand under her chin to raise it up again.

"We know this isn't a fun thing to go through. I'm just thankful that you came home. I worried you were stuck where you were, worried you would be stubborn and not make the move." She looked down again, this time in shame, knowing her original thought was to go back after one year. Jason picked up her chin, "Rosey, I need you to know that I am here no matter what, no matter how bad this thing gets. Please don't stop talking to me, ok."

"Dad," her voice held sadness in it, "Can you at least make it until I get married?" A tear slid down her cheek. That was what she wanted more than anything.

"For you, my Rose, I will try my hardest. What else is worrying you?" he asked, squeezing her hand.

Rose went on about the classroom and the kids, and then about her friends in Charlotte, divulging everything on her mind, even returning to Gibson and where things stood with him. "Follow your heart, Rose. Let it lead you and I promise, you will be fine." She looked at her dad and smiled, then threw her arms around him, hugging him as carefully as possible.

After dinner, she got her dad settled in to watch the Tigers' game. Sitting on the couch, Rose pulled her legs underneath her and just watched him as he cheered on his favorite team. Things are going to be fine, dad, she thought, and I am going to follow my heart.

CHAPTER SIXTEEN

Rose

The next morning, Rose was wandering around her house trying to decide if she should go to church with her dad or not. She pulled six outfits out of the closet but wasn't happy with any of them. Jason had begged her to go with him before she left the night before. Trying to oblige him, she had said she would think about it.

It had been at least ten years since she had set foot in a church. She missed it, but she wasn't sure she was ready to face the women and the questions. When she finished talking herself into it, she called her dad to say she would be there in a half hour to get him.

Rose pulled her hair into a low ponytail and slid on a scoop neck white dress with green flowers that fit her curves but not so tight that she looked slutty. She found her green heels and clutch, then headed down the stairs. Walking out the door, she was careful to lock it behind her.

When she turned to head down the steps, she tripped. At that exact moment, Gibson was heading up the walk. She saw the ground coming fast and let out a small scream. Just before she hit the ground, his arm was around her. She looked up into the eyes of a god. He lifted her to her feet but didn't let go. They were standing so close that their breath mingled, and she could smell the mint he had been sucking on. She had never wanted to be a mint so badly in her life. The way his arm wrapped around her made her want to stay there forever.

"You ok?" he asked with gentle concern. She shook her head to get out of her daze.

"Uh, yeah, I think so," she stuttered, glancing at his lips before his eyes, "Stupid heels."

Gibson smiled at her, squeezing her a little closer. Pulling his arm away, he said, "Glad I was headed over here to ask about mowing your lawn again."

"My lawn could use another mowing soon," Rose said, but then smashed her hand over her mouth seeing the toothy grin on his face. He wiggled his eyebrows at the last part. She smacked his arm, letting out a little laugh. That wasn't how she meant it.

"My pleasure," he said slyly

"Gibson Oliver Titus, you know what I meant," Rose yelled, laughing.

"You look amazing. Got a date?" His eyes slid from her shoes to her eyes.

"With my dad and church."

"Oh well, hopefully the single guys can smell me on you. This dress is something I'd like to keep to myself." Gibson grabbed her in a hug, pretending to shield her from the world.

"Is it too saucy, you think?"

"I'm kidding. You look beautiful. Almost makes me want to join you. Except that I have two hooligans in the house that I'd have to get ready too." He didn't want to let her out of his embrace. His heart was pounding, wishing he could take Rose back in the house and lock her in her bedroom, strip her out of the dress and show her how she made him feel. Then again, he knew that the town was already talking, so maybe letting her flaunt was a good idea. Show all the guys the babe he was talking to.

"Um, Gibs, do you think you could wipe that drool off your face? I gotta get going. Dad's waiting." Rose mock wiped Gibson's chin. When her finger touched his lip, he playfully bit the tip, sending shocks through her body. She had to look away or she would have jumped him right there in the front yard. She fumbled for her keys instead. He stepped back and motioned for her to walk past. She smiled shyly.

Then, in a low voice, Gibson said, "Enjoy church."

She felt like she was melting right there into her shoes. "I'll see you later?"

"You know where I am." Turning, he walked back to his house.

Church was interesting. All the older ladies were oohing and ah-hing over her and her dad. All the young men couldn't stop staring at her, almost as if they had never seen a girl before. Some of the younger ladies were giving Rose death stares, trying to pull their husbands and boyfriends out the door. Others were trying to get her attention so that they could catch up on the last ten years.

The pastor's wife, who was around fifty years old, swooped in and pulled Rose to the side. In the sweetest southern drawl she had heard since leaving North Carolina, Isabelle Slow said, "I am just so proud of you for uprooting yourself and coming home to take care of your daddy. You are definitely one of the good ones, sweety." Then she grabbed Rose in a hug before walking away. Rose searched the foyer for her dad. When she found him encircled by women of all ages, she smiled. He could still draw them in.

"Hey daddy, you ready to go?" Rose said, walking up and grabbing her dad's hand. He turned and gave her a thankful smile.

"I am Rosey. I love church but it tires me out." They said their goodbyes to the ladies; all of them promised to bring dinner during the weeks to come.

"Wow, I never knew how much of a rock star you were, dad," Rose said, elbowing him in the ribs with gentle movements.

"Well, women always fawn over a sick guy." Jason shared a tired smile. "Can you drop me at Bri's? She's making Sunday dinner for me, and I told her I would come to her this time."

"Of course, dad. I hope she isn't expecting me, though. I kind of wanted to spend some time at home..." she hesitated.

"Only if you want to. I know you're getting close to school starting though, so I didn't think you would want to," Jason shrugged at his daughter.

"You're right, I guess. I do have a lot to do and let me tell you, church tires me out too," she laughed.

Bri tried to talk her into staying, but Rose explained again how tired she was and winked at Bri knowing she would talk to her aunt later about everything.

Gibson saw her pull into the driveway as he was finishing up her front lawn. He wiped his face with his shirt before waving at her. As Rose stepped out of her car, she started walking across the lawn to him.

"Just finished up. Wanted to get it done before the sun got too hot today. How was church?" he asked.

"Well, apparently, I'm either a cheap hussy who wants to steal ALL THE husbands," Rose's arms motioned around the neighborhood with her arms, "or I'm the sweetest daughter in the world," she said.

Gibson laughed. "Well, you could easily be the Pied Piper leading all the men out of town dressed like that, but I'm going to put my money on the sweetest daughter," he joked.

Rose laughed too. "I'm not sure if I'm proud to be called the Pied Piper or not."

"I was just going to make some sandwiches for the kids and me. I can make four if you want. They aren't fancy, just pb and j."

"Sure, let me go change and I'll be over."

"Sure thing, gorgeous. See you in a bit," he said, pushing the lawn mower home.

Rose knew she should spend her time getting ready for school, and a twinge of guilt sped through her, knowing she had just said a tiny lie to her dad. Gibson drew her in like a bee to a flower. She craved his touch more every day, and she just couldn't resist.

Fifteen minutes later, she was walking through the side door of the Titus home. She heard the kids in the living room, and Gibson was at the counter, dirty and sweaty from the mowing, but still looking sexy as hell. The kids hadn't heard her yet, so Rose walked up behind him and wrapped her arms around his waist. "Hey," she whispered. He turned around and looked down at her, squeezing her back and kissing her gently.

"Glad you made it," he said into her ear. Letting her go, he hollered to the kids, "Guy's come get your sandwiches."

"ROSE!" they both yelled, rushing into the kitchen.

"We didn't know you were coming for lunch!" Oliver said in a voice WAY above inside voices.

"Oliver, come on dude, quiet it down. We aren't on the playground." Gibson laughed at his son and ruffled his hair.

"Oops, sorry dad."

"Can we eat outside, dad? Pleeeeeeaaaassssseee!" Chloe asked.

"I suppose. Here're your plates." Then he handed one to Rose.

"Shall we?" The kids bound out the door to the patio ahead of them, scrambling into seats around the table.

"My grandma made the jelly, Rose." Chloe had a look of pride on her face.

"Wow, I'll bet it's the best jelly in the county." Rose loved these interactions. She had prayed since she was a little girl to become a teacher, to get married and to have kids. So far, only one dream had become a reality.

"Dad, I wanted chocolate milk." "Me too!" Both kids were shoving their cups toward Gibson.

"I forgot, come on you two let's go put some chocolate in that milk." He pushed back from the table, and as he passed Rose, he lightly ran his fingers across the back of her neck, raising goose-bumps across her body and tying a knot in her stomach. The effect that man had on her was insane.

After finishing their sandwiches and clearing their plates, they walked to the ice cream shop downtown. The kids in the middle and all holding hands... a family.

Gibson looked over the top of the kids at Rose. "You ready for the rumor mill to really start churning?" he asked with a smile.

"I thought it already had," she responded with a wink.

"What's a rumor mill?" Chloe asked. Gibson and Rose just laughed.

Gibson held the door to the little cafe, letting the kids fly in first to look at the flavors. Rose followed, but as she crossed the threshold, Gibson swooped behind her, wrapping his arms around her waist. The movement startled her at first, but then a smile crept across her face, and she reached for one of his hands.

Someone cleared their throat to the right of them. Turning, Cody and his family sat in a booth enjoying the sweet treat as well.

"Well, well, well," Cody said, "I guess you weren't lying, Gibs. You did get the girl... again."

Rose turned her head slightly to look up at Gibson. "Got the girl?"

Gibson released a breathy laugh, "Yeah, uh, I mean, Cody's my best friend. I told him we were, uh, seeing each other again."

"And what, you didn't believe him, Cody?" Rose set a hand on her hip, cocking her head at their friend.

"I just didn't think you would actually listen to Lacey is all, let alone Gibson here." Cody's laugh filled the cafe.

"Hey, what's that mean? I thought you were my friend." Gibson was laughing, too.

"Well, I did want to deck her, if that's what you're wondering. And there's something about this guy, I just can't resist his charm." When she looked at Gibson again, the laughter slowed, and a peaceful smile replaced his giddy one. He squeezed her closer. Cody wrapped an arm around his wife and squeezed her, too.

"Get off me," his wife said, playfully pushing him away.

"Dad!! Are we gonna get ice cream?" Chloe was spinning around the room, impatiently waiting for her cone.

"Sorry, guys, here I come. See you guys later," Gibson and Rose waved as he pulled her to the counter.

Ice cream was exactly what the day had needed. The sun was beating down on them and by the time they made it home; the kids were sticky from the treat and tired from the heat. Gibson popped the air on in the living room letting the kids veg on the floor in front of cartoons, eventually falling asleep. Rose and Gibson sat at the table.

"So, how's school stuff coming along?" Gibson inquired.

"I'm almost ready. My room is set, the lessons seem pretty spot on. I'm just oddly nervous. It almost feels like my first year all over again," she explained.

"Really? Why? You know everyone here, and even if you don't, they aren't unlike everyone else in town." He sat back in his chair, removed the baseball cap he was wearing and rubbed the back of his head with it, before replacing it.

"I don't know. It's a new area for me. I'm so used to my inner city school, my kids needing me. A lot of those kids had no real stability, and I became that for them. Most of these kids already have that, so the dynamic will be different. I'm not sure I know how to act or what to watch for."

"The same thing, silly. There are plenty of kids around here that don't have stability either. It might be a different type of stability they need, but you remember how farm life can be. Parents who work way too much sometimes or don't make a ton of money because of the market. They're all going to need you. You'll remember as soon as you start." Gibson could see it in her eyes that something more was churning in her mind. "What else?"

Rose started picking at her nails then, "Well, after dad fell this summer, I questioned how it will be during the school year. Bri started a side hustle, and it's picking up. I'll be at school all day. What if that crazy man tries to climb a ladder again or something?"

Gibson leaned toward her then. "Rose, I have a secret." Her eyes darted across his face, questioning him. "I stole his ladder. He won't be climbing that thing alone ever again."

Rose laughed. "You did what?"

"I mean it. Go look in the garage. It's laying on the floor," Gibson shrugged, throwing his arm over the back of his chair.

Rose slowed her laughter. "That's great. I hadn't even noticed when I was over there." Then lowering her voice, she held his stare, "Thank you. At least that alleviates one fear."

"So, what else can I do to help?" he asked with a twinkle in his eye.

"I don't know," she said thoughtfully, "I am glad to have you right here. At least I know after a rough day, I can come sit and just be with you." She unconsciously traced the muscle on his forearm.

"You'll have me forever that way, Rose, no matter how things turn out with us." He grabbed her hand. "I'll always be right here."

CHAPTER SEVENTEEN

Rose

She texted Grace as she walked back to her house. It was about six and she knew her friend would be ordering take out or walking to the cafe. She never cooked for herself unless there was a man involved.

So, I think things are starting

to speed up a bit with Gibs.

Immediately, her phone rang. "Um, why?" was the first thing out of her friend's mouth.

"He slept over Friday night."

"Excuse me. What?"

"No, not like that. We slept, like slept-slept, well after a heated make-out session. He took me to dinner, we stayed out for a while, then something snapped when we got back to the house."

"Ooh, this sounds juicy. Keep talking. I want to have to take a shower afterwards."

"Ew, gross Grace," Rose said, but continued anyway. When she finished with the breakfast part, Grace was completely silent. "You still there Gracey?"

"Yeah," her friend said, "I don't know how you can do that though."

"What?"

"You have this gorgeous guy, and he is gorgeous, by the way. You have him half naked and then you shut him down. Then you make him lay in bed with you and don't jump him in the middle of all of this? Have I let you down somewhere?"

Rose laughed, "No. I just know that I truly want this to work. I don't want to rush into bed with him."

"Ok, whatever you say. I'm just saying, sounds like you're on the slippery slope that Alaina warned you about." Grace hesitated, "I say ride that bitch down the mountain on skis. Oh well, I gotta go. My noodles are ready." Rose heard the sexual tone in Grace's voice.

"What's the noodle's name?"

"Hank? I think? Maybe?" Grace's questioning tone made Rose laugh then.

"You might want to figure that out, Gracey. Love you. Thanks for the fake advice."

"My pleasure, love you more."

When she hung up, she noticed a text had popped through from Gibson.

Movie later this week?

I promise to be on time, even if

I have to drive my tractor home. :)

> *I could probably free up some*
>
> *time for you. When ya thinking?*

Thursday? The old theater is playing

your favorite, Notebook.

When did they start playing

movies again?

Is that a yes? We can walk down

together. I'll check what time it's

playing and let you know.

Sounds good. So you're saying I

have to wait until Thursday to see you?

There was no response, but she heard the screen door of Gibson's house open and shut. Then she heard footsteps in the driveway and up her porch steps. Then a pounding on her door. She laughed as she approached the door and saw him trying to peek through the window. Before she finished opening the door, he pushed through, grabbing her in a hug. Then, wrapping his arms under her bottom, he lifted her to his face. She wrapped her arms around his neck.

"You can come see me anytime I'm home," and then he kissed her. She pushed into the kiss, not wanting it to end. When it did, he slowly set her down. "Can't stay. The kids are getting ready for bed. Left 'em brushing their teeth." He pecked her lips again and ran back out the door. Her hand absently lifted to her lips. This was in no way a slope. It was more like a cliff, and she was ready to dive face first. She just hoped she wouldn't crash and burn.

CHAPTER EIGHTEEN

Gibson

Mondays were always the hardest for Gibson. He hated leaving the kids behind and weekends were always so busy that sleep was at a minimum. Today was no different. Brandi had gotten to the house five minutes late. He had left the chores list for the kids and had even gotten groceries. As Gibson pulled on his work boots and grabbed his wallet, Brandi asked him, "So, Mr Titus, my mom says that you're off the market. Is that true? My cousin is really into you, and I thought maybe you could take her out sometime."

He stopped in the kitchen and turned to look at her. She was a sweet girl, but maybe this town was going a little crazy with all of this. He had never been what people would call the most eligible bachelor, but now that Rose was back, it sure seemed like women were crawling out of the corners.

"Brandi, I don't think I was ever really on the market."

"I didn't think you were, Mr Titus. Have a good day." she smiled at him and walked to the living room.

"I will. Hey, I gotta make a stop after work. Is it ok if I'm a little later than normal?"

"No problem for me," the teenager responded.

"Great, thanks. See you tonight then." He walked out the door, jumped in the truck, started it, and then just sat in the driveway, staring at Rose's house. Things were heating up, and he was excited to see where things were going to go.

Rose

Ugh, Monday, Rose thought the second she opened her eyes. *The last Monday of my summer break.* Feeling the knot of anxiety bind up again in her stomach, Rose forced herself out of bed to start getting ready for the day. She was going to spend most of the day in her classroom. Last night her dad had said yes when she had asked him if he wanted to join her at the school today. She had to stop there anyway to load her book nook in the trunk.

She pulled on some jeans and a tee shirt before pulling her hair into a ponytail. Then rolled out the door with a huge mug of coffee and headed to pick Jason and the book nook up.

Rose knew that her dad loved being included in his daughter's work. He loved helping, feeling needed and missed when she was young, helping her with school projects. Now she could let Jason help with a project for her classroom. It was a full circle.

Hefting the large item into her Honda had been rough. Fortunately for Rose, one of her dad's neighbors was home and willing to help. Getting it back out of her Honda took a bit of work. She had wrangled Kendall and the school custodian into helping her. They loaded it onto a cart that was used to haul lunch tables and rolled it down the hall. The cart had tried skewing all over, making it a three-person guiding job. When they made it to the room, Jason guided the other three as they tried to position it over the masking tape "X" she had stuck on the floor.

"Thanks for your help, guys. This looks great in here." She was clasping her hands together and the childlike look on her face made Jason smile.

"Thanks for letting me help, Rosey," he beamed at his daughter, noting that she appeared much happier than she had when she first arrived. Rose rushed over and squeezed him.

"All I needed was Iron Man to help put the finishing touches on."

"Iron Man, huh? Is that what you've called me all along? I kind of think of myself as Batman, but if Iron Man is what you think, I'll live with it. I am smart like Tony Stark." His eyes twinkled.

CHAPTER NINETEEN

Rose

Tuesday, her dad had a follow up doctor's appointment. When she got to Jason's house to pick him up, Gibson's truck was in the driveway. *What's he doing here?* It was the middle of the day on a Tuesday. *What is going on?* She slammed her car door and ran up to the house.

"And then she said, 'Man, you need a hobby.'" Gibson's voice danced to her ears, followed by her dad's laugh filling the house. Smiling, Rose walked to the kitchen.

"Um, what's going on here?" she asked, with her head cocked to the side.

"Honey, Gibson and I have lunch every Tuesday. Didn't I tell you that?" her dad was smiling, and Gibson was too,

"Um, no, I'm pretty sure I would remember that if either of you did."

"Oh yeah, we've been doing this for a few years now. Ever since I got diagnosed."

"Yeah, I take a long lunch on Tuesdays. The guys at the farm have never given me crap about it. Plus, I mean, my dad owns the place, so what can they say?" Gibson winked at her.

"Ok then." She said, circling her finger between the two men. "This is a weird bromance then?" Her dad and Gibson looked at each other and smiled a strange smile.

"I guess so," Jason responded. "He is one of my best friends, I guess."

Rose shook her head, still so confused. "Well, I hate to break this up, but dad you have an appointment in twenty minutes. We have to get going."

Gibson slid his chair back from the table and took the two plates to the sink. He patted Jason on the shoulder. "I'll see you next week." He walked up to Rose and looked at her, calling over his shoulder, "Jay, you might wanna close your eyes for this." Rose heard her dad laugh as Gibson leaned in, placing his hands on both sides of her face, and kissed her. She felt her body go limp for a moment. This was definitely the edge of the cliff, and her dad was somehow helping push her over.

Gibson released her, waved at Jason, and was out the door. Rose was still standing frozen where she was. *Dad and Gibson, friends?*

"Earth to Rose. You ok?" Jason called to her.

"Uh, erm, yeah. I just can't think right now. I'm so confused."

Jason smiled at his daughter, "Confused or…"

Rose stuck her tongue out, before finding his shoes and handing them to her dad. "Get your shoes on, we gotta get going," Rose pushed, still looking at the front door through which Gibson had just left.

The doctor gave her dad a good report. Jason still had to use the sling, but the cast did indeed come off. They checked his Parkinson's symptoms, with the doctor taking a lot of notes, which Rose knew wasn't always a good thing.

"So, I know we just upped your meds, Jay, but there's a new Parkinson's medication trial that just started, and I think it might be beneficial to you. I'm going to send you home with some information. I want you, Rose, and Bri to look it over. Let me know what you think. You would have to stop your current meds for three weeks, but it would cut back your meds immensely and should curb a lot of these progressing symptoms." Rose's eyes lit up as she looked at her dad. Her dad was holding the pamphlets but wasn't smiling like she thought he would be. They thanked the doctor and left the office.

"Dad? What are you thinking?" she asked him when they got in the car.

"This trial," Jason started, "It seems too good to be true. I mean, I would love to be off so much medication, but what if it doesn't work? What if I start sliding faster?"

Rose hadn't even thought that far ahead when she had heard the offer. Taking her dad's hand, she looked him in the eye. "So, we do what you want to do. I say we talk to Bri too. Maybe she has some thoughts that would help. Then we do what you want to do. It makes me excited to think that maybe you will get to see all the dreams that you want to see."

He smiled at his daughter and squeezed her hand. "You're right, Rosey. I'll call Bri and see if she can come over tomorrow. I know she has a party for her new thingy she's selling tonight."

They got back to Jason's house, and she made tacos for dinner. While they ate, Rose pushed for info on this bromance that was revealed today. Her dad tried to explain.

"Gibson's been one of my biggest allies since I got diagnosed, besides Bri and you, of course. He was the first person to come to the house after I was diagnosed." Jason took a bite, the taco crumbling as he did. "He was still married then, but it was the beginning of the end. Coming here was like a place where Gibson could get away from Lorna, but it helped me too. I was pretty depressed at first and Gibson was in a bad place too."

Rose's heart felt like it could burst. "Dad, I had no idea! You never said a thing about this while I was in Charlotte. This is," she thought for a minute, "This is something I didn't expect, like AT ALL, but I'm glad he's been here for you. You need more guy friends."

"I didn't want to get you upset. I guess I felt a little like a traitor. But he was a godsend, kinda like a son. Now my best guy friend. I know that's a little weird, but you know I don't get out much. The neighbors come over now and then, but nothing that's a bromance, as you call it." Jason winked at her. The boyish smile on his face made Rose smile.

"Well, I'm glad, dad. I mean, I thought maybe it would be John Titus, not Gibs."

"Well, what you don't know, Rosey, is that after you left, Gibson came and talked to me. I didn't ask him too, he just showed up." Jason was looking down at the table, but he could feel the burn of his daughter's eyes on him. "He wanted to talk about what had happened. I still don't know everything, just that he wasn't the only one in the wrong. He loved you so much though, that he wanted to try to let you go be you." Jason finally dared to raise his eyes to meet his daughter's.

"Why does no one feel like they can tell me things?" Rose felt her blood boiling.

"Rose, hear me out. You needed to go to North Carolina. You needed to spread your wings. What you didn't need was interference. You wouldn't have become the woman you are today without those chances." He reached across the table and tapped his finger. "I needed you to go. We were becoming too codependent. I knew you felt the need to stay and be my babysitter. But what you absolutely needed to do was go and find yourself without the noise of me or Gibson or even Holly."

"Dad, I appreciate this, I really do, but why didn't you even bother to tell me he had come to you? Why couldn't you have done that?"

"Because Rose," Jason's voice got very fatherlike when he spoke, "you would have come running home before it was time. Because you were happy, you were forging your life. Because I knew if it was meant to be you would find your way back at the right time."

"But dad," Rose tried to interject.

"No, what I did may not sound right to you, but it was the right thing at the time. You go on and believe what you will, but I did what I thought was right for the only person in my world that mattered. Still the only person in my world that matters."

Rose knew it was true, but still couldn't help feeling a little hurt. "Um, so, speaking of Gibson, dad," she was hoping for a little advice, "I feel like I'm about to topple off the top of a cliff with my heart again. I feel like things have moved way faster than I wanted them to, but my feet are right there at the edge. Alaina called it a slope. It's not a slope. It's a cliff, and it makes me excited and nervous. Grace told me to jump."

Her dad listened intently to Rose's fears and excitement, but he said nothing. Around seven, she noticed the signs that it was getting close to bedtime for her dad. It was just like clockwork. He would tire at the same time every day. She got him settled again and kissed him good night. Right when she was ready to walk out the door, her dad said, "Rose, I have a parachute right here if you feel that you're about to hit the bottom."

"What dad?" she asked.

"I'm just trying to say, jump off the cliff, Rose. You won't be sorry. I promise. And if it goes wrong, I'm here. Dive, sweety." She hugged her dad. "Now get out of here and let me watch my game.

I'll see you and Brianne tomorrow." Rose drove home in a cloud of emotions.

Gibson

Gibson spent the rest of his day at work on the tractor. Lucky for him, it was the tractor with GPS, so when he caught himself daydreaming, the tractor was still moving in the line it was meant to be moving. He couldn't stop thinking of the look on Rose's face when she had found out about him and Jason's friendship. Although he was a little surprised that neither he nor Jason had told her about it; it just never came up. He was remembering how good she tasted every time they kissed.

He had told his parents about what had been happening. His mom almost cried because she had been so sad when Rose had left. His dad had slapped him on the back. Neither of his parents knew the entire story about why Rose had left town, but they both knew it was mostly Gibson's fault and Gibson was still nervous he was going to mess things up again.

Gibson had always loved working on the farm. When he had been married to Lorna, he had found reasons to stay late, probably to help him ignore the fact that Lorna wasn't where his heart was. Now that Rose was home, he couldn't wait to get leave.

When he finally made it home Tuesday night, Brandi was chomping at the bit to get out of there. She warned him, "The kids are pretty wound up. You're going to need to take them to the park or something to get them settled down."

He figured out after she left it was her own fault for giving them too much sugar that day. That happened sometimes when you left a teenager in charge.

He had hoped that Rose would stop over and that they could all go to the park together, but her car wasn't home. He let out a sigh that was obviously too loud because Chloe came running, wrapped herself around her dad's leg and said, "Daddy, are you sad?"

He reached down and picked his daughter up. "Clover, I just missed you guys so much today." His daughter wrapped her arms around her dad's neck and squeezed him with all her might.

"I missed you too, daddy. Brandi let us eat Oreos and M & Ms ALL DAY!" Yup, they're wound alright. Chloe was still carrying on about cookies and ice cream when Oliver rushed in and slammed into his legs.

"Hey dad! You made it home! Did you get to see Elsie today? Did you hear that we got to eat all the sweet stuff today?" Elsie was Oliver's favorite cow on the farm, and Gibson knew he was in trouble tonight. These kids were going to need a run at the park for sure. He peeked out the window again, but Rose still wasn't home. He told the kids to grab their sandals and off they went to the park, then to the Hot Dog Barn for dinner.

They started home right around seven. Gibson could see it in the kids' faces that the sugar had shot through them. The hot dogs they had at the stand had settled and they were ready to fall asleep. He had to carry Chloe from Main Street and Oliver's little feet were barely moving to keep up. Scooping Oliver up at the intersection before the house, Gibson carried them both the rest of the way.

Rose

Rose's breath caught when she saw Gibson carrying both his children. His brawny arms held tightly to their little bodies and both kids' heads were laying on his shoulders. His chin rose with a smile when she waved to him. She ran to get the door for him and then closed it behind him before walking back to her house. As soon as she closed the door, her phone rang.

"Hey," Gibson said, sounding tired.

"Macho man, I'm guessing you went to the park?"

"Ha, yeah. Brandi let the kids have entirely too much sugar today. They were wired when I got home."

"Ah, are they asleep now?"

"Chloe is, Oliver is fighting it, but I think he'll be out soon. How was the rest of your day?"

"Fine, dad got some news today at the doctor's office. Actually, is there a chance you can come with me to his house tomorrow? I mean, I know it's not Tuesday, so maybe that crosses your bro code? But he was told about a trial today that could help reverse or at least slow down his symptoms. He wants to talk to Bri tomorrow and wants me there, too. He's not sure he wants to do it."

"If you think it would help, I could break bro code and come with you. I just have to see if my mom can come watch the kids. I'm sure she won't care. She's been begging for the last three weeks," he laughed, but then stopped, "Do you want him to try it?"

"I'm not sure. I had high hopes when I heard about it, but then dad wasn't so sure, so it made me wonder. I'm going to head there around six. Will you be home in time?"

"Girl, remember, I work for my dad. If I tell him I need to do this with you, he won't bat an eye. I'll talk to you later. Ollie just wandered out here. Good night."

"Good night."

CHAPTER TWENTY

Rose and Gibson

Gibson was home at five thirty on Wednesday. When he got to her house, he looked like a god and smelled like the woods. She pulled him in, giving him a gentle kiss, then said, "Thank you for coming with me. I'm hoping you being there will help him be comfortable when we make whatever decision today." Rose locked her front door, waved at Mavis, who was out with the kids next door, and together they walked to her car.

When they got to her dad's, Bri was just pulling in as well. She had brought her husband, Tom. He raised an eyebrow at Gibson and Rose holding hands but didn't say anything. Bri elbowed her husband because Rose had told her a little about what was going on earlier in the week. Entering the house, Rose prayed her dad didn't feel ganged up on.

The five of them had a long conversation. Rose made a pros and cons list to help with the decision making. All of them voiced their concerns for both sides. It turned out that having Gibson and Tom there helped. Something about having a couple of men that her dad trusted calmed his fears a little more. In the end, Jason gave in, deciding to try the trial. He still looked like he wasn't sure it was the right decision but understood all the information and the insights that the other four had given.

Around eight, they all got ready to leave her dad's house. Jason was a bit sad to see them all go. It had been a while since so many people were at his house. He used to love having barbeques, so this was a bittersweet visit knowing they were only there for medical talk.

"Jason, remember you and I are going to call the doctor." Bri reminded him with a hug.

"I know. To tell him to sign me up." Jason's voice wobbled slightly.

Rose squeezed her dad tight and kissed his cheek. "Dad, I promise you that if things start to go bad, we will get you off the treatment. I'm excited though." She winked at her dad, who gave her a tired smile.

Gibson shook Jason's hand before grabbing Rose's hand heading out to the car. For the first time as adults, they had done a big thing as a team. And to Rose, it felt so right. Gibson drove them home, Rose chattering the whole way.

"If this works, he'll get to see so many things that he wouldn't have been able to. He might be able to get back to work part time, he could drive again. He might get to walk me down the aisle." She snapped her mouth closed as her face turned red. "I mean down the line if I ever get to that." Gibson smiled, lifting her hand to his lips.

When they got to the house, Gibson handed Rose her keys and asked, "So, are we still on for tomorrow? Or did you count this as our date?"

"That was a pretty lame date if it was," she grinned, still on cloud nine about her dad being willing to give the trial a go. Gibson reached up, pushing a stray strand of hair behind her ear. Cupping her head in the spot, he pulled her in for a kiss goodnight. Rose sighed, wrapping her arms around his neck. When they parted, he pecked her lips again.

"I'll see you tomorrow night, then. Don't be late," Gibson joked.

Standing on her tiptoes, not speaking, Rose begged for another kiss. Gibson leaned in, gently brushing her lips with his again.

"Right, look who's talking," she quipped. He shrugged with a smile as he turned to head home.

"Hey Gibson," she yelled, stopping him in his tracks and causing him to turn. "Thanks again. It means the world to me that you came tonight." He nodded his head to her and then continued home.

CHAPTER TWENTY-ONE

Rose and Gibson

The next evening, Gibson was on time, in fact, a few minutes early. Rose was still doing her hair when she heard him knock. She ran down the stairs and opened the door before running back up the stairs.

"Um, did a ghost just let me in?" Gibson said, stepping through the doorway, looking around.

"I'm almost ready," she yelled down the stairs. "You're early!"

"Hey, I was told not to be late. What do you want from me?" He joked as he started up the stairs.

"Don't come up here. I'll be right down." Gibson turned on his toe and walked back down the steps mouthing 'OOOKKK'.

He heard her heels on the steps. What he saw when he turned caused his hand to shoot to his heart. She was wearing a blue dress this time; the color was close to the color of the sky at twilight. The hem hit just above her knees, and it clung to every curve of her body. Her hair was curled, but she had wrapped half of it into a bun at the crown of her head. She looked like a page out of a magazine.

"We're only going to a movie," he said after catching his breath.

"I know, but I don't get to wear any of these dresses anymore, plus I got the exact reaction from you I was hoping for. Now wipe your chin, Titus. Let's go." She brushed past him out the door. He followed her like a puppy dog, watching those hips sway, almost not able to walk. His thoughts were upstairs between the sheets, wanting to watch those hips move above him. She turned to see where he was, catching him as he snapped his gaze from her butt back to her eyes.

"Are you coming?" she giggled. He took two steps and was beside her, grabbing her hand. He wasn't letting her go anywhere looking like that without his hand firmly in hers.

When they got to the theater, there was a line for everything. The entire town had turned out for the screening and once again, Gibson and Rose were the center of attention.

"I can't believe people. Have they never seen a couple on a date before?" Rose asked with a huff.

"If they're going to talk, let's give them something to talk about." Gibson draped his arms over her shoulders from behind. Rose reached for his hands before looking up and over her shoulder at him. The look in her eyes caused him to lean down and peck her lips. She smiled and puckered for another one, which he obliged. When she turned back forward, every eye was on them, before quickly turning away. She smiled a saucy smile at the crowd. Gibson left himself wrapped right where he was through the ticket line and the popcorn line.

It truly was her favorite movie. She always cried and laughed at the same scenes. When the scene started with the boat and the swans, Rose snuggled in a little closer to Gibson. The rain started in the scene, and she laid her head on his shoulder. They got out of the boat and Noah said her favorite line, 'It wasn't over. It still isn't over.' When Noah kissed Allie, Rose sighed and looked up at Gibson, who was already looking at her. He smiled and whispered, "Man, I feel him." She smiled back and kissed him, one sweet peck. He wrapped his arm a little tighter around her.

They hit the bar after the movie, but only stayed for one drink. It was a Thursday, but because of the movie, it was packed. Not the quiet place they had hoped for. Plus, Gibson had to work the next morning. They held hands, walking back to her house, repeating all the cliché lines from the movie.

"Should we lie in the middle of the road like they did?" Gibson asked, walking out into the street.

"No, Gibson, get back over here," she yelled at him. He laughed and ran back to her side, lifting her off the ground with no effort at all. Rose laughed, leaning her head back and kicking her leg out as she did. Placing her feet back down on the sidewalk, he grabbed her hand again.

They talked the rest of the way back to the house. Gibson voiced concern because Oliver's birthday was in a few weeks, and he wanted to have a birthday party for him but did not know where to start with Minecraft decorations. Rose talked about her dad a bit and work. Gibson talked about the new teenager who started at the farm, laughing about something to do with the milker that she didn't understand but she laughed, anyway.

When they got to her house, she unlocked the door, letting them both inside. She wanted to have a nightcap and he couldn't pry himself away from her. Gibson watched as she sashayed to the refrigerator, pulling out a bottle of white wine. His noticeable wince caught her eye, so she grabbed him a beer. She tried to reach the wine glasses but couldn't reach without climbing on the counter, and that wasn't happening in this dress.

"Hey cowboy," she said using a southern drawl, "can you help me?" She batted her eyelashes at him.

"Well little lady," He tried to mimic the drawl, "I suppose I can do that." He wandered over to the cupboard and grabbed one for her. As he handed it to her, their fingers brushed, lighting her skin on fire. She poured her glass, glancing at him as she took the first sip. *God, he's gorgeous.* Rose watched as he sat back down at her table and leaned back a bit. The muscles of his shoulders strained against his shirt. *Three months has to be enough time, right? We've had many deep conversations and really gotten to know each other again. Forgive me Alaina.* Setting her glass on the counter, she walked towards him, swinging her hips sensually. Gibson gulped as she stopped in front of him to take his hand. He stood obediently when she pulled.

"Gibson, I need to tell you something," she murmured, sliding her hands up his chest to his shoulders.

His voice was a low grumble when he responded by wrapping her in his arms, "Ok, what's up?" That grumble made her insides twist as parts of her body came alive. She had to say this first, though.

"I think... I think I love you..." She felt the squeeze of his arms. Looking up, Rose saw the fire in his eyes again.

"Thank god you said it. I love you too," he leaned down and kissed her.

Pulling back from his lips, she put a hand on his cheek. With a devilish smile she said, "I also want you." The wolf inside of his body roared, grabbing her, and setting her up on the counter. His mouth covered hers in a passionate kiss. Her hands wrapped in his tee shirt. She tugged slightly on his bottom lip, and he let out a moan. He pulled the skirt of her dress up a little and pulled her closer to him. His jeans were holding back a bulge that rubbed against her as she unconsciously wrapped her legs around his waist. The pressure caused her body to pulse against him. Pulling her off the counter, he walked them toward the living room. Slowly letting her slide down his body before they got there, she felt every part of his desire growing against her. She pushed into the kiss deeper, unable to get enough of his mouth.

When Rose pulled back for a brief breath, their chests were both heaving. Gibson cautiously asked, "Wait, are we still taking things slow?"

"Oh, god, I hope not," she responded, grabbing the button on his pants, "Unless you think we should." She stole a look up at him but he was shaking his head. His hands ran up her back finding the zipper on the back of her dress, letting it slide off her body to the floor. Gibson took a step back to take in the beauty that was beneath those clothes. She was breathing heavily, internally thanking herself for choosing the matching black lace bra and panty set. With one hand, he pulled his shirt over his head, revealing his tan body, rippled with muscles. She took in the view as he let it drop to the ground, thanking God again for this farm body.

He put one hand on the wall above her, hesitating before leaning in to kiss her again. This kiss was more romantic than the frenzy that had just occurred as his fingertips traveled up her body, exploring again, making his way to her chin. Every touch was deliberate and gentle, heating her entire body.

Her hands worked the button on his pants. When it finally freed itself, she struggled to push them down his hips. He took his hands off of her, helping his pants to the ground without separating from her mouth.

Her fingers traced down every muscle on his body ending just above his boxers. Pulling from their kiss, she looked him in the eyes pulling back his boxers. Her eyes darted down for a second as she took his member in her hand. When she started stroking, she looked up again, biting her bottom lip. There was no need for her help. He was fully erect already. But her hands on him pulled a gasp from his lips. His eyes got fiery. Pulling her hand away, Gibson easily lifted her up onto his waist. The fact that his length rubbed against her again sent waves of pleasure through her body.

"Where to?" he whispered in a voice that drenched her in so many ways.

"Up stairs?" The quiet question came out of her mouth before she met his mouth again.

Before he took the first step, he pulled back from her mouth, his voice raspy as he asked, "Oh god Rose. Should we be doing this?"

"Stop asking," she replied a little too urgently, pushing her lips to his again.

That was all he needed to hear. Starting up the stairs, he steadied himself on the wall with one hand as they ascended. He traveled her neck and collarbone with his mouth while carrying her as if she was as light as a bird. When Gibson set her down at the top of the steps, she took his hand and led him to the bedroom.

He switched the light on, wanting to see every part of her. Rose unhooked her bra with one hand, slowly removing each strap until it fell to the ground, allowing her hands to trace over her bare skin. Gibson swooped in, lifting her again with one arm onto the bed. Laying her down, he took one of her nipples into his mouth, ripping a quiet moan, almost a cry, from her. Gibson pulled and tugged on both breasts before abruptly standing up.

"Shit, my pants are downstairs. Protection," was all he could muster. She let out a small giggle, watching him in his boxers run out the bedroom door. The realization set in for Rose that she was about to give herself away for the last time. She knew this was it and that if this didn't work out in the end, there would never be another.

She heard him rushing up the stairs, two at a time, back to the bedroom, and heard the wrapper crinkling as he came through the door. Gibson stopped short in the doorway, his chest heaving from running and took in the sight of Rose laid out on the bed, smiling with a blush on her cheeks. Looking him in the eyes, she tugged her panties off and threw them at him with a smile that made his heartbeat go wild.

As he moved across the room back to her, he yanked his boxers off. When he reached the bed, she sat up to meet him. He threw the rest of the condoms on her bed stand before rolling one onto himself. Their mouths collided before he entered her. She let out a low moan as he did, which added to their arousals. He moved in and out of her with a passion she had missed with all the other men she'd had. It was want and need, but also love.

When she wanted more, she rolled him over and slowly lowered herself on top of him, with enough pressure to hit her spot, grinding against him to heighten her arousal.

When he couldn't handle it anymore, he rolled her back onto her back. With slow, deep thrusts, he felt her clench around him. Her fingernails were deep into his arms as she climaxed. The feeling of her shuddering around him pulled him over the edge with her. They laid in the afterglow talking and flirting before doing it all over again and again. So much passion and love was twisted together that night. They filled the entire night with ten years of missed time.

They took a breather at three in the morning so Gibson could call into work. He didn't want to ruin whatever was going to continue happening. She laughed as she took him into her mouth while he was leaving his voicemail, causing him to groan quietly. When he hung up, he growled at her before the love making started again. When the sun began to rise, they finished simultaneously, falling asleep in each other's arms.

When she awoke, it was to Gibson stroking her face. His dimples on full display.

"Hey," she said sleepily, rubbing her eyes.

"Hey," he whispered, kissing her lips, "Sleep ok?"

"Best sleep I've had in ten years," she responded, smiling.

"Same," he smiled back at her, "Should I go make coffee?"

"Not yet," she said with a grin that made him raise his eyebrows. She straddled him and brought them to heaven again. Once they both came back down, he got up and pulled on his boxers. Looking back at her with her hair ruffled made his chest tight. God, he loved her.

Rose climbed out of bed and walked out of the room, putting nothing on. The way he followed her was almost like there was a string attached between them. She put on her apron in the kitchen. The cloth barely covered her body, causing his manhood to jump.

"What can I get you, cowboy?" she asked, winking, and using her southern draw again. It took every part of his brain to not to climb over the counter and take her right there on the kitchen floor.

"Coffee... black. Apparently, I'll need all the caffeine possible to get through this day."

Rose smiled and turned to get the filters out of the cupboard, her bare butt swinging at him in the process. He couldn't handle it and flew around the counter to grab her, spinning her to face him. "Now? In the kitchen?" she laughed.

"I hope you don't mind, I can't help myself. That apron makes me hungry for you." His eyes smoldered.

Gibson's hands were wild again, traveling over her body, stroking her nipples with his fingertips. Rose moaned as his fingers plunged into the crevice between her legs, stroking her. She dropped the filters, grabbing his arms to steady herself. When she came, he covered her mouth in a kiss that told her he wanted to be inside her. He lifted her onto the counter but stopped short.

She looked at him in desperation. Gibson whispered, "No protection." Rose kissed him and put one finger up. Jumping off the counter, she walked to the half bath and opened a drawer. Then threw a box at him.

"I was prepared just in case," she said slyly. The response pulled a low groan from him as she hopped back on to the counter. He quickly tore the wrapper and covered himself. With a grab of his arms, Rose tugged him back to her. Wrapping her legs tightly around his waist, he plunged into her, grabbing her bottom in the process. The need was the same as the night before, and he couldn't get enough. The angle allowed him to hit her spot easily, sending her up and over the edge of climax again. Her moans, and the feeling of her clenching around him, created a pressure in him. Another hard thrust and he toppled over the edge. When they finished pulsing, he helped her down, kissing her as he did.

"Ok, now let me make the coffee," she said, laughing. He sat down at the bar and watched her, moving every part of her, hoping he could make it through breakfast.

They spent the next six hours after breakfast lying in bed, with an occasional wandering hand or finger, talking, watching movies, and binging tv shows. Spending time, just the two of them. They napped, occasionally waking each other up with a kiss. Neither of them ready to face the world again, or to leave the other's side. Around dinner time, she heard his stomach growl.

"What kind of girlfriend am I?" she said out loud.

"I love hearing that out of your mouth," he said, laying on his side, one hand on her stomach.

"Girlfriend?"

"Yeah, makes my world feel complete again."

She kissed him gently, "I hear your tummy growling. Should I go make something to eat? I think I have some bread. I could make grilled cheese. It's nothing special, but it's food." She stroked his face and his goatee.

"Well, I don't want to put clothes on, so going out is out of the question."

"Oh well yeah, clothes are a non-starter for me too," she replied with a wink, climbing out of bed.

He stayed the entire night Friday as well. They made love twice that night. This time, they were slow and controlled instead of fast and frenzied. Certain that the neighborhood had heard everything, but neither of them cared. In fact, maybe if they did, they would stop staring. If they could just stay in this nirvana forever, they would. Unfortunately, Lorna called around eight the next morning, just as his tongue was circling and Rose was seconds from climaxing.

"What!" Gibson shouted into the phone, instantly regretting it.

"Oh, yeah, hi to you too. Um, Oliver is puking, and I don't have the mental ability right now to deal with it," came Lorna's voice.

"Are you fucking kidding me, Lorna? He's your kid, be a mom for once." Rose sat up and mouthed 'what?'

"Yeah, well, I'm not the full-time parent here. You are. I'm bringing him to you right now. I'm about 5 minutes away," and she hung up.

"Shit. Argh, I want to finish that…" he said licking his lips, looking between Rose's legs, "But the bit…" Gibson let out a long sigh, "Lorna is bringing Oliver home because he's sick. She said she's right around the corner." He practically jumped off the bed and pulled his clothes on. He turned back to Rose who was still sitting, waiting, and gave one kiss between her legs and one on her mouth. "I'll finish this later. I love you," he said with a low growl. She heard him run down the steps and out the door.

"Love you too!" she yelled after him trying to decide if she needed to finish herself off.

Gibson

Gibson made it to his house just before Lorna rounded the corner and pulled in the drive. He tried to act nonchalant walking out the door. Lorna had climbed from her car and was standing at the front of her car with her hands on her hips when he did.

"Come on," she hissed, "I can't lift him myself. I had to have Bart put him in the car for me."

"Who the fuck is Bart?"

"None of your business."

"Well, according to the court, it IS my business." Gibson walked down the drive to the back seat of her car. He peered in and saw Oliver laying on the back seat, not belted into a car seat. In fact, he saw no car seat at all in the back seat for either kid. His anger surpassed a level that any man should ever reach.

"What the hell is wrong with you, Lorna?" he asked, whipping open the back door. "Don't you know it's against the law to not have him in seat? And where's Chloe?"

"I'm going to keep her until tomorrow. She's not sick."

"So, who is she with right now?"

"Bart, you dummy. Like I'm going to leave her home alone."

"Again, who the fuck is Bart?" Gibson's voice was gruff.

"He's the guy I'm seeing. You'd like him." Lorna didn't seem to care that she was making Gibson angry.

"What happened to Gus?"

"Gus was no fun." she sighed like a teenager, "Bart is... well he's more fun."

"Come on buddy, up you go." Gibson delicately lifted his son out of the car. "Jesus, Lorna, he's burning up! Didn't you give him anything?"

"I don't have the money for that stuff. Plus, letting them sweat it out is good for them," she said with a sneer.

Gibson couldn't believe his ears. He kicked the back door of her car shut and started walking up the driveway to the house, but stopped when he got to Lorna's side. "I'm going to suggest to you that you drive fast back to your house and make sure that OUR little girl is ok with this dude you left her with. And I swear to God if either of them says one bad thing to me about this week-end, the court will know it and your rights will be done." Lorna huffed at him. When she did, Gibson caught a scent in the air she released. "Is that alcohol on your breath?" His eyes grew dark. His heart raced more, feeling like it was about to bust out of his chest.

"Well, I'm done here. Bye, baby." Lorna kissed Oliver's head and turned to get in her car.

"You drove MY SON home after drinking?" he yelled. The look on Lorna's face answered him. "You're finished, Lorna. I'll be over shortly to get Chloe. She'd better be ready in fifteen minutes because if she's not, the cops will be coming." He turned and walked into the house, slamming the door behind him.

After getting Oliver some Tylenol, Gibson tucked him into bed, putting a trash can next to him on the floor. Then he called Rose.

When she answered, he was breathing hard and not in a good way.

"Gibs? What's going on?" Her voice filled with concern.

"Rose... ugh... Lorna... I'm hoping you can come over right now and watch Oliver for a bit. I have to go rescue Chloe," he huffed into the phone.

"Yeah, I can. Let me throw some clothes on quick and I'll be over."

Gibson was grabbing his keys when she walked in. He stalked towards the door like a lion had taken over his body.

"What's going on?" Rose's eyes searched Gibson's face.

"I'll tell you when I get home. Oliver is asleep. I just gave him Tylenol. I don't know if he will throw it up. Thank you for coming." He kissed her forehead and was out the door, leaving her standing in the kitchen.

As he slammed the truck door, he jammed it into reverse, burned out the driveway backwards, then slammed it into drive. He tried to keep an even head and made it to Lorna's in ten minutes. She was standing at the front door with her hands on her hips.

"I didn't think you were serious," she hollered as he slammed the truck door.

"I'm always serious when it comes to my kids," he hurled at her. "Where is she? Let's go." His hand was motioning for her to get Chloe.

He heard a man's voice come from behind Lorna. "What's he doing here?"

Lorna turned towards the voice, and scoffed, "He thinks he's taking my daughter home early."

"No, no, not THINK, I KNOW it. Come on, Lorna. Let's go," he started towards the door.

"Take another step, dude. I dare you." The man came into view. He was shorter than Gibson, but about the same weight. He opened the front door and stepped out onto the stoop.

"Ha, are you trying to scare me, little guy? You must be Bart," Gibson said in an arrogant tone.

"Not trying, asshole. Get off our property. You can get the girl tomorrow when it's time for her to leave."

"The girl?" Bart's nonchalant mention of Chloe caused Gibson to pause. "Nuh uh, that's not how this is going to work." Gibson stepped closer to the house and then saw Chloe's sweet face in the front window. He beckoned to her then. "Come on, Clover. Let's go." She looked a little sleepy, but smiled and turned away from the window. He heard her little feet running towards the door, but her mother stopped her before she could open it. Her little smile turned down into a frown and he could see her little lip shaking.

"But mommy, I want to go with daddy," she said in her tiny voice.

"Come on Lorna. Let's not make this any harder than it has to be," Gibson pleaded.

"Hey, dude, I told you to leave." Bart took another step towards Gibson.

"Look, I'm not sure when you started squatting with her, but this has nothing to do with you. So, if you were smart, you'd shut the fuck up before I close your mouth for you."

The standoff went on for about a minute before Gibson grabbed his phone and threatened to call the cops. Enraged, Bart ran towards Gibson. He swung once, connecting with Gibson's chin, and causing Gibson to stumble backwards a few steps. The nasty grin on the little guy's face pissed Gibson off and, unlike what would normally happen, Gibson went after him. He landed a blow to Bart's nose, and then one to the side of his chin. Bart stumbled and fell to the ground. He heard his daughter crying and Lorna yelling at them both to stop. Gibson stalked to the door, opened it, and scooped his daughter up into his arms.

Hugging Chloe, Gibson gave her a kiss, trying to console her on the way to the car. He set her into her car seat, whispering gently to her, trying to calm her sobs. When he shut the door, he turned around and said, "Lorna, I warned you not to fuck things up. It's just too bad you can't do anything good for your kids. I'll be questioning them both and recording it. If I find out that anything was going on here... so help me, Lorna."

She nodded at him and slunk to the floor behind the door. He knew what that meant. There was more to the story.

When he pulled into the driveway at home, he peeked again at his Chloe in the back seat. Her eyes were heavy with sleep, but she was still shuddering from her crying. He got out of the car and pulled her out of her car seat. Wiping her tears off her face, he told his daughter, "I'm so sorry daddy got mad at mommy and Bart."

In her tiny voice, still wobbling, she replied, "It's ok daddy. I didn't wanna be there anymore, anyway. Mommy kept being mad at me, Bart is mean, and I haven't been asleep since we got there. They play their music really loud. I'm so tired, daddy." Laying her head on his shoulder, she whispered, "Thank you for coming, daddy." It took all his might not to shed a tear as he walked into the house.

Rose was sitting at the table with a mug of tea in her hands, rubbing the side of it with her thumb. Hearing the door open, she looked up. The sight of Chloe's tired face caused Rose to stand. Her gaze slid to Gibson's chin, which had a hint of yellowing to it already. He was still puffed up in Lion-mode, but he smiled a weary smile at her and mouthed 'Hang on'.

Gibson walked past her, bringing Chloe to her room. Rose over-heard them talking and then heard Gibson sing a quiet tune to his daughter. When he backed out of her room, he opened Oliver's door and peeked in.

"Anything happen in there since I left?" he asked Rose as he sat down with her at the table.

"No, he's been asleep the entire time," she answered. "What happened over there?"

"Oh god Rose. What a mess." Gibson dropped his head into his hands. Then told her about Lorna dropping off Oliver and ending with the fight at Lorna's house. When he finished, Rose put her hand on his.

"I'm sorry this happened. What can I do?"

Gibson just shook his head and squeezed her hand. "I'm not even sure yet. I'm going to have to call the courts on Monday. I think I should probably call the cops right now and let them know what happened and why." Shaking his head over and over, he rested his forehead on his free hand's palm.

Rose got up and went to the freezer to find an ice pack, only finding a frozen bag of peas. She handed it to Gibson and walked to Chloe's room. He watched her while holding the bag to his chin. Quietly, she opened the door and peeked in, then squeezed through the opening, leaving the door ajar. He stood from his seat to see what she was doing.

When he got to Chloe's door, he saw Rose sitting on the side of Chloe's bed holding her hand, delicately pushing hair off Chloe's face. They were whispering to each other, but he couldn't make out what they were saying. He watched his woman lean down and squeeze his daughter. It was the sweetest exchange he had seen since before Lorna had gotten wrapped into drugs. He caught Chloe's face with a small smile on it. Rose laid Chloe back down, kissed her little forehead, and stood from the bed.

Gibson quickly ran back to the kitchen and grabbed his phone, pretending to scroll. Stealing a look, he saw Rose peek into Oliver's room. He must have still been sleeping because she immediately wandered back to the kitchen.

"So, are you going to make that call?" she asked. He wasn't sure what she had just asked because he was still reveling in the fact that his girlfriend obviously had as fierce a love for his kids as he did. "Gibson?"

"Huh? What?" he responded, absentmindedly.

"The cops, are you going to call them?" Rose's voice was calm.

"Oh yeah, but I think I'm going to step outside to do it. I might get loud. I'm still pissed."

"Go, I don't know that I want to hear everything again, anyway."

The cops, of course, said they couldn't do anything but took the report just in case Lorna called as well. They told Gibson to get all the information he could from the kids without prompting, and to call the friend of the court first thing Monday morning. After the phone call, he sat at the patio table for a bit, replaying the day.

The screen door squeaked behind him, and the tiniest steps walked behind him. He turned and saw Chloe standing there, rubbing her eyes. He gave her a small smile, opening his arms. She climbed up on his lap and snuggled into him. How could I let it get so out of control in front of her? He stroked his daughter's brown hair, feeling her breathing start to slow, and he knew she was asleep.

Not wanting to move her, he picked up his phone and was about to text Rose when he heard the door open again. Another small set of feet was walking towards him. Looking over his shoulder, he saw Oliver walking towards him. The poor kid still looked like he didn't feel good. Gibson adjusted Chloe a little and Oliver climbed up as well. These two were everything to him.

Oliver looked up at him and asked, "Daddy, can I just stay with you forever?"

Gibson squeezed his son slightly. He couldn't answer that question yet, so he responded, "I'm going to try my hardest to make that happen, buddy."

Oliver smiled at him before laying his head on his father's shoulder. The three of them sat together for a couple more minutes before he heard the door a third time.

Rose settled into the chair next to him and smiled at the sight. They looked so sweet, all snuggled together. She pulled out her phone and snapped a picture. Gibson smiled at her. She reached her hand out and laid it on his arm. She just wanted him to know she was there. After a moment, she stood. His eyes followed her before he asked in a hushed voice, "Where ya going?"

"I don't want to overstay. You've got your hands full today," she whispered, brushing Gibson's hair away from his eyes.

"What if I want you to stay? I think the kids would be happier if you were still here when they woke up," His eyes pleaded with her.

"I mean, I'll stay if you want. How about I go make us some sandwiches or something?"

"How about you take Clover here and I'll take Ollie and we can go put them in bed for now. I don't think anything is going to wake these two for a while." She reached down and stole Chloe from his arms. The little girl made the sweetest sigh as she wrapped her little arms around Rose's neck and squeezed.

"Oh really, nothing?" she whispered with a grin.

After getting both kids tucked into their beds, Rose and Gibson snuck back out to the patio. He grabbed a couple beers on the way, popping the tops and handing one to her.

After a brief silence, Rose asked, "So ok, do you think Lorna is using again? I mean, I saw her at the store the other day, remember? And she appeared drunk. I mean who knows what else was going on."

Gibson took a swig of his beer and stared into the backyard before answering, "I hope she isn't, but if I'm being truthful, Rose, I did smell alcohol on her today, and her eyes had a look to them that I haven't seen in a while. And that Bart character, he smelled weird."

Rose smiled, trying to make a joke. "Well, you smell weird, and I don't think you're a druggie."

He grimaced, "I know, but he smelled like something I've smelled around her house before, when her first boyfriend was cooking and selling meth."

Rose winced. "Ok, but do you think she's doing things in front of the kids?"

"Rose, she drove my son here with alcohol on her breath. Not 'oh shoot I woke up hungover' breath, like she drank a bottle of whiskey before deciding her son was too sick to take care of." His eyebrows were furrowed, and the vein on his neck popped out and pulsed.

"Ok," she started, "So what do we do?"

Her mention of the word 'we' made him turn to look at her. She was staring at him with those to die for eyes. She was all in, and he hadn't even had to ask. He reached over and brushed his thumb across her cheek. As he did, she turned her face into his hand and kissed his palm.

"WE," he emphasized, "are going to fight for our kids." His use of 'our' made her heart thump a bit off course. This time, she scooted her own chair closer to him and took his hand.

"Yes, we will, but how do we start?"

Rose and Gibson

Gibson called his parents that afternoon and told them he was going to have to take another sick day on Monday. He rolled through the story, leaving out the part where he had hit the guy living with his ex. Rose ran home to grab some pizza rolls out of her freezer to make the kids when they woke up.

While at home, she heard a car pull in next door, so she peeked out to see who was there, expecting Mavis and John, since they both sounded like they wanted to come and snuggle with the babies. It wasn't. It was a rust bucket hatchback, but she couldn't see who was in the car. Walking out the front door, Rose began crossing the lawn when she saw Lorna step out of the driver's side and some greasy guy get out of the passenger's side. Lorna looked ready to roll someone and the guy's expression said he was not there for a good reason.

Rose rushed across the driveway as Gibson was coming out of the house. He shielded his eyes from the sun and then puffed up. It was almost sexy, but a little scary. This looked like the beginning of something bad. Rose was at Gibson's side in an instant and he whispered to her, "Keep the kids inside and call the police. Go, now!"

Rose backed towards the door and into the house. The kids were still tucked in their rooms. She prayed they would stay there. Picking up his cell phone, she dialed 911. She wasn't even sure what she needed to say but when the operator answered, she relayed that two people were at her boyfriend's house and that there had been an issue earlier. Rose gave the address. When the operator said an officer was on the way, she peeked out the front window because the voices outside were getting louder.

"I want my fucking kids back, Gibson." Lorna was swaying and pointing her finger at him. Rose felt her body temperature rise. She wanted to jump in front of him and take the woman on herself, but she stayed where she was.

"Isn't that poetic," Gibson said gruffly, "Now that you have a bit more liquid courage, you think you can take care of them. Brilliant."

"I'm not leaving until they are in my car, you knob," she said with a stagger backwards. Bart thought it was smart to get in front of Lorna.

"Dude, give us the kids. It's our weekend with them. We got some stuff planned." Bart sounded lost in his own brain.

"First of all, MY kids are not YOUR kids. What was your name again? Bart? Second, not happening." Gibson's arms crossed in front of him in defiance. "Not happening at all. You two lunatics shouldn't be taking care of yourselves, let alone MY kids."

"Gibson," Lorna tried her pleading voice, "Come on, I only get them every other weekend. I need them."

"You made that choice and apparently they aren't as important to you as your drinking is. What new drug are you trying now?" he chastised her, moving his gaze between them.

Lorna lunged towards Gibson. Rose wasn't expecting her response to Lorna's assault, but she pushed open the front door and lunged at the woman before Lorna had made it to Gibson.

"Rose! Don't!" Gibson was too late. Rose stood in front of Lorna, took one balled up fist and slammed it into Lorna's nose. Lorna stumbled and fell to the ground.

"I think it would behoove you to get your sorry drug addicted ass off our property and fast. The cops are on the way and if they catch you here with your blood alcohol level where it is, you're a sure thing for jail." She glanced over at Gibson, who was smiling a victory smile. Bart had slithered into the car again. He undoubtedly didn't want to mess with any of this. Just then they heard the siren and Lorna scrambled to her feet.

"This isn't over, ya know. You ain't nothing to those kids, bitch. They're mine. And you," she pointed at Gibson, who was still smiling at Rose, "you're worthless. We'll see who wins this." She got in the driver's seat and swerved backwards into the street. The cop was just rounding the corner and saw her car leaving. He didn't even stop at the house, just followed her down the road.

Gibson walked over to Rose and took her in his arms. "Um, that's another Rose that's new to me." His smile never faltered, looking down at her.

"Yeah, well, sometimes the new city girl comes in handy," she said, shaking her hand. He grabbed that hand and kissed it, before grabbing her chin and kissing her.

"I guess we are a united front. Are you sure you're up for this?"

"Listen, you have my back. I have yours. Plus, I love those kids, I have since the day I met them. I just didn't realize they were yours. That makes it even better." He crushed her mouth with his, bending her backwards in a dip you would only see in a movie. Bringing her upright, they both looked to the front window. Two little faces pressed against it with goofy smiles stretched across them.

"Guess we'd better go face the music," he said, grabbing her hand.

Around dinner time, there was a knock on Gibson's door. He figured it would be the police, and it was.

"I'm Officer Bigelow, this is my partner, Officer Lang. Do you mind if we come in and ask you and your kids some questions?"

Gibson sighed, but let them in and sat them at the table. Rose was pulling the pizza rolls out of the oven and getting them onto plates for the kids. They were about to sit and watch a Disney movie.

Jumping up and down, Oliver asked, "Are you a real cop?" Evidently, Oliver was just suffering from no sleep, which had caused his fever and his vomiting. There was no flu bug, just a mother who had no care for anyone but herself.

"I am," Officer Bigelow responded with a smile.

"Ooh, can I see your badge?" Oliver pressed

"Sure, here it is." The officer pointed to his chest.

"It's shiny like jewelry!" Chloe exclaimed.

"It sure is. Do you guys think you can tell me about your mom's house?" the officer asked.

The kids stopped short and looked at each other. Oliver was the first to speak. "She told us not to." The officer raised his eyebrows.

"I wonder why?" he asked carefully.

"Mommy says that if we talk about her pretty vase and her fire that we can get in trouble," Chloe said.

"Chloe!" Oliver shouted. "Shh!" He put his little finger to his mouth and Chloe closed hers with a chomp.

"Ok, so we won't talk about those things. What did you guys do when you were there?" the officer asked.

"Mommy told us to go play in our rooms. She and Bart were playing kissy face and didn't want us to see it," Chloe spun on her toes, telling her story. "She told me we were going to be princesses, and I was so excited. Then I got tired, but mommy told me we were going to sing. Oliver and I got to use a microphone and everything!"

"Mommy told us that she forgot to make dinner, so we were going to have to wait for breakfast. My tummy was growling, but she told me that it was good for me," Oliver interjected. "I asked why we couldn't eat some of her secret potion that she was making. She yelled at me and told me that only big kids could taste it and that I'm not a big kid yet. I told her that I was too but then Bart grabbed my arm and told me to go sing some more."

Gibson hung his head and swayed, trying to contain his anger. He hadn't talked to the kids yet, and this story was making him angrier by the minute. Rose tried not to cry.

Chloe jumped onto the chair next to Officer Bigelow and looked him in the eye. "I told mommy I was tired and wanted to turn the music down, so I did. Bart and mommy got really mad at me. She told me that they were having too much fun and to never touch the turny thing again." In a small whisper, almost inaudible, she said, "And she even smacked my hand."

Oliver picked up the story. "I told mommy I wanted to go home. She laughed at me. She told me daddy was never going to let me come home because I was being naughty." He stole a look at his dad then, and Gibson couldn't handle anymore. It took two steps, and he was with his kids. He wrapped them both in his arms and said, "I will always come for you. I will never not be there if you need me."

Oliver beamed at his father. "I know daddy. I told mommy that she was wrong. That's when Bart turned the music up louder and they had those things you have at the doctor when they give you a shot. They got to try that magic potion. They put it in the shot thingy. I was so mad so I ran to my room and slammed my door."

Gibson couldn't believe how fast Lorna had spun out of control again. Worst of all, she wasn't even hiding it around her children. The kids finished their story and Rose took them into the other room to eat and start the movie.

Gibson sat down at the table and told the officers his part of the story. How he went to get his daughter after a drunk Lorna had dropped Oliver. How they showed up at his house high and drunk hours later. The officers nodded, continuing to take notes. When they got ready to leave, Rose walked back into the kitchen.

"Um, I hit her," she said bluntly. "I hit her and I'm not sorry. She was going for Gibson, and I wasn't going to let it happen. You might need that in your report." The officers smiled at her and flipped the notebook open again.

"I'm going to need a copy of the report to take to the friend of the court, if possible," Gibson requested.

"Sure thing. This is going to be an ongoing investigation, but for now, Mr Titus, don't let those kids go with her."

"It wasn't going to happen, anyway." Gibson shook both officers' hands and led them out the door. The day had taken a toll on his little family and vegging in front of a movie sounded great, but first he had to process what his sweet children had just told the cops.

Rose had already started the movie when he lowered himself onto the couch next to her.

"So, what are we watching?"

"Lion King dad!" Oliver said. The excitement bubbled from him because they didn't have to watch a princess movie for once. Chloe was pouting but knew she had lost the battle. She had climbed onto Rose's lap, had her legs draped over Rose's and her arm around Rose's neck.

"Ooh, that's a good one," he leaned over and wrapped his arm around Rose's shoulders. Oliver hopped up onto his dad's lap and sat facing forward.

By the time the movie was over, Chloe was asleep and had a bit of drool on the corner of her mouth. Oliver was rubbing his eyes, forcing them to stay open. Rose stood, careful not to wake Chloe, and carried her to her room. Gibson stood, wrapped his son's arms around his neck, and carried him to his room. They both backed out of the kids' rooms at the same time. They turned and faced each other with a small smile.

"I should go," said Rose

"It's been a rough day. Do you want to stay here tonight? No strings. Just would be nice to hold you."

She smiled and thought for a minute, "I don't know Gibs. I don't know if the kids would understand."

"I don't think they need to. They already love you as much as I do. Pllleeeaasssee," he said, mimicking his daughter.

She smiled and shook her head. "You don't think they've had enough for the weekend? I mean, come on, Bart? Eww."

"Yeah, but you're Rose," he said, wrapping his arm around her. In his daughter's voice again, he said, "The princess next door that is sooooo beautiful!"

She giggled and wrapped herself around him. "You have a way of convincing people to do things they probably shouldn't."

Pushing her back, he feigned shock on his face. "What do you mean?" Then he leaned in and whispered, "Just stay. Please."

She looked at him, their mouths so close that she could almost taste him. Glancing at his lips and back into his eyes, she nodded. She couldn't will herself to leave, even if she wanted to.

Gibson kept to his word, giving her a tee shirt and shorts, and curled up behind her, holding her close. She knew he was hurting and was more than willing to be his teddy bear.

In the middle of the night, she had heard him whimper in his sleep. Careful not to wake him, Rose had nudged him to roll away from her before wrapping her arms around him. The response that came from him was a huge breath of release as he grabbed her hand.

When the sun came up, the bed was much smaller than when they had gone to bed. They were facing each other, but there were two brown-haired angels lying between them. At some point, the kids had climbed into bed with them. Rose was shocked and embarrassed at first, but then she noticed how they were strung out on top of both her and Gibson. It was at that moment she realized this was where she wanted to be for the rest of her life. Chloe opened her eyes and sleepily in her tiny voice, "Rose, are you going to be my mommy now?" Rose had stroked the girl's hair. As much as she wanted to say yes, she withheld not knowing how to respond. She just squeezed the little girl.

CHAPTER TWENTY-TWO

Rose

Monday came with a somber feeling. Rose's first day was meant to be exciting, instead fear and anxiety filled her. It was Oliver's first day of school too, and she had promised Gibson that she would keep a close eye on him and bring him home after school.

Rose had stayed home the night before. She needed to get her head in the game and wanted to be sure everything was ready to go. She had chosen her outfit and packed her lunch so that she didn't feel rushed in the morning. Simple black slacks with a royal blue sleeveless shirt. It was still August, and she wanted to be comfortable. It took her two trips to her car that morning, but oddly, she still left on time.

Gibson

"Hold still, Ollie!" Gibson was struggling to get the perfect first day of school picture. Oliver was not happy with having to wear his backpack and, to be truthful, it was a little big for him. But it was the Spiderman backpack he had begged for.

"Come on, man. Just hold still and smile," Gibson begged his son. Finally, Oliver shot him the toothy grin he was looking for.

"I want a picture too, daddy!" Chloe whined.

"Ok, Clover. Get in there with your brother," Chloe squealed, and Oliver rolled his eyes.

Gibson had called Chloe's new daycare the night before and told them he was keeping her home. He didn't feel safe leaving her anywhere yet. He corralled his kids into the car. Looking next door, hoping that Rose had made it out the door on time. The weekend had them both frazzled.

Pulling into the school parking lot, he found Rose waiting and smiling at them. She put her hand up and waved. Oliver climbed out of his car seat and leaned between the front seats. He grabbed his dad's neck in a hug. His little hands pulled his dad's face towards his, looking him directly in the eyes, and said, "Daddy, I love you. Please take care of Chloe today. Rose will take good care of me. You don't have to worry."

Gibson smiled and rubbed his nose against his seven-year-old's nose. His heart ached, knowing his son completely understood the situation.

"I love you too, buddy. Here comes Rose to get you."

"Hey Ollie, are you ready?" she asked, pulling the backdoor of the car open. "Hey Clover! Take care of your dad today." She winked at the four-year-old.

"I will, Rose!" Chloe said with a giggle as she bounced her legs against her seat.

"Gibson," Rose started. He looked at her. "Good luck today. We will see you around four." Then, checking that the kids weren't looking, she mouthed "I love you."

Gibson smiled and said out loud, "Rose, I love you too." Shooting a wink at her. The two kids stopped and stared at their dad and Rose. Chloe clapped and Oliver pretended to throw up. Rose blushed as she closed the door. This was definitely a cliff dive.

Alaina was going to kill her, but Rose didn't care.

———————

"Hello, hi, yeah, my name is Gibson Titus. My case number is," Gibson had finally gotten through to Friend of the Court. "I need to report an incident." The woman on the other end of the line put him on hold, so he peeked in on his daughter, who was watching cartoons on the couch.

"Yes, I'm still here. Ok thanks." The receptionist transferred him to his caseworker. When she answered, Gibson rambled the entire story again, including that the cops had told him to keep his kids from Lorna. The response was that they were scheduling a meeting with the referee. He agreed. Once the call ended, he leaned back in his chair and rubbed his face before pushing himself up to go snuggle on the couch with his daughter.

———————

Rose

Rose's first day was going so well. She did, in fact, have a couple of her old classmate's kids in her class. Holly's daughter looked just like Holly. Thomas' son was obviously her friend Lydia's child, too. When lunch came along, she texted Gibson to check in.

How's it going? Did you

get through to Friend of the Court?

Yeah, magistrate meeting

next week. How's Ollie?

He's fine. He's an amazing

reader!

Well, I tried, unlike his

mother. LOL

See you soon. XO

XO

When recess was over, Rose looked over her class counting heads. She felt her heart drop. She was one child short, and it happened to be Oliver.

"Um, guys. Does anyone know where Oliver is?" Trying not to sound too frantic.

"I think he had to go potty," one boy said.

"Ok, everyone sit and don't move," she said, running out of the door.

She ran down the hall and knocked on the boy's bathroom door. Opening the door a crack, she called inside, "Oliver Titus?" No answer. "Oliver, it's Ro… I mean Ms. Harper." No answer. Rose felt her heart jump into her throat. "Oliver!" She yelled again. Still no answer. She ran to the office, her mind racing.

"Kendall, is Oliver Titus here?" she asked, her breathing almost making it hard to speak.

"Hey, Rose!!" Kendall said in her bubbly voice. "Yeah, he's in with the nurse! He took a spill outside."

Rose's body released all the tension she was holding. "Oh, thank God!" she breathed. She rushed to the nurse's door and sure enough, there was her beautiful, brown-haired boy. Wait, what did she just think? Hers?

Oliver looked at her with those big brown eyes. He had alligator tears streaming down his cheeks, and his bottom lip jutted out. "Rose, I tripped playing kick ball. Everyone laughed at me and my knee was bleeding."

She stooped next to him and wiped his eyes. "Oh, buddy. I'm so sorry. But look at this cool band-aid you get to sport! I'm so glad you're in here. I was so worried!" She took his hand as they walked back to the classroom.

The rest of the school day was uneventful. After cleaning up her desk at the end of the day, Rose left the school with Oliver, feeling better about the entire event.

When she pulled in her drive, Gibson was waiting for them on his lawn. She had already texted him, letting him know what had happened. Oliver climbed out of his seat and ran to see his dad. Gibson hugged his son, telling him to head inside and grab a snack. When the screen door closed, he turned to Rose. She could see he was upset by the expression that sat on his face.

"So, what was he doing outside? Out of your sight?" Gibson said, trying not to raise his voice.

"Oh, hi to you too. I had a great first day. Thanks for asking."

"Rose."

"It was recess. I had to eat sometime! And Kendall was aware of what was going on. She was on recess duty." Rose placed her hands on her hips.

"I see," he said, rubbing the bridge of his nose, "And you thought that after the weekend we had 'Why not leave someone else to watch Gibson's kid. Sounds like a great idea.'"

"Gibson, he's safe. What do you want me to say?" she flung her hand in the air.

"Yeah, he's safe, no thanks to YOU!" he roared. Rose recoiled from his tone. "Rose, you KNOW what could have happened!"

"Listen, don't sling your shit at me! I did what I could do. So, I had one brief period where someone else had him. Oh, dear lord, Gibson. I'm not perfect."

He let out a snort. "Obviously not," he said with too much arrogance.

"You know what. Fuck you! I don't need to stand here and listen to you belittle me." Rose turned on her heel and started toward her front door before whipping around again and pointing at Gibson. What she said next she instantly regretted, "You think you're so perfect, then why aren't those kids OURS? If you could have kept your tongue out of someone else's mouth, we wouldn't be dealing with your drug addicted ex, and they would be safe EVERY FUCKING DAY!"

Gibson flinched. "Well, if you would have just listened to me back then, we wouldn't be dealing with any of this, and they'd be safe EVERY FUCKING DAY!"

This time it was Rose that flinched before whipping back around, leaving him fuming, standing completely still, and glaring at her. He winced when she slammed her door, then again when he heard the deadbolt. Hanging his head, he kicked a stone in the driveway. Then, releasing a sigh, he retreated to his house, like a child who was just scolded by his parents. *Shit*, he thought.

She wiped the tears that were hot on her face. "ARGH!" she screamed through the empty house. She paced from one end of the house to the other. The tears continued.

"How could he think I don't care?" she said to herself. "What a dick! Argh!" She picked up her phone and called her dad, knowing it was wrong to pull him into the middle of this. She should have called Grace or Alaina. But she just wanted her dad.

When he answered, she was still crying. "Rosey, breathe. What's wrong?" The concern in his voice made her cry more. She took a few breaths before pulling him into the muddy mess that had formed.

"That rat bastard," was Jason's response, "I'm calling that boy."

"No daddy. Don't," she pleaded, "I shouldn't have told you." She put her head in her hand.

"Rosey, you did nothing wrong. Give him some time. He'll see that. You two have come so far. He's stressed, and he has every reason to be. But he shouldn't have taken it out on you."

Pushing through the backdoor, she sat on her back steps. "You're right. Ugh, dad, I was so scared when I couldn't find Ollie. It was like he was my flesh and blood," she sighed, shaking her head.

"I know that feeling all too well. Look at you being all mom-like." She heard him smile.

"I guess so," she said, wiping her face. Then, remembering that her dad had his appointment to talk about the trial that day, Rose changed the subject, "Sorry daddy, I should be asking you how today went. Did they give you a start date?"

"My consultation is Thursday," Jason hesitated, "But I can't start until I've been off my current meds for at least three weeks."

Rose winced at the response, "I remember, daddy, three weeks. Remember the doctor told us that the other day." Oh daddy, I'm losing you.

"I'm scared to do that, Rose," he admitted.

"That's understandable, dad," she told him, "I'd actually be worried if you weren't nervous. But dad, this is going to work. I just know it!" They talked a few more minutes before hanging up.

As she stood to go inside, she caught a glimpse of Gibson standing at his door. Instead of throwing the traffic finger at him, like she desperately wanted to, Rose turned and walked inside. About an hour later, she heard the familiar ding of her phone. She was binging a new show that Grace had told her about. She picked up her phone and looked. It was Gibson.

Hey, can we talk?

She set her phone back down and pressed play again. Then the ding again.

Come on, Rose.

She flipped it over again to ignore it. Ding.

Seriously?

This time she sent the shrugging emoji back and turned back to the tv. She heard his door open and close. She heard the footsteps on his driveway and then silence. Shortly after, a knock on the door.

"I'm not buying anything," she yelled, not leaving her couch.

"Rose, open the door," Gibson said calmly.

"I'm good," she replied.

"Rose, open the door!" she heard the kids yell.

He actually brought the kids. What a jerk move. He knew she couldn't ignore them. Walking to the door, Rose unlocked it with the pace of a snail. Then, almost as slowly, she opened it, fully aware that her face was still red and puffy from crying. When the little family saw her, all their faces fell.

Oliver was the first one to grab her around her legs. "Rose, it's ok. My knee already doesn't hurt." She bent down and squeezed him.

While Rose was still stooped, Chloe reached her little hand to Rose's cheek and wiped where her tears had been. "You can stop crying now. We are here to take care of you." Rose squeezed Chloe too. She didn't want to look at Gibson, so she stood up without taking her gaze off the kids.

She felt his finger on her chin, but she didn't budge. Then Gibson's hand pulled gently and though she didn't want to, Rose looked at him. He gave her a sheepish smile, grazed her cheek with his thumb and said, "I'm so sorry, Rose." A single tear rolled over her cheekbone that he swept away with his thumb. Leaning in, Gibson dropped a cautious kiss on her lips. "I overreacted," he said when he pulled back. She nodded and looked at the kids again, trying not to show her pain.

"Can we come in?" he asked, trying not to push too much. She didn't budge.

"Please, Rose? We want to talk to you!" Oliver said, swinging on her hand. She couldn't deny those kids, or Gibson for that matter, so she stepped aside, and the group walked past her into the house. She and Gibson talked while the kids bounced between them. They were careful to talk in words the kids couldn't understand.

"I'm sorry I took it out on you," Gibson started, "I'm just so on edge."

"I know that babe. You have to know that when..." she looked across to the kids, "The olive oil went missing, I wasn't sure what I... was going to cook with." Her eyes said, 'please understand what I'm trying to say'.

"I understand. But the olive oil is one of the most important... ingredients in my... kitchen." He winked at her.

"I know. I tried to be sure that I didn't lose the olive oil, but you have to understand that as a... chef... sometimes I need a small break. That's why I had the only sous chef that I trust the most to keep track of the olive oil. Please know that the oil was always my priority, even above the other spices and cooking items in the kitchen that day."

"I know that." He pulled his chair closer to her. "I had no right to even think otherwise." He grabbed her hand. She forced herself to look at him. His brown eyes had a hint of sadness. "Rose, I will never doubt you again. I know that... my spices and oils are as important to you as they are to me."

"Are we still talking about..." she winked at him.

"Well, Ms. Harper..." He knew then that the stop he had made the prior week was absolutely the right decision.

CHAPTER TWENTY-THREE

Rose

That week was full of new things. Jason and Rose had gone to the University of Michigan for his consultation, where the group had approved him into the trial. Rose was thankful that Jason had stopped his meds when the doctor had told him on Monday and only had a little over two weeks left until he could start the trial meds. Rose and Bri took turns staying with Jason for the next few days. Withdrawal was rough on him. He was nauseous and overly tired. Rose hated watching this, but Jason reminded her it was for the best. His shakes slowly came back harder than she had seen before. His mind started slipping again, calling Bri, Rose and Rose Bri occasionally. He even slipped calling Rose Dana and one time called Gibson by his dad's name. Watching this was almost too much for Rose. More than once, she broke down at her house when she got home. Most nights, she either stayed with Gibson or he and the kids stayed with her.

"I don't know if I can do this," she said to Gibson one night. It was a Saturday, almost to the end of three weeks. Mavis had taken the kids for the weekend, knowing that Rose and Gibson had needed some time alone. Rose cried silently in Gibson's lap. He consoled her as best as he could, stroking her hair and holding her close, letting her vent.

She sat up and looked at him. "I need you to love me. I need to feel you in every way tonight."

He resisted at first. "Rose, you're vulnerable. I wouldn't feel right about it."

The answer just made her more determined. Pushing him back onto the couch, Rose climbed between his legs. Looking at him through her eyelashes, she pulled his gym shorts down, revealing his member. She stroked it while looking up at him. Gibson tried to move her lips to his face instead, but she pulled away. She licked her lips before taking him into her mouth, pulling his member in and out. He wanted to stop her, but it felt so good. He let out a low moan, grabbing the back of her head. She swirled the tip with her tongue, teasing the crevice before swallowing him again. Rhythmically pulling him in and out of her mouth a few more times before she stopped. Gibson snapped his eyes to her. She could taste that he was close, but wanted to leave him wanting more.

She had hoped he would take her right there. Instead, he pulled Rose's lips to his lips and kissed her. He was ready and so was she, but he wasn't going to let it happen yet. She had teased him, so he wanted to repay the favor. With a gentle push, she fell back to the couch, and he pulled her shorts down around her ankles.

"Gibson," she said in a throaty voice. He pulled her hands above her head and kissed down her body, starting with her mouth, then moving to her neck. He took time there, nipping a bit at the skin. Then to her collarbone, running his tongue and lips lightly across it, breathing hot breath on the trail he'd left.

A shiver ripped through her body. He pulled her tank top up, exposing her breasts. The air hitting them caused them to harden. He firmly licked each nipple with the tip of his tongue, then tugged on them slightly with his teeth. She let out a groan that made his member pulse, but he still wanted to take his time and make her feel every ounce of need that he felt when she left him.

Gibson kissed down her belly, dipping his tongue into her belly button with a firm movement. Then he kissed her inner thighs, moving closer to where she wanted his mouth. He kissed all the way around it before running a firm lick over her nub, dipping his tongue inside for a taste. Rose sighed and grabbed his head. He pulled back before going in again with a double lick. She groaned louder, writhing in pleasure. He sucked and licked, twirling around her nub. She was swelling, and it was sexy as hell to him. He pulled back to see her reactions. Her eyes snapped open then wanting more. Instead, he grabbed her face in a kiss. Leaning over her, he put both hands on either side of her. She begged again, "Gibson."

The need in her voice caused them both to ache. He leaned into her with only the tip at first. She pulsed at the first touch of him against her. Taking his time, wanting to feel every inch of her, he slowly started sliding inside of her. She pulled on him, wanting all of him causing his manhood to jump again at the change in depth. He kissed Rose again, completely entering her. Rose's body flushed with fire.

Moving in and out of her, Gibson tried to drive her wild, being sure to not only kiss her face but to trace her neck and collarbone again. He kept his slow and steady pace for what seemed like a beautiful eternity to her. With each thrust, she lifted her hips, wanting more. She tried putting her fingers on herself to speed things up, but he grabbed them and placed them over her head.

Finally, to her pleasure, he started rocking faster, causing her eyes to close. Gibson thrust harder, and her back started arching. He pulled her nipple into his mouth again, flicking it with his tongue. Rose let out a throaty moan. His movements brought his name as a whisper from Rose's lips until he felt her clenching. Gibson was ready too, so he grabbed her hips and thrust solidly. Rose cried out his name in pleasure as he let out a moan, finishing simultaneously. He grabbed her into his arms; their hearts pounding in sync. When he pulled her hair gently to look her in the eye, she captured his mouth with hers.

"God, Rose. I don't remember you being this naughty."

She smiled at him and said, "This isn't naughty. Just wait. I'll show you naughty." They laid on the couch for a few more hours watching tv together. But around eleven, she pulled him upstairs.

"I want to give you a proper thank you for taking care of me tonight. Do you think you can handle another round?" Pushing him onto the bed, he nodded at her. She stripped all her clothes off in a slow striptease. Then started by touching her own body in front of him, touching her breasts, traveling her fingers between her legs, and dipping them inside herself. Then stopped shooting him a devilish smile.

Ok, I can handle this kind of apology, he thought. The response under his shorts was immense. She turned then, grabbing a ponytail holder from the bed stand. *Oh boy, this just got serious.* She had a determined look on her face as she pulled his shirt over his head. Then began kissing her way down his torso. She was paying him back, and he knew it. Pulling his shorts down, she rubbed her crevice against his groin before pulling his boxers down. She smiled, looking at him as she gave him a tight, slow stroke. Then looking at him through her eyelashes, she slowly took him into her mouth, pushing her tongue against his length as she pulled him in deep. She bobbed her head, firmly running her tongue in a circular motion, teasing his head. He squirmed slightly before she swallowed his member fully again. She moved down his shaft, pulling him in deeper until he hit the back of her throat. Moving slowly back up, she dipped her tongue into the crevice at the top.

"Rose," he pleaded. She shook her head before she pulled him in again and moaned, being sure that he felt the vibrations. She pulled with her mouth a few more times and then stopped. He looked at her with needy eyes, trying to push her back down below. She swerved around his hands, licking up what was already dripping from him. He moaned again as she straddled him, not sitting at first. Starting slowly, just like he had done, she hovered above his erection, allowing just the tip to feel her. Gibson's hands shot to her waist, trying to finish the move. She put her finger up, waving it at him, telling him no, lowering herself a little more. Rose kept her pace slow, taking him into her bit by bit until he was fully inside her. As she started rocking her body, he tried to move beneath her. Each time he tried, she would stop her movements. His breathing was ragged.

"You're the devil." he said, trying to keep his composure. "Fuck, I love the devil though." Rose laughed and moved again. His body was tense, wanting her to finish him. She rocked against him, getting into a steady movement. Groaning as her motions were bringing her closer, she put her hands on his chest for stability. Feeling his member beginning to pulse, she moved faster, using her fingers to help her meet his climax. He let out the most beautiful moan as he climaxed, helping her tumble over another orgasm. She collapsed onto him, and he held her as they pulsed together, falling asleep with him still inside her, reveling in their love and lust for each other.

CHAPTER TWENTY-FOUR

Gibson

The following week was Gibson's Friend of the Court meeting. He figured it was going to be easy and that Lorna wouldn't show up. To Gibson's surprise, Lorna showed up, looking a mess and apparently drunk or high. He couldn't decide.

"Hey Gibs!" she shrieked at him as he walked through the door.

"Oh, uh, hi," His answer was short, sounding annoyed. He walked to the counter and checked in. Then found a seat as far away from Lorna as he could find.

She skipped to him, acting as if nothing had happened. "Where are my babies?"

"Well, MY son is at school and MY daughter is at the farm with my parents."

"Well, that's stupid. I wanted to see them."

"And you thought bringing them here would be a great time to spend with them?" His voice was a lion's growl.

She shrugged, "I wanted to give them some mama sugar," she was practically spitting as she spoke.

"Huh ok," Gibson flipped his phone over to check the time.

"Waiting for some nudes from that whore?"

He felt a growl in his throat. "First, she isn't a whore and second, no, I was checking the time, not that it's any of your business." He stood and walked across the room, forming his left hand into a fist as he did. She was provoking him on purpose.

"You are worthless, you know!" she yelled across the room.

"So, you've told me. Yet you're the one who lost custody of the kids." he shot back, shaking his head.

Lucky for him, the receptionist called them back for their meeting. This meeting was just the start, but Gibson hoped they would terminate Lorna's rights right away.

"So, what brings us to a meeting?" The referee asked.

"Well, sir, the weekend before last, Lorna here had the kids for her weekend. She called me the day after she had gotten them to tell me that Oliver, our son, was sick and that she couldn't take care of him." The referee nodded, taking notes. "So, she brought him home, and I could tell she was drunk by the way she was stumbling." Gibson shot a look at Lorna, whose cheeks flushed. "I told her to get Chloe, our daughter, ready and I would come pick her up too. Lorna here had left my daughter with some new guy she's been seeing. Didn't make me happy."

"Ok, I see that there is a police report, too. I have read through it all, so I know the rest of the story. What are you hoping to get out of this meeting?" The referee was looking at them both.

"I want her rights terminated. It's obvious she doesn't care about the safety of her children, sir. If she doesn't want to take care of them, why make them go over there. Plus, according to the kids, they're cooking something in there, drugs. I don't want my children around that."

"Ms. Titus," the referee started. Gibson flinched at the use of his last name. "What do you have to say about this?"

"He's being a worrywart. I'm not 'cooking' anything more than dinner over there. I just wasn't feeling well myself and watching Oliver puke all over wasn't helping." Lorna tried defending herself. "I love those kids and I do want to do what's best for them."

"Ms. Titus, I want to believe you, but I can't. I want you to show the court that you are truly invested in your children. You sit here and tell me you are, and yet I can tell that you're high right now."

"Am not." Lorna fought back.

"Ma'am, please don't interrupt me again or I'll deem you in contempt and you'll go to jail right now. I know you think no one can tell, but they have trained me to see the effects of many drugs. You are under the influence. It's actually illegal for you to be here right now in your condition, but I know that Mr. Titus is a hard-working farmer who really can't continue to take time from work to come to these meetings. He is, of course, supporting your children." Gibson smirked.

"I help too," she whined. "I got a part-time job at the gas station now."

"Ma'am, I've warned you, but since you've offered this information, maybe we should re-look at your child support payment. But first, as part of the agreement that we will sign today, I would like you to start going to AA again. I also will need you to abstain from any illegal drugs when you are in the presence of your children. If you can clean up your act, we will look again at this case." Lorna looked like she was going to puke.

"Sir, AA isn't good for me. It never works. The people there don't know me, they don't understand me." Lorna was whining and carrying on.

"Ms. Titus, you don't have a choice in this. It's part of the original agreement that was signed a few years ago when you turned the kids over to Mr. Titus. It's going to remain in the agreement this time. Now, child support." He said, not allowing her to interject again. "I'm fairly certain that twenty dollars every two weeks isn't helping him much. We should look at raising it since you're up to part time now."

"Sir," Gibson interrupted, "I don't want anything from her. I really don't need it and I'd rather she kept it since she boldly told me she doesn't even have cheap Tylenol at her house for the kids."

"No matter, Mr. Titus. It's the view of the court that both parents should be contributing. If you don't need it, put it into an account for the kids." Gibson nodded. After the amount was decided upon and written into the order, the referee turned back to Lorna.

"Ok, next are the living arrangements. Ma'am you have here that you live with a Gus Marden?"

"Oh, no, not anymore. I kicked him out a month ago. He didn't like me... never mind. No, he doesn't live with me anymore."

Gibson eyed Lorna and said, "But she does live with some guy named Bart now. What's his last name, Lorna?"

She shot him a look that he knew meant she wasn't sure, or maybe she couldn't remember right now. "It's, um... um... Mung. That's right, Bart Mung." She looked relieved.

"Mmhmm, ok, and what does Mr. Mung do?" the referee asked.

"He's, um, an entre... what do you call it? An entrepreneur. He, um, sells... things."

"What? Drugs?" Gibson quipped at her.

"Mr. Titus, it would be nice if you could let me ask the questions." The referee was pointing a finger at Gibson.

"Sorry, sir."

"Ms. Titus, I can tell what an 'entrepreneur' sells by his clientele. I'm guessing that's how you met Mr... um... Mung. I don't like it, but I can't tell you who you can date. What I can tell you is that in no uncertain terms will I allow these children around an 'entrepreneur' of that type." Lorna nodded and shot a look at Gibson. He was sitting back in his chair, smiling.

"Mr. Referee, sir." Lorna said, snapping her head forward again. "You should ask Gibson here about his living arrangements then too."

"Ok," he nodded "Mr. Titus. Are you living with anyone?"

"No sir. My girlfriend lives next door. She's an elementary school teacher. In fact, she's Oliver's teacher this year. Lorna would know this if she ever paid attention to the school notices that come in the mail or listened to her children." He didn't even need to steal a look. He knew she was glowering at him.

"Well. That seems like an outstanding role model to have around." He winked at Gibson. "Now let's discuss visitations."

The result of the meeting was Lorna getting three hours one day every two weeks of supervised visits to begin with. Gibson got to choose which day of the week worked best for him. If Lorna could prove that she had been attending AA meetings and could stay clean for the first 6 months, the court would allow her more time.

Gibson wasn't happy, slamming his truck door and watched Lorna slink into the Escort with Bart waiting for her inside. He gripped his steering wheel but didn't start the engine, needing to calm his mind before heading to the farm to pick up Chloe. After finally feeling composed enough to pull away from the courthouse, he watched as the brown hatchback headed in the direction of the farm.

"Oh, come on," he said out loud. "Where are you going?"

He watched as the escort turned on their blinker to head down his parent's dirt road. This wasn't happening. He hit the gas, spinning his truck tires, and kicking up rocks, swerving around the little car. He sped down the long, winding drive back to the farmhouse that sat next to the old red barn. The barn that only stood as a monument in front of the many newer barns that housed the cows. The lawn was flawlessly manicured, so the brown escort was a stark contrast as it pulled down the drive.

His mom appeared in the door, and he motioned for her to stay inside. She did, closing the door. He heard the distinct sound of his father's truck hurdling across the farm toward him. Lorna stepped out of the hatchback, wobbling a bit, and stared at Gibson, then looked at the house.

"What?" she asked.

"What do you mean what?"

"Why are you looking at me?"

"Um, because today the referee literally told you that you only get to see the kids once every other week and that Bart," he said, flipping off the driver of the hatchback, "wasn't to be near them."

"Well, today is a day, and he's not getting out of the car." She was trying to negotiate.

"Lorna, get back into the car. You don't get to see them until next Wednesday. You know that."

She laughed and started walking toward the front door. Gibson's dad, John, had just pulled up and was climbing out of his truck.

"Lorna Louise Titus, if you take one more step towards my house, you're going to regret it." John said in a booming voice. Lorna stopped. No one had called her by her full name since she was little. She turned with fire in her eyes and stomped towards John. Gibson took one step sideways to plant himself in front of his dad.

"What are you going to do, Lorna? Take a swing at the old man? I suggest you take a walk back to your car and get out of here before my mom calls the cops." She looked up at him with a blank look on her face, almost as if she had forgotten where she was. Like a zombie, she turned and walked back to the car. Bart threw the car in reverse, backing into the lawn, before spinning the tires and driving off. John put a hand on his son's shoulder. They both nodded at each other and walked to the house.

CHAPTER TWENTY-FIVE

Rose and Gibson

That weekend, Rose and Gibson took the kids to Jason's for a while. Her dad loved having them around and it forced him to spend some time in the backyard instead of in front of the TV. The four of them piled out of the truck and the kids ran up the porch to Jason. He hugged them both, telling them there were cookies on the counter for them.

"You made cookies, dad?" Rose said, hugging him.

"No, Walmart made cookies. I just put them out," Jason said, giving her a funny look and reaching for Gibson's hand. The two men shook hands and Jason led them into the house. It had been three weeks since he had stopped his meds, and it showed. His trembles had become harder. He was fumbling harder with words, but his spirit was still there. They spent a good four hours with him. The kids played on the swing set Jason had built all those years ago. Gibson had spruced it up over the last few months. The kids loved playing on it, and it made Jason smile.

"So, this is the week, Jason. You ready?" Gibson asked. Rose had been spending more time at her dad's as his trembles and other symptoms had returned while being off the meds.

"Yes, but mostly because I can't even drink a beer without spilling it down my shirt," He tried to make jokes at his own expense.

"Well, maybe Rose needs to buy you some straws then," Gibson said, tapping Jason on the shoulder. The two of them went back and forth a bit longer, inserting a few dad jokes before falling into farm talk. Once the kids started getting a little restless, they packed them up and headed home.

"Rose, can you stop over in a little while? I have something I've been meaning to give you. I just keep forgetting," Gibson asked, kissing her cheek.

"I can come now if you want."

"No, I gotta get the kids settled. You know how they are after your dad's house," He smiled.

"Yeah, sure, I have some spelling tests that need correcting and a few other things to do, anyway. How about I come over in an hour?"

"That works perfectly. See you soon."

As she was finishing up her last test, she heard the kids outside. Then she heard her doorbell ringing. No one uses the doorbell. Normally, the kids would just run into the house. As she walked from the kitchen table to the front door, she could see the outlines of two little heads bobbing up and down. Opening the door, Rose was met with the smiles from Oliver and Chloe. Chloe was wearing a princess dress, and Oliver was wearing black pants and a white shirt. They were both very giddy.

"Hello Rose," Oliver said, trying to sound older than the six that he was, "Dad wanted us to see if you were ready to come over yet."

"Well, don't you two look fancy," she said, taking in the sight, "I guess I could be ready." She pulled the door closed behind her as she walked outside. The kids held their hands out to her, pulled her down the stairs and across the yard. They pulled her to the front door, which was also weird, and the kids hurried inside. She followed inside, turning to close the door behind her.

When she turned back around, Gibson was down on one knee with Oliver on one side of him and Chloe on the other. The kids were beaming. Gibson's eyes were shining, a smile pulling his dimples out. The house was lit with candles that were strategically placed around the living room, and pink rose petals covered the floor. Rose couldn't grasp what was happening at first until her eyes landed on the tiny black box in Gibson's hand. He looked at his children and Ollie spoke first.

"You make daddy happy AND we love you so, so much!" he said beaming.

Chloe followed, saying, "You read me my favorite princess books!" Her little squeak made Rose smile. Both kids were jumping up and down, hanging on to their dad's shoulders.

Then Gibson spoke, "Rose, you know I love you. I always have. I literally fell for you fourteen years ago." The memory made them both laugh. "These last few months have been wild. But this last weekend solidified what I knew the minute you walked back into my life. I wanted to fight for us. It also made me glad I made the decision to buy this ring a few weeks back. I need you more than anything in this world. My little family does, too." He smiled at his two children. A tear trickled down her cheek. "Rose, will you please be my wife?" Rose's hands covered her mouth. The kids were still jumping and then Chloe yelled in her tiny four-year-old voice, "Be our wife!" Rose's smile burst into laughter. She kneeled in front of them, put both hands on each side of Gibson's face, and before planting a kiss on his handsome face, she whispered, "Yes." After a fairytale kiss, she reached out and grabbed both kids in a hug.

Looking at the ring after Gibson had placed it on her finger, she smiled. Rose twisted her hand from side to side letting the diamond sparkle in the light. It was a simple round stone, but it was perfect in her eyes.

They called her dad first. He laughed because he knew it was coming, just not when. It was one reason Gibson had been at her dad's a few weeks ago the day she had found out about their bromance. He had been there to ask for Jason's blessing. She jerked her head to look at Gibson when that fact became known, but that he had asked was no surprise to her. He had always been a bit old fashioned.

They called the girls in North Carolina. Grace screamed with excitement. Rose knew she was thinking about bachelorette parties. Alaina said she was happy, but Rose heard her hesitation.

They called Mavis and John next, who, of course, were happy for them. Mavis was excited to have another daughter-in-law. The last call was to her aunt. When they hung up, Bri was talking about bridal showers. After they finished the calls, Gibson looked at his crew and said, "Let's go to Chucks for dinner!"

"YAY!!" the kids yelled.

CHAPTER TWENTY-SIX

Rose

Three weeks later, Rose woke up feeling nauseous. She didn't have a fever though and figured it had to be tied to something she had eaten the night before. Being a recent addition to the school, Rose didn't want to use any sick time, so she got ready, throwing up once prior to leaving for school.

Later that morning, she was standing in the teacher's lounge talking with the second-grade teacher, when she suddenly felt queasy again and hot. She put her finger up to the other teacher and ran for the trash can. She looked up at the other teachers in the room and said, "Those leftovers must have been bad."

She gingerly walked to the office and told Kendall she needed to go home. Kendall could see on her face that Rose wasn't well. The feeling hit Rose again and she grabbed the office trash can. Standing back up, wiping her face with a tissue, she told Kendall, "Bad leftovers."

She got into her car, shooting a text to Gibson, letting him know she wasn't feeling great and that she could not bring Oliver home from school. He texted her back, concerned, but that it was fine. He'd have Mavis grab Oliver and Chloe after school.

She got to the corner of Main Street, and that's when it hit her. She was late, not late to the party, but late. *No, no, no, that can't be.* Her mind was racing, counting days backwards in her head.

She opened her calendar on her phone and sure enough, she was three weeks late. *It has to be stress,* she thought, trying to wipe anything else out of her head. She ran inside the house when she got home and threw up again, before climbing into bed sleeping for an hour. When she woke, she felt a bit better, but got a little woozy when she stood. *Ok, so three weeks, but we always use protection!*

It was then that it dawned on her that four weeks ago she had seduced Gibson in the best way, but they hadn't used protection at all that night. They had been having too much fun teasing each other back and forth, that in their frenzy it had slipped their minds.

She put her head in her hands. "How could we be so stupid!" she said out loud to herself. She peeled herself off her bed and walked down the steps. Grabbing her keys, she made the drive to the lone drugstore in town. Lucky for Rose, it was only the old man working when she got there. *Surely, he won't say anything, right?* After making her purchase, she got back into her car and drove home.

The wait was endless. She kept looking at the timer on her phone, but it seemed to only go down by a couple of seconds each time. She paced around the house, a pit in her stomach. They were just engaged. There wasn't even a wedding date set yet. She didn't want to be pregnant yet.

When the timer sounded, she closed her eyes, reaching for the stick. Her hands were shaking, not wanting to look. Forcing her eyes open, there it was, two blue lines, pregnant. She took one more test just to be certain, ending with the same result, two blue lines. She sat down at the table, staring at both sticks in disbelief.

"How am I going to tell Gibson?"

She picked up her phone and called Alaina. No answer. She called

Grace and there was no answer there either. She didn't want to tell her dad or her aunt anything yet. Just needing a friend to talk to, she sent a text to Gibson. Her hands were shaking the entire time.

So, um, are you busy later?

He responded almost instantly.

Never too busy for you. ❤

Are you feeling better?

She smiled but then typed.

A little bit. Can we make dinner at my place tonight?

Sure. The kids always love that.

You're not contagious are you?

She laughed at that one because no; she was definitely not contagious.

No, I feel a lot better after some sleep. But I do have to talk to you about something.

Everything ok?

It will be, I think.

Ok, I love you. See you in a while.

I love you too.

And that was it. She tried to keep her mind busy by cleaning and getting a few items prepared so that the kids could help as much as they wanted with dinner. She cleaned and cleaned some more. Then she tried to sit and watch TV, but every commercial was baby food and diapers, and it genuinely made her stomach hurt. The engagement felt so new and was a lot already, but now a baby too? She went to the fridge to grab some wine, but as she reached in, her hand stopped. She couldn't even drink it out because she's pregnant. *Pregnant.* She just kept saying it in her mind.

After what felt like an eternity, she heard the truck pull in next door. She heard Gibson walk to his house with the kids. The side door slammed, followed by the two kids hollering and yelling as they ran towards her front door. They threw open the door and yelled, "ROSE!!!!!"

She smiled at the two of them. "Where's your dad guys?"

Chloe was holding her nose. "He fell into some cow poopy. He said he was going to take a shower but that we could run over here. So, we did. We ran over here, Rose." Chloe was giggling.

"Well, I'm glad he decided to take that shower." She loved watching these two sweet faces smile and laugh. She put a hand on her belly, catching a glimpse in her mind of the little life growing inside her. He or she would more than likely look just like these two. The thought made it a little easier to deal with being pregnant.

"Rose, how come you left school early? Grandma had to get me from school in the farm truck." Ollie was looking up at her with his big brown eyes.

"Oh, I got a little sick and had to come home, buddy. I'm sorry about that." She helped the kids climb on the bar stools and gave them each a plate. She placed little pieces of dough on each of their plates. They both looked at her, confused, and she said, "We're going to make our own pizzas for dinner!"

"WOOHOO!" Oliver yelled, throwing his hands in the air. Chloe was already pulling hers into a circle, or what was meant to be a circle. Rose pulled the bowls of toppings she had prepared out of the fridge, setting them on the counter. Then she helped them both shape their crusts, trying to let them do it themselves. She heard her front door open followed by his footsteps quietly moving towards them.

"There's my family," he said, a smile on his face. "What are we up to?"

"Rose says we get to make our OWN PIZZA!!" Chloe said, throwing the diced peppers that were in her hand into the air. "Oops. Sorry Rose"

Rose laughed, "It's ok sweetie. The kitchen is going to be messy for a bit. We'll just clean up once we're done."

His hand raised to her shoulder, and he whispered in her ear, so quiet so the kids couldn't hear. "It's been messier." Then nipped her earlobe, which gave her goosebumps. She elbowed him playfully and turned to look at him.

"Well, hey there handsome."

"Beautiful, how are we feeling?" He bent down, landing a gentle kiss on her cheek.

"Better now that you guys are here." She stepped away, grabbing him a ball of dough and a plate.

The little group laughed together as Gibson and Rose tried to help the kids spread the pizza sauce on their crusts. The kids took fists full of veggies and meat from the bowls to sprinkle on top.

"Whoa, whoa, whoa," Gibson exclaimed, laughing. "I don't think you need THAT much pepperoni, Clover." Chloe looked up at her dad before forcing some into her mouth. "Come on, Chloe."

"Oliver, you could use some peppers for your dinosaur eyes and onions for his teeth." Rose took some of the cheese out of his hand.

"Ooh, that's a great idea!" Oliver said with a smile.

Once they were all done putting on their toppings, Rose put all the pizzas in the oven and set the timer. Gibson took the kids into the living room and got a board game out for them to play. When he had gotten them going, he walked back to the kitchen, finding Rose wiping the counters off and putting away the left-over toppings.

"Well, that was fun," he said to her, plopping down on a barstool.

"Mhmm, it turned out pretty good I think," she said thought-fully, still wiping at the counter.

"We should do that again."

"Mhmm, we should."

Gibson took note that she wasn't paying attention. "I really think the hippos made it all better."

"Yes, the hippos helped," she said absentmindedly.

"Rose." He said it so tenderly that she stopped and looked at him. "What's wrong?"

She felt a tear trickle down her cheek. She put both elbows on the counter to prop her chin on her hands and stared at her fiancé, pursing her lips tightly. "I have to show you something," Sighing, she stood again and reached into the drawer next to her. She pulled a baggie out, the white sticks inside, and handed it to Gibson.

"What's this?" he asked, pulling it across to him.

"We goofed," she shrugged, not knowing how else to put it.

"Goofed? What's that mean?" He turned them over and saw the

blue lines. Holding the baggy tight, Gibson stared at the sticks for a few seconds. Rose had pushed away from the counter and backed herself to the refrigerator when he raised his head. "Is this what I think it is?"

Rose nodded slowly, trying to gauge Gibson's reaction. The dimple on his left cheek peeked through just before a smile spread across his face. "So, we're... I mean you're..."

She nodded again, placing a hand on her stomach. She turned and started fidgeting with the cupboard door, like she didn't know how to open it.

"Rose, what's wrong. I think this is great news!" Gibson stood and walked to her side. He pulled at her chin. When she looked at him, her eyes were sad. Gibson cocked his head to the side slightly, asking, "Aren't you happy?"

"I mean, it's not that I'm NOT happy. I just really wanted things to go in the order they're supposed to go," she started. "You know, engaged, wedding, then... baby," she whispered the last word.

"Sometimes things don't go in the order we want, but Rose." She looked away again, so he gently said, "Look at me." Hesitantly, she turned back to him. "We already know we love each other and that we're going to be together forever. So, we add another little one to the family first. Big deal!"

She nodded at him but said, "I don't want people to think we are getting married because of this AND I don't want to have an enormous belly in all of our wedding pictures."

"So, we get married sooner," he said with a chuckle. "Is that the biggest problem you're having with this? Who cares what people think?"

She leaned into him, wrapping her arms around his waist, breathing in his scent, and savoring in the warmth of his body.

He lightly ran his hands up and down her back, waiting for her to respond. When she pulled back, she was smiling.

"You're right, Gibs. The only important thing is that we love each other, and we are finally getting our happily ever after." She peeked around him to spy on the kids. They were still happily playing their game. "But let's wait to tell the kids... or anyone... until I go to the doctor. And maybe until closer to the wedding?" He nodded and kissed the top of her head. She wasn't sure how it happened, but everything she had wanted when she was younger was coming true, right down to her prince charming.

The next week was a blur. Rose had to find a doctor that would take her as a new client as well as allowing for an appointment after school. She and Gibson moved quietly through the process together. He was having the hardest time keeping it a secret and so from Monday until her appointment on Thursday, he would shoot random texts to her:

So, what do you think of

the name Tristan?

Stop it.

Is that a no?

Or:

We should name it after my

mom and your dad

Mavson oooohhh or Jasvis

What is wrong with you?

When she walked into the doctor's office, she prayed that no one she knew would be there. Luck was not on her side though, as the physician assistant was Lacey, of all people.

"Good morning," Lacey was saying as she backed into the room with her computer. When she turned, both Rose and Lacey froze. "Rose?" Rose felt her face flush, and some sort of anger washed over her.

"Lacey? Um, I didn't know you worked here." Rose was flustered. She wasn't sure if she wanted to bolt or cry. Their secret was going to be out for sure. She knew Lacey was conniving. "Maybe I should find another doctor." She said, standing.

"No, Rose, wait. Please don't."

"I can't work with this office. I don't even trust the second person I've interacted with."

"Rose, please give me a chance." Lacey was pleading with her. Pleading like a child, and this was a win for Rose, plus Rose realized Lacey already knew what was up, so even if she found a new doctor's office, Lacey still had the goods.

"Lacey, you HAVE to keep this a secret. We want to tell our story on our own." Now Rose was pleading, and she didn't like the feeling, so she firmly added, "Besides, if this gets out, your perfect little husband will know everything about you still pining away for Gibson." There, Rose thought, I've got her.

Letting out a quiet laugh, Lacey said, "I couldn't tell anyone, anyway. There's a thing called HIPAA, remember. And Henry already knows that I have a little thing for Gibson, Rose. It's not like we don't live in a small town. But I promise you can trust me. I've been doing this for years. In fact, when Holly got knocked up with Harrison a few years ago, no one knew until three months before her due date when she started showing." Lacey was grinning in self-esteem. Rose had no choice but to stay where she was.

Oddly, the appointment went well. She loved the doctor, and she had the choice to get a vaginal ultrasound to see if they could hear the baby's heartbeat. Just like someone knew she needed to hear it, Rose's breath caught in her chest when she heard the fast-paced pitter patter echo into the room.

Closing the door of the Honda, she was still on cloud nine. She looked down at her stomach and said, "You have no idea how loved you are already. I wasn't sure at first, little one, but the music of your heart took those fears and threw them out the window." Grabbing her cell, she called Gibson.

"You ok, babe?" The cows were groaning in the background. He wasn't on a tractor today.

"I heard it." She brushed a tear from her cheek.

"Heard what?"

"The baby's heartbeat, Gibson. I heard it." No response. "Gibson?"

"Yeah," he choked up, "I'm here."

"It's really real. We're having a baby."

His smile was evident in his voice as he said, "I love you."

They wanted to plan the wedding before giving the baby news to the world, but this was getting harder and harder to do. The moment she had heard that heartbeat, she immediately wanted to tell her dad. Now it was her shooting odd texts off to Gibson.

What if we only told your

parents and my dad.

Rose, we have to do this how

we planned. This was important to

you, remember. Plus you know Mavis,

she won't be able to keep her mouth shut.

I know but what if I just

dropped some hints….

Rose, stick to the plan.

We have 3 months to put this together.

You're right… I swear I'm

fat already though.

Even if you think you are,

you're still sexy as hell to me.

CHAPTER TWENTY-SEVEN

Rose and Gibson

That Saturday was Oliver's birthday party. The decision to have the party at the park was a disaster. Of course, it rained. All the party favors got drenched, the food basically melted except for one batch of Walmart cookies. It was a disaster, but one would not have known it watching the kids dance in the rain, slide down the slide, and jump in mud puddles. It might not have turned out the way Gibson had hoped, but his son enjoyed it. Even Lorna had made an appearance. Albeit only for fifteen minutes, she tried. While Lorna's appearance made Gibson happy, he could still see his son shy away from the woman.

Rose

The following Friday, Grace and Alaina flew in from Charlotte. The girls were going to go dress shopping. Rose and her dad had driven to the airport to pick them up.

She was getting the girls settled into the spare bedroom in her house when Alaina suddenly stopped and looked at Rose with a quizzical look.

"Rose?"

"What's up, Alaina?"

"Are you pregnant?" The blood drained from Rose's face as she stammered, "W... why would you ask me that?"

"You are totally pregnant!!!" Alaina screamed.

"I don't know what you're talking about."

"Shut up, fool. You can't lie to me about this. Look at me, I have a baby strapped to my front. My boobs are sagging to the ground. I just went through this."

"Ok, shut up," Rose threw her hands in the air in defeat. "We haven't told a SINGLE soul yet, not even our parents. You HAVE TO KEEP IT QUIET!"

Grace, still confused, stammered, "Wait... no wait... like pregnant?" Alaina and Rose laughed. "Come on, man! This means no bachelorette party!"

"No, Gracey, we still have to have one... people will suspect otherwise. I'll have to just pretend to drink somehow."

"I mean, we don't HAVE to have a party. We could just do a shower. I mean, you guys ARE rushing this along." Alaina suggested.

"No fucking way," Grace yelled. "Every bride deserves a kick ass bachelorette party. I've got this."

"Ok girls, no more talking about this. Let's talk about meeting my fiancé!" As if she had summoned him, the doorbell rang.

The girls bound down the stairs together. Rose swung the door open, and Gibson scooped her into a hug that ended with a kiss on her lips. The kids pushed past like it was nothing new to them and plopped on her living room floor with the Candyland board game. When Gibson finally set Rose down, they turned to her friends.

"Guys, this is Gibson Titus. Gibs, this is Alaina and Grace." She pointed to each of them. Grace shook his hand, but Alaina threw her arms around his neck. Rose rolled her eyes.

"Nice to finally meet you both in person." Gibson's eyes sparkled.

"So, let's all go sit at the table and chat a little. Oliver, Chloe, are you guys ok in here?" Rose asked. The kids nodded, but Chloe got up and ran to squeeze her. Rose picked her up and squeezed her back, setting her back to the floor.

At the table, Alaina was too fidgety. Rose kept shooting her glares, once caught by Gibson.

"What's going on?" He asked, side eyeing the girls.

Rose hung her head and shook it. Letting out a sigh, she said, "Alaina over there…," she paused, eyeing her friend, "figured out our little secret." Gibson looked from Rose to Alaina and then to Grace with eyes as wide as Texas.

"She figured it out?" he tried to keep his voice down. Alaina was now bouncing in her seat. Grace was doing her best to hold her down. "How?"

"Yeah, I swear to you, I didn't say a thing." Rose looked at him.

"It's written all over her gorgeous face, Gibson. Look at her, she's glowing!" Alaina couldn't contain herself. Gibson's face swung back to Rose's.

"It is, isn't it?" He cocked his head to the side and gave her a goofy smile. She slapped his arm. "What? You are damn fine but this glow."

"Oh, shut up. They both know to be hush-hush." Gibson pulled her chair closer to his and put his hand on her leg.

"And I'm sure they will be. But she's right, this glow on your face is something to be reckoned with." He flashed her his bedroom eyes.

"Hey, Titus, slow your roll." She frantically looked around the table. "My girls are here, and the kids are right there."

"What are you talking about?" His eyes got more intense as he inched his face closer to hers.

"Now THIS is what I came to see," Grace was watching intently. Rose shot her a look before turning back to Gibson.

"Down, boy," she giggled, and his mouth turned to a smile just before he planted a sweet kiss on her cheek.

Alaina sighed like she was watching a romance movie and Grace grunted, "You two are something all right. Couldn't you have let it smolder for a bit?"

They spent a few more hours chatting. The girls grilled Gibson, even though they knew almost everything. Gibson asked them about their lives. Grace was especially interested in any single friends that Gibson had. She wanted to know her options for the night of the wedding.

"Knock it off, Grace," Rose had smacked her friend.

"Rose, a girl has needs. If you found a dude here, why couldn't I?"

"She has a point," Gibson played along. "I do have a few guy friends that have needs too."

"Don't egg her on, Gibs. She's a mess without Alaina or me around to keep her in check."

By the end of the night, the girls were more than satisfied with the man their friend had chosen. He lifted the kids into his arms, telling the women good night, and walked his little family home.

The girls stayed up late talking. Rose had missed her friends and had missed out on so much in the short time she had been home.

The next morning, Rose's Aunt Bri pulled up in her overly huge Chevy suburban. Why she needed anything that big for her two kids was beyond Rose's imagination, but she was thankful for it that day. The girls piled in after securing little Beatrice's car seat and headed to the bridal shop in the next town. It was known around the world even though it was nestled into a small town. Holly was waiting for them when they pulled up.

The poor salesgirl had to bring a million dresses in and out of the dressing room until they finally got it right. As Rose stepped out of the dressing room, her aunt looked at her and started crying. The girls froze, so she spun to look in the one hundred eighty-degree mirror.

Rose gasped as the salesgirl set the veil on her head. It was perfect, and she felt her own eyes well up. It wasn't white, more of an ecru, the satin underlayment covered by a layer of lace, with tiny crystals sewn into it. Strapless with a sweetheart neckline and just above the waistline, the dress spread gently outwards, complimented with a taupe crystal enhanced belt. There was no over the top train and the bottom hem was scalloped following the lace. Perfect for her country wedding.

The veil was cathedral length, though. The lace pattern and crystals matched her dress almost exactly, adding just enough city to the country vibe. Her dad had given her his credit card, allowing her to buy the dress on the spot. Her Aunt bought her the veil because it completed the entire ensemble. She only needed to find shoes and a tiara, but she wanted to see what she could find elsewhere. Normal shoes were not going to cut it.

They also found the bridesmaid dresses at the shop. The girls had to buy off the rack because there wasn't enough time for alterations. They had no problems, though. The color of the dresses was a pale rose color, in a nod to their friend's name.

Alaina's dress hung off her shoulders a bit with a sweetheart cut to the bodice, but fit to her body flaring just at the end with long pleats accentuating the skirt. Grace's was a spaghetti strap with a vee cut bodice ending just above her waist, showing just enough cleavage to not be slutty. The dress hung to every curve of her body, like a glove to a hand, and had a slit that went to the top of her thigh. Holly's dress was more of a halter look with a twist to the bodice and swung out at her hips, falling slightly looser than the other girls' dresses. They looked perfect. Just enough city to mix with the country.

They headed to the next town to find shoes and jewelry, where Rose fell in love with a pair of heels that made her two inches taller and had crystals covering the toes. The three bridesmaids decided on cowboy boots, just for fun.

The weekend was too short, and Rose was not ready to give her friends back to North Carolina. They hugged and cried with the reminder that they would be back again in just over a month for her bachelorette party and the wedding. Those girls were truly her sisters, blood or not.

CHAPTER TWENTY-EIGHT

Gibson

That Wednesday was the day Gibson chose as Lorna's supervised visit day. He was to drop them off at the social services building at four in the afternoon to spend three hours with their mother. He was nervous about letting them go, but the social worker assured him they would be safe under her watch.

Gibson told the receptionist they would wait in the car and to let them know when they could come in. He hated making his kids sit in that dull, smelly building any longer than they had to. So, sitting in the parking lot inside the truck, Gibson, Rose, and the kids waited for Lorna's car to pull in. Of course, she was late, pulling in at four thirty when she was expected at four. They watched as she climbed out of the car with Bart in tow. Rose put her hand on Gibson's arm as he gripped the steering wheel too tight.

"Let them go in, Gibs. The case worker knows he isn't allowed. They'll kick him back outside." Rose wasn't sure herself but wanted to try to calm him. Gibson's phone rang then.

"Mr. Titus, the children's mom is here. You can bring them in."

"Like hell I am. That man she's with isn't allowed near them."

"She didn't come in with anyone. Please bring the kids in." Gibson looked at Rose. What was this, some sort of ambush.

"Listen, what was your name again?"

"Sheila."

"Sheila, listen. We watched her walk through the door with that man. You need to sweep the building. He's there."

"Sir, I assure you, if he's in the building, he won't be allowed near the kids. Now please bring them in so we can get this started." Not waiting for a response, Sheila hung up. He turned to his kids and saw the fear on their faces. This was going to kill him in so many ways.

"Guys, Ms. Sheila says you will be fine. I believe her," I think, "So let's go see mommy!" He opened the truck door as Rose did too. She opened Oliver's door and held her hand out as he jumped down. Gibson opened Chloe's door and held his arms out to her. She climbed into her dad's arms and pulled his face to hers.

Nose to nose she whispered, "I'll stomp on his foot if he's in there, daddy." She rubbed her little nose against his. He squeezed his daughter and the four of them walked inside, like the squad they were.

The visitation seemed to take forever, but Gibson wasn't leaving that building without his kids. Rose napped on his shoulder. The pregnancy was taking all of her energy lately. He scrolled Facebook, checked his emails, texted his dad, texted Rose's dad. Watching his fiancé sleep, he rubbed her belly gently, hoping no one would notice. Anything to keep his mind occupied. He looked at the old-fashioned black clock on the wall. Seven o'clock. He started to get antsy as he watched the clock move. Five after, then ten after. He shot out of his seat, which jostled Rose awake, and went to the desk.

"Um hi. Yeah, my kids' visitation should have ended ten minutes ago. Why aren't they out yet?"

"Sir, she was late, so we have to give her the full time that she would have gotten."

"Uh, no, that's not how this is going to work. She loses out because she wasn't on time. We don't reward people for their faults in my house."

"Unfortunately, sir, the court doesn't care about your rules. She showed up, so she gets the full amount of time."

Frustrated, Gibson started pacing, never taking his eyes off the clock. Quarter after, twenty after, twenty-five after. As the clock hit seven thirty, the doors burst open with the kids running for his arms. Wrapping them tightly into him, he let out a sigh of relief. Lorna walked past him as he stood.

Gibson cleared his throat. "Lorna."

She spun to look at him. "What?"

"Try to be on time next time, please."

"Whatever. Next time, don't bring your whore. Bye, kids. Love you both." Rose flinched at the name calling. Gibson noticed that Lorna's eyes were clear, but he was sure that in the time it would take her to get to the car, that would change.

"Let's go home guys. You can tell us about how it went on the ride home." Chloe was rubbing her eyes, signaling that they would only hear from Oliver on the way.

They got the kids home and in bed by nine. Rose was so tired and thankful for the one outfit she had left at Gibson's house. It meant she didn't have to go home and could go straight to work in the morning. All she wanted to do was crawl into bed. Instead, though, she climbed onto the couch next to her man. He raised his arm above her so she could snuggle into his side and draped his arm around her.

Letting out a sigh, he grunted, "I wish there was a way that they never had to go back there." Rose was quiet, knowing that there wasn't a need to agree. He knew she felt the same way. "God, Rose, if only we could have made this family together from the beginning."

She felt the knot of guilt form in her stomach. "I feel like I'm to blame for ruining us, Gibson." She pushed herself up and turned to face him, crisscrossing her legs on the couch.

He looked surprised to hear the revelation fall from her mouth. "Don't blame yourself. I feel like we ruined it together. I know you feel like that because you wouldn't let me talk to you, but Rose," he shook his head, "If I wouldn't have gotten so blitzed that night, I would have realized what Lacey was doing. I could have just stopped or not started drinking. I should have stayed with you that night. I should have not worried about the party and worried more about you. I was too young to deal with what we wanted back then. It was all me." The look of sadness in his eyes made her reach for him.

"And if I wouldn't have been so stubborn, we could have talked long ago and made this family together from the start." She kissed his cheek. "Let's not talk about it ever again, ok? We've hashed this out, we're obviously growing our family now." She looked down, putting a hand on her stomach. "And we are facing this world together with our united front again." He placed his hand on her stomach too and smiled at her.

"Wanna go pretend to make another one?" Gibson wriggled his eyebrows at her. When Rose had found out she was pregnant, she had been afraid of intimacy, thinking they could hurt the baby. After talking to Alaina, though, she had given in. Pregnancy had her wanting sex more often.

She faked a yawn and stretched, shooting him a wink. He took that as a yes and scooped Rose up from the couch, carrying her through the bedroom door. With a gentle tap, he kicked it closed behind him. He lowered her feet to the ground, reached behind his neck, and pulled his shirt off. She scurried across the room from him, stripping clothes as she went. He couldn't help but follow her, walking out of his jeans and boxers. He caught her by her waist then and finished removing her bra and panties himself.

Lifting her onto him, he kissed her fiercely, and backed them against the wall. He moved in and out of her with perfect rhythm while standing there. She held on, legs wrapped around him, digging her nails into his arms in pleasure, biting her lip to keep from screaming. He gently nipped at her neck, and she nipped at his. She rode him all the way to climax, doing her best not to explode too loudly. She knew little ears were next door.

CHAPTER TWENTY-NINE

Rose

It had been six weeks since Jason had started the trial medication, and so far, it was going well. While that first week on the drug had caused bouts of nausea and extreme fatigue, his tremors were slowing.

The second week, his energy returned, and his speech was getting better. Excitement rose inside of her as Rose watched her dad getting better. The normal shuffling was becoming a clear walk again. His sentences were quicker, and smile was stronger.

This weekend, Rose was sitting at her dad's table showing him the wedding plans that had been made so far.

"Dad," she said, causing him to look at her, "do you have any of grandma's jewelry at all? I'm trying to find my 'something old'." He said nothing but smiled at her. He pushed out of his seat and walked to the old desk in the living room. Opening one drawer, Jason pulled out a small box.

"I was going to wait to give this to you until the wedding day. But I know you have a lot on your mind, rushing through to get this planned. This was the necklace your great grandma wore, and your grandmother wore. Aunt Bri wore it at her wedding too." He gingerly opened the box to reveal the most beautiful antique diamond and pearl necklace. It took her breath away when she saw it, and her eyes instantly welled up.

"May I?" she asked, holding out her hand. Her dad nodded and passed it to her. Holding her breath, she ran her fingers over the piece.

Jason told Rose, "My grandma wore this almost one hundred years ago, when she promised herself to my grandpa. Their wedding was right here in the backyard. Of course, grandpa's family owned the place then, and it was still a working farm." Rose was still staring at the piece in awe of the age and the importance of it.

"Is Bri ok with me wearing this?" she asked.

"Bri told me to give it to you. She doesn't have any girls. You're the next one in line, Rose," He leaned in to his daughter and kissed her on her head, "Your grandmother would have loved to see you wear this."

Throwing her arms around her dad's neck, she whispered, "Thanks, daddy."

That next week, Rose was sitting at the Titus farm, working through one crucial detail. Someone had the church booked the weekend of the wedding, and the golf course was too, leaving them with no venue. Rose was sitting with her head on the table, hands grasped behind it.

"What are we going to do, Mavis?" She asked her future mother-in-law, "We only have seven weeks until the wedding."

"Well, honey, let's think this through." Mavis set a glass of tea in front of Rose and settled into the seat next to her. "What are your must haves?"

"I don't even really care at this point. It needs to be beautiful and have some type of altar for us to stand in front of or at or under." She knew that her voice sounded whiney, but at this point she didn't even care. Mavis placed a hand on Rose's back, gently rubbing it.

"Rose, I think I have an idea," Mavis said excitedly, causing Rose to lift her head. "Now hear me out. What if we have the wedding here at the farm?"

"What? How?"

"We get a big white tent, tables, strings of white lights, white folding chairs…"

"I'll build you a trellis," John had walked in and overheard the idea. Rose looked between the two, a small smile creeping across her face.

"I love this idea. But are you guys sure? Your lawn will take a beating."

John placed a hand on Rose's shoulder. "The lawn doesn't matter to us, Rose. All that matters to us is that you two get your happily ever after. You both deserve this." Rose stood suddenly and grabbed them both in a hug.

"You guys are amazing. Thank you for doing this," Her smile broad across her face, lighting her eyes. Gibson walked in just then and gave them all a questioning look.

"What's happening here?"

"Gibson, how do you feel about getting married here at the farm?" Rose's eyes sparkled as the words fell out of her mouth. His parents were both beaming.

"I think that's an amazing idea!"

"And I'm going to build a trellis for you both to stand under." John's pride was electrifying.

"We'll need more flowers, and some tule…" The women had begun to iron out the details together.

When the pair left the farm after dinner with the kids, Rose's fire was lit again with planning. Although they had knocked one item off the list, it seemed six more items took its place. She was bubbling and carrying on. Gibson decided it was a good chance to ask her about his suit.

"So, since we're getting married at the farm now, do you think I can wear jeans?" He stole a glance sideways. He watched as she lifted her head from her checklist, turning her face towards him. From the drawn-out movement, he knew the answer.

"Gibson, we've had this conversation four times. You are wearing a navy suit and tie with a cream shirt underneath."

"Yeah, but the farm… Don't you think jeans would…"

"NO! You are wearing the suit," she smacked him on the arm playfully, "I don't need any additional stress from you."

Gibson laughed but said, "Are you sure I can't persuade you to change your mind?" His hand was on her thigh, slowly creeping up her leg. She smacked him again.

"That's not going to help. Knock it off."

"Fine," he said, pulling his hand away. Glancing in the mirror, he smiled at the kids, "How was granny's today?" The kids took off describing everything they had done.

CHAPTER THIRTY

Rose

There was only one month remaining before their wedding and Rose was feeling the crunch. One night while talking to Gibson in her kitchen, she quietly suggested that they tell their families about the baby, "We're going to need them to help us keep it on the down low at the wedding. People will be expecting to see me drink, or at least have a glass of champagne, and if I'm being truthful, I want my dad to know so bad it hurts." She smiled at Gibson, who nodded. Jumping into his lap, Rose squeezed him, before giving him a look. Gibson had become accustomed to this look. It meant 'take me to bed'.

He loved her, but pregnant Rose was something more. She wanted it so much, and it was fun knowing they couldn't get pregnant. They experimented with so many positions that it made him want to stay home more often than go to work. It was almost becoming a problem.

A weekend prior to this, the kids were at the farm with their grandparents, so she had come to see him on the tractor. If corn stalks could talk, the ones on those eighty acres would have been able to tell stories. She had climbed into the cab and rode him for almost half of the acreage. Again, he was thankful for the GPS in that cab. She was almost insatiable.

The next evening, they drove to her dad's house. The kids ran to Jason, calling him grandpa, which apparently was music to his ears because his smile widened further than Rose had seen in months. She grabbed her dad's hand and walked into the house.

The kids ran around to the back to climb the swing set.

"What are you kids up to? I wasn't expecting any company tonight, although I am glad to see you all." He was moving around the kitchen, grabbing glasses and filling them with water.

"Well, dad, we have some news to tell you. Come sit down." Rose pulled a seat out at the table. Jason eyed her before gingerly sitting down. "We haven't told the kids yet because... well... mouths." A small laugh escaped her mouth.

"Jason, how do you feel about being a grandpa?" Gibson blurted.

"I love it! Your kids are such great kids, Gibson." His eyes twinkled.

Rose twisted her hands together before phrasing the question differently. "Dad, how do you feel about another grandchild?"

"Oh, I can't wait for that to happen!"

Jason still wasn't getting it, so Rose reached across the table, taking his hand, and said, "Dad, I'm pregnant." Jason's smile faltered for a brief second while he took in the information. Then his smile grew again as he looked from Rose to Gibson.

"WHAT?!?!" he exclaimed. He jumped up abruptly and circled the table to grab his daughter and Gibson into a hug. "Oh my god. This is great news!! How far along are you?"

"Ten weeks." Rose felt relieved and happy all at once. "But dad, you cannot tell anyone. We're going to make our announcement after the wedding. Like I said, the kids don't even know yet."

He nodded, pulling her into a hug again. "Rose, Gibson, I'm so happy for you both. This is my dream come true!" For the rest of the night, her dad didn't stop smiling.

The next evening, Rose met Gibson at the Titus farm. Mavis was pulling brownies out of the oven when Rose walked into the kitchen.

"Mavis, is John around?"

"He'll be in shortly. What's going on, love?"

"Oh, Gibson and I need to talk to you guys about the wedding." She tried to sound nonchalant, but Mavis caught wind of the tone in her voice.

"Uh huh. Sure. I've been waiting for this wedding talk for about two weeks now." She winked at Rose, whose face had paled.

"I don't know what you're talking about."

"Sure, Rose. I'll wait for the men to come in." She winked again, just as the boys stampeded in the door. Rose looked at Gibson and then at his mom. He mouthed 'What?'

"So, Gibson, Rose says you guys have some wedding news for dad and me?" Mavis got right to the point.

"Uh, yeah mom." Gibson hesitated, eyeing his fiancé. "So, Rose and I..."

Before he could finish, Mavis interrupted him, "ARE PREG-NANT!"

Gibson's mouth dropped open, gaping at his mom. "How did you know?"

"Oh, come on you two. Your dad and I have had four children and have seen all of them have children. This old grandma sensed it two weeks ago. Right, John? Isn't that when I told you my suspicions?" John nodded at his wife.

"Ok then," Gibson looked at Rose, who looked shocked. "Um, yeah, so the kids don't know, actually only Jason and Rose's two friends from North Carolina know. We, um, want to keep it a SE-CRET," he put a ton of emphasis on the word and pointed at his mom, "until after the wedding." His mom made the motion in front of her mouth as if she was zipping her lips, shooting them both a wink.

"Well, that took the excitement out of the announcement." Rose felt a bit deflated. Mavis walked over and grabbed her in a tight hug.

"It doesn't make it any less exciting to us, though, Rose. We couldn't be happier for you both." John nodded again and stood to shake his son's hand.

They stopped by Bri's on the way home and told her and Tom as well. Everyone had the reminder that the kids did not know for obvious reasons and that they were waiting until after the wedding to tell anyone.

The invitations went out; the flowers ordered. John finished the trellis, and it was perfect. The wedding was falling together and inching closer and closer. Rose's and Gibson's friends planned the bachelor and bachelorette parties for the week prior to the wedding, with Rose's friends coming in that Friday and staying through the wedding.

CHAPTER THIRTY-ONE

Rose and Gibson

Three nights before the parties, Rose was cleaning the house, preparing for the girls' return to Michigan. When suddenly she was in her own thoughts. She turned off the lights and crawled on the couch, wrapping herself in the blanket that her grandmother had made her years ago. Tucking her legs under her chin, she let her mind take over, knowing full well she shouldn't. She ignored a text from Gibson and let two calls from him go to voicemail.

When he burst through her front door, he almost missed her sitting in the dark. He stared at her for a moment, before he heard her say, "I don't know if I can do this."

His heart stood still, but he walked to her and sat. "What, Rose?"

"I just... these parties... It scares me. It's bringing me back to high school." She stared into her hands. He reached out to her, but she shrugged away. "I thought I had worked through all of this, Gibson. But now I'm afraid of what's going to happen."

"Rose, you know me better than that." He tried to sound gentle.

"I know, I mean I think I do. But what if you get drunk again? What if your brain goes nuts again? What if..." He pulled her arm gently, making her fall towards him. She had gone down the road alone, with no lights on. He wrapped her in his arms and kissed the top of her head.

"Hey, I will make you a promise. I will keep my drinking to a minimum, and if there is a stripper, I'll stare at the wall above her head."

"I'm being serious, Gibson. I really am worried."

He angled her face up to look into his eyes and held her there. "I am going to say this one time. You are my person. There is never going to be, and never has there ever been, anyone who could take your place. I have wanted to be your husband since you fell out of that school bus fourteen years ago. I knew it then, and I know it today. I am yours and always will be. I promise you, nothing will happen." He let her chin go then. She felt two tears roll down her cheek. She knew he was right, and even though her brain wanted her to ignore the truth, she knew better.

She laid into his chest, "My heart knows that. It's this pesky brain of mine." Turning her face to see him, she whispered, "And those should be your vows. Thank you for always loving me." They sat in the dark for a few more minutes before he had to wander home.

CHAPTER THIRTY-TWO

Rose

Two days later, after school, she made the trip again to Grand Rapids, to pick up her friends from the airport. Grace was giddy because Alaina had given her full reign of the party. This made Rose a little worried.

Rose's aunt had offered to watch Alaina's daughter while they went out, so they dropped everyone's stuff at the house before bringing little Bea over to Bri's.

While the girls were getting ready in Rose's bathroom, the door-bell rang. Rose opened the door, finding Kendall and Holly standing on her porch. When they started walking in, she noticed one more body behind them. Lacey. Rose let her pass, eyeballing her as she did, then pulled Holly to the side. Kendall went straight upstairs to meet Alaina, feeling the fight that was brewing.

"Um, what the hell, Holly. Why is SHE here?" Rose hissed at her friend.

"Rose, come on. We needed a DD, and she volunteered." Holly grinned.

"I'm sure she did." Rose turned towards Lacey, scowling at her. "Well, won't this be a blast? Partying for my bachelorette party that should have happened long ago, with the girl who is the REASON IT DIDN'T!" Rose's voice got louder than she expected, but she didn't care. She spun to face Holly again, who was cowering a little at the tone of Rose's voice, "WORST IDEA YOU HAVE EVER HAD!"

"I'm sorry, Rose. I just thought that because you guys had talked, that maybe..."

"You were wrong, Holly. Get rid of her." Rose spun on her heel and went upstairs, leaving Holly, Lacey, and Grace standing in the living room. All of them with their mouths open. Even Grace, who didn't have the pleasure of seeing Rose mad like this very often but absolutely loved it.

"So maybe I'll just go," Lacey started, "She's right, we haven't totally patched things up yet."

"Hold up, blondie," Grace held up her hand, "I think we need to take you upstairs."

"Do you want her to punch me or something?"

"Well..." Grace looked at the ceiling. "No, not really. But I DO think that you should at least plead your case." She grabbed Lacey's hand.

Holly looked as confused as Lacey did, but at least there wasn't blood yet.

They walked into the bathroom where Alaina, Rose and Kendall were fixing their makeup and hair. Grace saw Rose's face in the mirror and held her hand up to her friend.

"Look, I know this isn't everything you wanted, but I think that Lacey should stay," Grace started.

"Grace, if you think..." Rose interjected.

Grace held her hand over Rose's mouth. "Hear me out, please. Lacey-girl here owes you an apology, and maybe being DD is part of that, BUT also if it weren't for her whorish ass butting in back then, maybe you and Gibson wouldn't even be together anymore. He said it himself. He was too immature to be an adult back then. Does it suck? You're damned right it does but think about it."

The four other girls all stood there in awe. Then all of their gazes swooped to look at Rose, who was trying to compose her thoughts into complete sentences. Turning to Lacey, she took a deep breath and in a quiet yet firm voice said, "Fine, you can stay. But Lacey, one false step and I'll pummel you myself. Now girls, if you please, I'd like to get this party started." The girls all cheered. They checked themselves one more time and hurried down the stairs.

Before Rose walked out the door, she stopped Grace. "Ok, what gives? I know you better than this."

Cocking her head to the side, Grace responded, "I'm not sure I understand the question." She shot a devilish grin at her friend.

"Spit it out, Grace. I know that you, knowing how I feel about Lacey, wouldn't have tried to pull us together."

"Rose, can't you just have fun. Alaina told me to play nice this weekend, so I am." Grace quickly turned, her brown curls smacking Rose in the face.

She's up to something. Rose followed her friend, shaking her head as she did.

Lacey's white minivan sat in the driveway. Ok, not a luxurious limo, but it would fit the entire group. Piling in, they took off for Main Street.

Grace had done a pretty good job with the party. While there wasn't a lot that she could do in the small town, she had rented out the back room of the bar. She had invited almost all the girls from Rose's high school class. She had lots of stupid party games, like Pin the Dick on the Cowboy and Ball Toss into Blow Job Betty, the blowup doll's mouth. The girls were laughing and carrying on until the lights went down.

A sultry song started to play, sending a shot of fear through Rose. *Oh no, not a stripper, please God, not a stripper,* she pleaded internally. When the lights came up, there on the stage was Gibson, in a cowboy hat, flannel shirt and jeans, tied to a chair, looking at Rose with a sheepish smile. Her eyes shot around the room, catching that all the husbands and boyfriends had entered the room. Grace had heard Rose loud and clear when she had talked to her the other day, telling her about her worries. She squeezed her friend and whispered, "Thank you," into her ear.

Grace nodded and started looking for a guy to dance with as the DJ started playing, landing her eyes on the man hanging around Lacey. A look of determination swept over her face before Grace pushed her breasts up with her hands, licked her lips, and made her way towards the couple, grabbing the man's hand and pulling him onto the dancefloor.

Ah, there's the plan. Rose shook her head at her friend. Then she turned her attention back to the stage. Gibson looked so hot tied up, so she waltzed up to him. Placing her finger under her own chin, she looked down at Gibson. Then, biting her bottom lip, she straddled her man, wrapping her arms around his neck.

"Well, if you're my stripper, I'm ok with that. But I'll have to warn you, my fiancé can kick your ass." Gibson smiled and tried to nip at her, but he couldn't reach.

"Ooh," she cooed, "I like this. You can't do anything, but I can do whatever I want." She took her pointer finger and pointed it at him before pushing it into his chest, traveling it down his front and stopping right below his waistline. Playfully, she drew the outline of what she knew was below his jeans before massaging the bulge that was clearly growing below.

Letting out a quiet groan, he said, "Don't start something you're not willing to finish in public."

Rose cocked her head to the side. "Who said I'm not willing." She brought her hand to his zipper, pretending like she was going to go after him.

"Seriously, do not move. You get me worked up just seeing you, but when you touch me, you make me stand at attention." His own suggestion caused his member to jump.

"Oh, Mr. Titus, I haven't even begun to touch you yet," her hand hovered at his waistband, "But, if you'd really like to continue with your party, I have a sure-fire way to, um, help you down again."

"God, Rose, please tell me because right now I just want you to untie me so I can take you to the bathroom, lock the door and release his enthusiasm into you." His voice was breathy and growling at her. He wanted so badly to touch her, to feel her. Evidently, his body did too as he felt his Wranglers getting tighter.

Leaning forward with a gentle shift that garnered another groan from his throat, she whispered into his ear, "Holly brought Lacey to my party..." She leaned back to see the look on Gibson's face. It was a look of horror and anger. "But according to Grace, it's ok, because if it weren't for her, we might not be here now."

He scanned the room. It was almost his worst nightmare, except that the hottest woman in his world was sitting on his lap, creating a bulge in his pants that he wasn't sure how he was going to remedy. When his eyes found Lacey, he felt his manhood softening. Sure enough, she weaseled her way in here.

Rose looked between her legs and, seeing that things had calmed down, she stood from his lap. She whistled at Cody, who immediately ran to the stage to untie his best friend. Gibson double checked his groin. Seeing he was safe, he stood, snatching his soon to be wife up and carried her down off the stage. When they reached the floor, he set her down before grabbing a microphone from the DJ.

Gibson cleared his throat, "Um, hey, guys." The DJ stopped the music, and everyone turned to look at Gibson and Rose. "Yeah, hi. Um, I just wanted to say thank you to all of you for pulling off this crossover bachelor-bachelorette party. I know it isn't the normal type of party, but when Grace and Cody came to me with the idea," he stole a look at Rose, who smiled sweetly at him, "I told them it was the best idea I had heard. I'm so glad that we were able to keep it a surprise for you, Rose. You know I love you and I've only ever loved you. Thank you for believing in us again." He leaned down and kissed Rose hard. After he released her, he shouted, "Let's party!" The DJ started again, and the group partied until one in the morning.

———————————————

After the party, Rose and the girls headed back to her house. She couldn't sleep, though. Grabbing her phone from the bed table, she texted Gibson, hoping he was awake. She needed something.

You awake?

Lying back on her pillow, she stared at the ceiling. The way he had groaned under her at the party had awakened her. It had taken all of her strength not to take him to the bathroom at the bar. She didn't want any of their times together to be cheap, though, even if it did sound daring. The vibration of her phone brought her back to earth.

You ok?

Yeah, just wondered if you

were up for a little something.

What about the girls?

Oh, they won't know I'm

gone. I can hear them both

snoring in the other room.

Come on over.

She didn't even answer or change her clothes. She slipped quietly down the stairs and out the front door, tiptoeing across the lawn to his drive. He was standing at the door, waiting for her in his boxers.

Yanking the door open, Rose stood in front of Gibson with a childish grin. "That felt like the time I snuck out to see you in high school."

Gibson smiled at her, "That was a pretty exciting night."

Rose nodded, "After grinding on you on the stage tonight, I've been trying to talk myself down, especially since the girls are here." Rose was pushing him backwards, stripping her clothes off as she did. Her voice was dripping with need. "I just couldn't, though. Something about you, tied up, wriggling beneath me."

Gibson leaned down, grabbing her up and wrapping her legs around his waist. His hands firm on her buttocks. Looking into his eyes, Rose leaned forward to meet his mouth with hers. Their tongues danced together as he walked them to the bedroom.

Setting her feet to the floor, Gibson removed his boxers. Rose took his arm, turning him to sit on the bed.

"I liked the way we were on stage. Let's finish that." Rose's voice was low and sensual. Gibson's eyes grew a little wider at first as she swung her leg over him, straddling him just below where his arousal was. She slowly moved herself forward, to grind a little against him. Rubbing his member against her crevice. He tried to pull her up and onto him, but she resisted, wanting more of the current motion. She continued rubbing against him, stimulating herself. He liked it too as he dove into her breasts and clenched her backside. She continued her outside dance a bit longer until she felt herself tipping the edge.

Not wanting to climax yet, she pulled herself up and onto his member. As she lowered herself, Gibson groaned her name, arousing her more. With both feet next to his waist and her hands behind her on his knees, she started pulling him in and out of herself. He held her hips, helping support her movements, leaning in to kiss her body. The new angle was something they had never tried together and hit places inside that she had never known existed. The position was both ecstasy and agony for Gibson. He had no opportunity to move, creating a need and want he had never known. She sighed as she sat upright, placing her hands on his shoulders to steady herself, riding faster.

He tugged at her nipples with his mouth as her breasts bounced in front of him. Rose started to clench around him, and he took that opportunity to grab her tightly to him and stand. The shift of his body against her caused her to cry out as she exploded. Turning her to the bed, Gibson laid her down and began thrusting into her, needing to release the built-up desire she had created. Rose cried out again as his movements found her spot inside, bringing her through another climax. He felt himself climbing to the top of his summit and as he toppled over the edge, he devoured her mouth.

Laying together in the afterglow, Rose's head on his chest, Gibson let out a soft laugh.

"What?" Rose asked.

His fingertips softly tracing her spine when he responded, "I've just been wondering if you've been studying the Kama sutra is all. Some of these positions lately have been very outside anything we've ever tried."

Rose felt her face flush as she playfully smacked him. "Mr. Titus, are you saying that you aren't enjoying it?"

"Are you saying that you have been studying it?"

"I guess you'll just have to find out," Rose pushed up from his side, shooting him a playful look. The look that crossed Gibson's face amused her. Almost a look of fear and shock. "I should head home. I don't want to get caught by the wedding patrol."

Rose leaned in, planting a gentle kiss on her beau's lips. He sat to meet her, running his fingers through her hair and down her back, squeezing one of her butt cheeks. Rose tried pulling away, but he pressed her backwards onto the bed, causing her to squeal. Hovering over his fiancé, Gibson studied her face. Her smile was the most beautiful thing in his entire world, and all he wanted was to be sure she never lost it.

He gently kissed her again. Rose released a tiny moan as he did. Then, pulling her up, he hugged her. Rose knew she had to leave, or this would continue until the sun rose. She kissed Gibson again, "Good night."

"Night. I love you," Gibson responded, stroking her cheek.

"I love you too," Rose responded before following the trail of clothing back out the door. The minute her feet hit the driveway she saw that the light of her front porch was on.

"Shit," she breathed.

Walking up her front step, Grace was sitting in one of Rose's rockers, tapping her finger on the arm, a devilish grin on her face.

"Walk of shame?" Grace chided, pulling her finger under her chin.

"Ha, ha, very funny. I have no shame when it comes to Gibson."

"Well, judging by the length of time you've been gone, I'm hoping that means you enjoyed yourself."

"You have no idea, Grace." Rose's mind wandered back, reliving every touch and movement in her head.

"You're right, I don't. But if you'd like to indulge me, I could sure use some ammo for my shower in the morning."

Rose shot her friend a look that read 'not happening'. Grace shrugged, standing from her seat. "Guess I'll just have to use my imagination."

"Gross, Grace." Rose side eyed her friend. "Wait, how long have you been out here?"

"Oh, not more than ten minutes, but I heard you leave," she said, following her friend back inside. "I know how long you've been gone." The tone of innuendo in Grace's voice made Rose roll her eyes.

CHAPTER THIRTY-THREE

Gibson

The week of the wedding was busy enough, but Gibson had to take the kids for their visit with their mom in the middle of the week, and it did not go well. Gibson was sitting in the waiting room, one hour into the visitation, when Oliver fled the room looking for his dad.

"Whoa, hey, buddy." Gibson said as his son climbed into his lap. "What's going on? You're not done yet."

"She's mad at me, dad, she yelled at me and said that I don't love her. All I did was draw a picture of you and me and Chloe and Rose."

"Oh buddy. It probably scared her a little. I don't think she meant to be mad at you. She's just trying to get used to all of this, like you and your sister are. It's different."

"Daddy, I do love her though, but she's scary now." Tears were streaming down his little face. "Her eyes are really weird, and she smells like a stinky butt. And when she tries to kiss us, her breath smells like puke."

Gibson tried not to laugh at his son's description, but seeing how she looked when she had arrived, he didn't figure she had showered in a few days. "Buddy, I'm sorry."

"Please don't make me go back in there anymore," Oliver pleaded.

Gibson squeezed his son, setting him in the chair next to him. He walked to the desk.

"Sheila, right?" The receptionist nodded. "Sheila, my son here, Oliver Titus, isn't feeling very well. I think, if it's ok, I'm just going to keep him out here with me for the rest of the time. I don't want him to throw up and get anyone sick." Sheila started to deny the request, but then Oliver pretended to gag. She quickly stood, pointing to the bathroom and ran to the back room to tell the supervisor.

"Well, that was a good show, son." He ruffled Oliver's hair, who shot a huge smile up at his dad. "But let's not lie like that again, ok?" Gibson's smile was sweet to his son, knowing that his little fake out allowed him to stay with him. They had to sit in the waiting room for another two hours, waiting for Chloe to come out.

Chloe was smiling when she came out. "Mommy told me she was taking us to DISNEY WORLD!" Gibson had tried to hide his rolling eyes.

"Well, that will be fun, if it ever happens." He had responded.

"I'll get to meet Cinderella, daddy! Isn't that so cool?"

He quietly groaned when he picked up his daughter, swinging her onto his hip. "Sure is, Clover. I hope it works out." Except that it won't. One more broken promise coming, Lorna would never take the kids to anything fun like that. It irritated him when she fed things into the kids' heads. He took Oliver by the hands and walked out to the truck before Lorna had even made it out of the back hallway.

CHAPTER THIRTY-FOUR

Rose

Three days later, on the morning of the wedding, Rose woke up with a start. She was certain she had forgotten something throughout the planning. Gibson and she had gone through the plans a million times that week with their families and her friends, but she still had an awful feeling. She heard the limo pull up outside her house and heard Grace, Alaina, and Holly enter the house. They were hooting and hollering, carrying on about how the limo driver was hilarious.

"Rose, you'd better be awake and ready to go! The hair appointments are in fifteen minutes!" Alaina had firm control over the events of the day, which was fine with Rose. All she wanted to think about was not tripping down the aisle and marrying Gibson. Also, hopefully not throwing up all over the place.

"I'm up here. I can't shake the feeling that I forgot about something." She heard Alaina say something to the other two girls and run up the stairs.

"Look, you haven't forgotten anything. It's pregnancy brain. Believe me, everything is set and ready to go," Alaina grabbed her friend in a hug, "You're going to be fine, leave today to me." Rose was so thankful that her friend was so organized, and always willing to take care of details for anything.

After getting her hair pulled up and into her tiara and veil, Rose watched as the girls got their hair done. That's when it dawned on her, "Um, where's Chloe? Shouldn't she be getting her hair done too?" Alaina was sitting in the chair and looked up at Rose with wide eyes.

"Shit," was all Alaina said.

"I've got this." Holly ran out the door and into the limo. Rose watched in horror as the limo tore away from the curb.

"I cannot believe I forgot about my almost daughter!" Luckily her makeup wasn't done yet because her eyes turned to rain.

"Rose, it's not like you left her home alone or something. She's with her dad," Grace smiled at her friend, trying to calm her fears, "And I'm certain that Gibson will understand." Regardless, Rose shot a text to Gibson.

Holly is on her way to get

Chloe. Is she ready?

Yes, ma'am. Sitting here

with her smile on.

See you soon. ;)

*I cannot wait. :**

Three hours later, Rose, Chloe and her friends were sitting in the limo heading to the Titus farm. Grace and Holly were sitting next to each other up towards the front. They were taking turns flirting with the driver for no reason. They were a pair; both had their minds in the gutter most of the time. Alaina sat across from Rose, watching her. Rose's leg was bouncing in anticipation under the skirt of her dress. Chloe was sitting next to her, holding her hand, and swinging her legs in her seat.

Rose's stomach was churning and shooting a look at Alaina,

spit it out, "Laney, why does it feel like I'm doing something I shouldn't be?"

Alaina reached across and took her friend's hand, "Rose, breathe. You're fine." Her thumb ran circles on her friend's hand. "You love him, he loves you. Truthfully, I'm more sure of you and Gibson than I was with me and Tate." Rose still felt nauseous, but nodded, looking down at the little girl holding her other hand.

"Yeah, Rose," Grace interjected, "Watching you and Gibs, knowing how you can't keep your hands off each other, you're like a movie. This wedding is meant to be."

"Why can't they keep their hands to themselves?" Chloe's little voice interrupted them, sending a laugh from the group.

Gibson

They had transformed the lawn of the farmhouse into a beautiful wedding venue. They had placed the white chairs in perfect lines, turning them away from the sun. Hanging off the end of each row, there was a bouquet of antique-rose colored roses wrapped with burlap. A cream satin runner covered the path to the brown trellis that John had built. The same antique pink roses covered the trellis with cream roses intertwined with them. Burlap and ecru lace wove into the spaces of the trellis.

Gibson was inside, pacing around his childhood bedroom, pulling on his tie. His navy-blue suit perfectly tailored to him. A cream rose pinned to his lapel. Oliver was watching him, mimicking every movement he made.

Cody came in then, "Hey man, you ready? The girls are right around the corner."

Gibson took a deep breath and nodded, grabbing Oliver's hand.

At the top of the stairs, he stopped short, the sudden movement pulling Oliver backwards. When he looked up at his dad, Gibson motioned for him to go ahead. Watching his son descend the stairs, he felt a rush of anxiety flow over him.

He turned to Cody and said, "Man, this is the day I've been waiting for since junior year. Now that it's here, I'm freaking out."

Cody smiled at his friend, clasping his shoulder. "Knock it off. She came back, like one hundred percent. Nothing is going to stop this now. Let's walk down that aisle and get you off the singles list."

"Yeah, you're right." Gibson lifted his foot to start down the stairs before Cody grabbed his shoulder, stopping him. Gibson looked at his friend again.

"Dude, remember when you married Lorna, and we had this conversation? I was wrong to have pushed you."

"No, it was the right thing to do. Or so I thought. You're right though. This time I know for sure this is it. God, I love her."

Cody smiled and smacked his friend on the back, "Then let's get out there, huh."

The two friends walked shoulder to shoulder down the stairs. Gibson's mom and dad were waiting at the bottom, beaming at him.

"Gibby! You look so handsome." Mavis was wiping a tear from her cheek.

"Mom, quit it. This is my second wedding." Gibson pulled his mom into a hug.

Into his chest, Mavis responded, "I know, but this time it makes sense." They all shared a short laugh.

The crunching of the stones in the driveway as the limo drove up broke the moment. Gibson felt his heart race as he double checked Oliver, making sure his clothing was straight. As the music started outside, he reminded his son to wait for Rose to tell him when to head down the aisle and stuck his elbow out for his mom. Mavis let out another small sob as she wrapped her arm through his.

"Mom, come on. You're going to have messy makeup now for the pictures."

"Shut up, Gibson. Just get us to the front." Mavis jabbed her elbow into his side and John let out a tiny laugh from behind them.

Walking down the front porch steps towards the trellis, he caught a glimpse of the bridesmaids stepping out of the limo. Chloe was waving at him, so he stuck his hand up, sending her a tiny wave. At the end of the aisle, he turned and kissed his mom on her cheek and shook his dad's hand before taking his place at the front.

Rose and Gibson

The front doors of the farmhouse opened each time a bridesmaid and groomsman walked out. Each girl held a bouquet of cream-colored roses wrapped in burlap. The guys each wore a navy suit a lot like Gibson's. First, Holly and Mitchell, next Grace and Thomas, then Alaina and Cody. The music changed and out of the doors popped Chloe and Oliver. The sight of them caused a grin to creep across Gibson's face. Chloe was throwing petals that matched the flowers that were creeping up the trellis all over the place, and Oliver was trying to pull her along.

Finally, the door opened one last time and Gibson felt his breath catch. His hand flew to his chest as Rose and her dad stepped on to the porch. She looked beautiful, and Gibson could hardly control himself. His smile was gigantic as a happy tear strolled down his cheek, all the anxiety fading away. He looked over at his friends and mouthed 'Babe'.

When Rose and her dad made it to the trellis, Jason raised her veil, leaving a gentle kiss on her cheek. He was smiling, but a couple of tears made their way down his face.

"I love you, daddy," she whispered to him.

"I love you too, Rosey," He placed her hand in Gibson's and moved to the side.

"You look amazing." Gibson's eyes dragged over her dress, up to her eyes.

She batted her eyelashes at him, smiling. "You clean up pretty good yourself." They turned to the pastor, and the ceremony began.

"Who gives this woman to this man?" The pastor asked.

With a catch in his voice, Jason proudly said, "I do."

The entire ceremony lasted all of twenty minutes, and Gibson did indeed say almost verbatim what he had told Rose a few nights earlier for his vows.

When it was Rose's turn, she felt a happy tear slide down her cheek. Gibson raised a hand to wipe it away. "Gibson, when I came home to our sleepy little town, I thought it was because my dad needed me. But I think it was also because my heart needed you. Even after all these years, I never stopped loving you. You knew we were meant to be. You were so patient with me, allowing my fear to melt away. When I finally allowed my heart to open again, you were there to catch my cliff dive. Thank you for holding my hand through all of this and for being my best friend. Thank you for finding a way for us. I love you." After a reading from the Bible, the pastor pronounced them husband

and wife. They turned to look at each other and locked into a kiss.

"Introducing Mr. and Mrs. Gibson Titus," the pastor announced. Everyone clapped. Alaina cried, as did Mavis. Chloe and Oliver both let out a loud "Whoop!" and did a little giddy dance.

They held the reception in the tent that had been raised on the same property. They had set it to face the west, so that the guests could enjoy the Michigan sunset. The sky did not disappoint that night either, lighting up in hues of purple, red, and pink.

As their first dance began, Gibson wrapped an arm around Rose's waist and pulled her hand to his chest. She laid her head against him in a state of utopia. They swayed together for a few moments before she looked up at him again. The hint of a smile sat on her lips. "Mr. Titus is that a tear I see?" she questioned.

"No, it's my allergies," He responded, wiping his face.

"Really. Interesting. I've never known you to have allergies."

"Must be something new this year. I've noticed that the cleavage your dress is holding looks amazing." His finger traced her skin.

"Ah, classic Gibson, changing the subject." She giggled at him. "Know what I've noticed?" She asked, pulling his hand away.

"What's that?"

"My groom has only kissed me once today. I'm not sure that's an impressive start to a marriage." She was grinning at him as he leaned down and kissed her. She stood on her tiptoes, wanting more, so he pushed back, massaging her lips with his, causing the guests to roar.

As the music changed, she found her dad sitting alone watching the event. "Daddy, it's our turn." She held her hand out, pulling Jason to his feet. His smile grew when he heard the song she had chosen. It was the same song they used to dance to when she was little. Little Rose would stand on his feet, holding his hands, as he turned them round and round in the living room.

She wrapped her dad's arms around her. He tilted his head so his cheek leaned against the top of his daughter's head. Feeling a tear trickle down her cheek, Rose pulled back to look at his face. "Daddy, I'm so glad that this worked out. Thank you for calling me home."

"Rosey, all I've ever wanted is for you to live a happy life. I just selfishly always wanted it to be here, near me. You have no idea how glad I am that this is where you decided to be." He pulled his daughter in again, and they swayed together to their song, Rose standing on his feet for the last chorus.

After cutting the cake, Gibson and Rose took the kids inside the farmhouse to put them to bed. Oliver squeezed both of them and climbed into his bed, easily falling asleep. Chloe hugged her dad but then said, "Daddy, can you go back outside? I want to tell Rose something."

Gibson shrugged, kissing his daughter on the cheek, "Ok Clover, good night. Babe, I'll be right outside the door so we can go back out together." Rose nodded and turned back to Chloe.

"What's up, Chloe?" She asked. The little girl's eyes were wide and there were almost tears forming along the rims. "Oh Chloe, what's wrong?"

"Rose?" Chloe started, but hiccupped. "Rose, do you care if I call you mommy instead of Rose? My mommy isn't really that good at being a mommy like you are." Gibson heard the request through the door but waited to hear Rose's response.

"Chloe, I think that if you want to call me mommy and daddy is ok with it, then that's ok. But remember that your mommy does love you and that she will always be your mommy."

Chloe nodded. "But she doesn't really love me. She loves the things that made her not my mommy anymore. I think I would be happier calling you mommy." Chloe's eyes were drooping.

Rose reached over and brushed Chloe's hair off her forehead. "Well, I love you, sweet girl. Let's talk to daddy about this when we get back from our time away, ok?"

Chloe nodded, sat up and hugged Rose, whispering into her ear "I love you, mommy." Rose's heart broke as she squeezed Chloe.

"I love you too, Clover."

Closing the door behind her, she looked up at Gibson. "You heard that?"

He nodded at her. "I think you dealt with that perfectly, but she's right, you know. You've been a better mom to these kids these last few months than Lorna has in a long time." Gibson pulled her to his side as he kissed the top of her head. "This conversation is over for tonight, though. We have a party to attend." She laughed, still hearing Chloe's little voice in her head.

Joining their reception again, Gibson twirled his wife onto the dancefloor, positioning them directly into the middle of the group. He pulled her tightly again and began swaying with her.

The dancing turned to the bouquet toss. All the single ladies grouped together, pushing each other around when Rose tossed the flowers at them. Grace caught the bouquet, immediately dropping the bunch to the ground.

"Not happening," her voice was flat. The girls all laughed at her.

The garter ended up in the hands of one of Gibson's cousins. Grace rolled her eyes as they forced her into a chair to have the garter tugged on her thigh by the cousin. He tried to act sultry with her but couldn't quite get the moves right. Then he pulled her up to share a dance with her. Grace kept space between them, and Rose knew it was because she already had her sights set on someone else. Around midnight. Rose sat down and looked around at the guests having fun. Alaina and Tate were dancing tightly to each other. Rose hoped that Gibson and she would be that tight still after their first few years of marriage. She found Grace tucked into a dark corner, making out and groping a guy she barely recognized. Grace caught Rose's eye then, with the man's face deep into her neck. She gave Rose a devilish grin and a wave before pulling his mouth back to hers. Rose shook her head.

Gibson had joined her in a seat just then, so Rose leaned over and whispered to him what she had just seen. Gibson stretched his neck finding the two, except now they were rushing out of the tent towards the old barn.

"Well, from what I've learned about Grace I'm not surprised," He shook his head.

Rose stood from her seat before settling on her husband's lap. "I am so in love with you." Her hands began creeping up his chest, stopping on his shoulders, tracing the bottom of his earlobe with her finger, and pushing into him with her entire body.

"Ah, Mrs. Titus, are these little signals that it might be time to go home?"

"Well, it appears that the barn is now occupied, so maybe taking this home is a better idea." Her voice was seductive, and her eyes said, 'take me now'.

The two quickly found their parents. Rose kissed her dad good night. She hugged Mavis and John, thanking them for keeping the kids. Gibson hugged his parents as well. Together, the newly-weds walked to Gibson's truck that had been fitted with strings of beer cans and a "Just Married" sign on the tailgate. He helped her into the cab before running around to the driver's side to climb in next to her. She snuggled into the center seat, tight to her new husband, as they drove back to his house. When they got to the side door, he picked her up, placed a gentle kiss on lips, and asked, "Mrs. Titus, are you ready to start the rest of our lives?" Rose giggled and nodded. With one more kiss, Gibson carried her over the threshold.

Setting her down in the kitchen, she launched for his mouth again. No one was around, no children, no friends, no one to hide from. They were finally alone after a long day. After releasing his mouth, she said, "I love this dress, but it needs to go."

"Mrs. Titus... I love how pregnancy makes you want me so much."

"Shut up and undo me," she joked.

Turning her back to him, he started fumbling with the buttons and zipper. "Rose, how do I get you out of this?"

"That top button, do that first, then unzip." She was madly pulling bobby pins and her tiara off her head and was on the verge of ripping the dress off herself. When Rose felt it start to loosen, she felt Gibson's fingers trail along her back, following the dress as it fell to the floor. She turned to him, in her heels, bra and panty. He clutched behind her neck, tilting her face to him, and devoured her mouth again. As she let a small sound escape from her throat, Gibson started backing her into the next room.

She pulled away from his mouth and turned her attention to his clothing, wanting him naked. She pushed his jacket off his shoulders, letting it fall, hurrying her hands to his tie, stripping it from his neck, and swiftly unbuttoned his shirt, ripping the last few buttons off. Then, reaching for his pants, she got stuck. Rose couldn't get his button undone, groaning at herself. He moved her frantic fingers out of the way and unbuttoned himself.

Slowing the pace of their movements, he trailed his fingertips up her arms and over her collarbone. "I will never get tired of looking at you, Rose."

"Even though this tummy is starting to push out a little? Pretty soon it will be five times bigger." Rose made a face, pushing her cheeks out.

Gibson let out a quiet, breathy laugh, "You have no idea how sexy pregnant women are then, do you?" Gibson wiggled his eyebrows at her as his hand trailed down her front to her belly.

"Let's go, lover boy. I have big plans for you tonight." She waltzed into the bedroom, throwing her bra at him. He hadn't even noticed she had removed it. He grabbed her from behind when she stopped at the bed. His fingers swept her hair over her shoulder, following the trail with his mouth. The feeling caused her to arch into him. His length rubbed between her buttocks.

Rose climbed on to the bed and beckoned to him as she removed her panties. Gibson ripped his boxers off and climbed on top of her. She kissed his face and traced his arm muscles, working her hands down around his member, firmly stroking him while caressing his body with her other hand. He pulled her hand away from him. With his mouth massaging hers, he entered her. He kept himself in a gentle rhythm, like the waves on the shore, slow to be sure that they didn't rush through their first time as husband and wife.

He pulled her up to sit on his lap. The sudden change in depth made her cry out in pleasure. Then, as Gibson grasped her hips, Rose started rocking. As she sat on his lap rocking against him, he pushed her gently to lean backwards, still holding her hips. Her body arched in a beautiful way, causing him to run his hands up and over from her neck to her waist. Leaning into her again with his mouth, Gibson feasted on her breasts. Every movement he made was more pleasurable to her than the last.

As he lowered her back onto the bed, he heard her groan, so he gave a quick firm thrust, causing her eyes to flip open before slowly sliding closed again. She worked her hips with him as he moved again from her lips down to her neck, sucking gently on the skin. She threw her head back with another small moan.

He had hoped he could keep at this all night, but apparently, that wasn't the case. He kept thrusting, a little faster and harder. Each time, she arched into him. He continued his firm movements until he felt her start to clench around him. He continued pumping as she bucked against him, crying out with want, "God Gibson, yes."

"Not yet, wifey." He said with a sexy grin. She moaned, getting louder with every movement he was making. He slowed his movements again, trying to back her down from her arousal just enough to drive her wild, but her moaning was turning him on more, causing him to pulse. He wasn't sure he could even handle the change in pace.

"Please, Gibson." she pleaded, writhing against him. As she said those words, he felt himself starting to fall over the cliff.

"Now?" He asked, teasing her, shifting his hips as he started to speed up again.

"Oh god!" she yelled again, starting to shudder. He knew he was pushing her buttons, his thrusting became more vigorous as she clenched tighter. He felt himself beginning to pulse and as he exploded, she yelled his name, exploding with him.

She kissed him as they vibrated together before rolling him onto his back, "Let's do that again."

ABOUT THE AUTHOR

Bethanie L Kramer

 Bethanie Kramer started her love for reading when she was four. As she grew, obviously her tastes changed in books, and currently she is enamored with historical non-fiction and romance, with steam. She has wanted to be a writer ever since second grade, albeit not this genre at that point. When she was in high school, she started exploring poetry and was published one time in tenth grade. She works full time as a financial specialist, living in West Michigan with her husband, youngest son, (oldest has flown the coop), and adorable dog.

Find Bethanie online:
Website: blkramerauthor.wixsite.com/website
Facebook: www.facebook.com/BLKramerAuthor
Email: blkramerauthor@gmail.com

89045278R00152